Seal My Fate

The Oxford Legacy
Book 3

Roxy Sloane

Cover design by British Empire Designs

Created with Vellum

The Oxford Legacy: Book Three

Seal My Fate

I came to Oxford to avenge my sister, but instead, I found a web of lies.

Ancient loyalties. Fortunes built on sin.

Riches they'd do anything to protect.

I'm the one who could bring their empires crashing down.

But can I destroy the man I love?

Time is running out...

THE OXFORD LEGACY TRILOGY:

1. Cross My Heart

2. Break My Rules

3. Seal My Fate

For the readers who know that the wildest fantasy of all is being chosen, every time.

Chapter 1

Tessa

"Where the hell are you?" I mutter, searching the dark garden for my cellphone. I'm naked in a robe, with a hot man waiting for me in bed; the last thing I want is to be on my hands and knees, hunting around the patio furniture.

Not when I could be on my hands and knees for him...

I smile, unable to keep the delighted beam off my face. Moving in with Saint is a major step, but already, it feels like home here, with him. And after everything we've been through in the past months, all the suspicion and doubt, it's a relief to finally be able to breathe easy and know everything is finally settled and—

There's a sudden rattling noise, from the far end of the garden, then the skitter of footsteps. I freeze.

Somebody's there.

"Hello?" I call out, trying to stay calm.

There's no reply, as I edge closer, peering into the dark. Maybe an animal's trapped there, or has built some kind of nest—

"Shhh, don't scream."

A voice emerges from the dark, so familiar that I swear I'm hearing things.

It can't be...

Then the intruder steps out of the shadows, and my heart stops beating in my chest.

"No..." I whisper, standing there in total disbelief.

"Yes. Tessa, it's me," the ghost replies.

But somehow, it's not a ghost. It's not a dream. Because the woman I'm staring at, I've known since the first day I drew breath. I would recognize her anywhere, even skulking in the shadows with dyed hair and anxious eyes, a year after I wept at her funeral and said goodbye for the last time.

Not dead. Not gone. Here.

My sister.

"Wren?" I stutter, frozen in place. Blood pounds in my ears, and I feel like I'm going to pass out. "How? How is this possible—"

"Shh!" She grabs my hand and yanks me into the shadows, sending a fearful look towards the house. "Keep your voice down. We don't have long."

"But... I don't understand..."

I stare at her, still not sure this is real. *How can this be real?* "You're dead," I blurt, gripping her arm. I clutch her, my legs weak. "You died, Wren. You walked into the water, and left a note, and never came back. What are you doing here? How could you—?"

"I said quiet!" Wren hushes me again. "We can't talk here," she says, already pulling away from me. "I'm sorry, I know this is a lot, but there isn't time to explain. Meet me tomorrow."

"What? Wren, no—" I try to hold on to her, like this is a dream that I'll wake from, but Wren wrenches back.

"I'm sorry, Tessa, but you have to trust me," she says,

glancing around again. Skittish. *Afraid.* "Tomorrow, two o'clock. There's a pub in Hackney called the Two Hearts. I'll be there. I'll explain everything, I swear."

I stare at her, open-mouthed, still numb with shock.

"But Tessa, you can't tell anyone," Wren whispers urgently. "Not even Saint. *Especially* not Saint. Promise me."

I shake my head dumbly. "Wren, no. This is crazy. Just come inside. We can talk—"

"No!" Her eyes flare with panic. She grips me by my shoulders and stares into my eyes, desperate. "You can't tell. Promise me! *Please.*"

I stutter. I've never seen her like this before, even in the worst of her downward spiral, when she was self-destructing and barely keeping it together. There's something raw and wild in her eyes, like a caged animal, willing to do whatever it takes to save themselves.

"Trust me, Tessie," her gaze turns pleading. "For old time's sake. I swear, I'll explain everything. You just have to trust me on this. Pinky swear?"

She holds up her little finger, the way we always did when we were kids. It was a sister thing, rare and precious, and only meant for the most important kind of promises, like when I wanted to sneak out with my friends to a rock show in the next town, or Wren accidentally scraped the paint on our parents' old Honda.

It seems absurd to be doing it here, in the dark shadows of Saint's garden, when my sister has just come back from the dead. But the old gesture pierces my shock and confusion, and I can't help holding my own pinky up to link with hers.

"Promise," I echo, still stunned.

"Good." Relief flashes across her face, and then she's backing away, into the shadows. "Tomorrow," she whispers. "It'll all make sense."

And then she's melting into the dark as if she'd never been there at all, leaving me standing there in the middle of the yard, my head spinning with a thousand questions as I struggle to process the impossible.

She's back. Wren's alive. As if my prayers have all be answered. All year I've been wracked with guilt, tormented by grief; I would have done anything to have my sister back again...

And now I do.

So why is she so scared? What—or *who*—has she been hiding from?

What the hell is going on?

Chapter 2

Tessa

I lay in bed awake all night, unable to sleep for even a second. My mind is still reeling, and my emotions ricochet from joy to anger and back again a thousand times over.

What happened to you, Wren? What the hell have you put us through?

The minute dawn breaks outside the windows, I slip out of bed and into the bathroom, but even the sharp shock of an ice-cold shower can't snap me out of my confusion. Wren hid from me. She lied. We grieved her, all of us, Mom and Dad and—God, do they know? How could she do this to them? Why would she torment us all like this, when all the while, she's been alive?

When all this time, I've been trying to avenge her death.

"'Morning, sunshine," Saint greets me as I reenter the bedroom. He's sprawled in bed, looking with his dark hair rumpled and his plush mouth curled in a grin. As he sees me, wet from the shower and wrapped only in a towel, his smile grows. "Damn, if I knew what moving in with you would be like, I'd have done it eons ago."

I muster a faint smile. "You didn't know me eons ago," I correct him lightly. "And asking me to live with you the first day we met wouldn't exactly have played too great. We're moving fast enough as it is," I add.

Saint searches my face, as if intuiting my mood. "No morning-after regrets, I hope?"

"No," I say immediately, crossing to the bed. I lean over and drop a kiss on his lips. "No, I'm happy to be here."

At least I was, up until the moment last night when Wren turned my whole world upside down.

"Good," Saint gives me a lazy grin, reaching up to stroke over my damp skin. "Because I'm not hauling any more boxes for you, baby. So it looks like you're stuck with me."

"What boxes?" I tease. "I had all of two suitcases, thank you very much. I travel light."

"Not anymore." Saint suddenly pulls me into his lap and wraps his arms around me. "You travel with me now," he promises, his mouth humming against the sensitive point right above my collarbone. "First class all the way."

He pulls my towel open, already skimming his hands over my curves as his mouth moves to claim mine in a slow, heated kiss. My body reacts to him in an instant, the way it always does, but my mind is a million miles away, still fixed on Wren's cryptic comments.

'You can't tell anyone... Especially not Saint'.

What does she mean? Why can't anyone know she's really alive?

How can I keep this from him?

Luckily, his phone buzzes loudly on the nightstand, interrupting us. "You should get that!" I blurt, slipping out of his embrace.

Saint gives a rueful laugh, checking the screen. "It's work. Hold that thought," he adds, as he answers. I quickly move to the massive walk-in closet, and dress for the day in good jeans and a button-down. By the time I emerge, he's just finishing up.

"... Be there soon."

"Ashford emergency?" I ask lightly, as he gets out of bed and stretches. Even in my anxious state, I can't help but admire the sight of his body, lean and powerful, carved like one of Rodin's finest masterpieces—and capable of bringing me to the heights of pleasure over and over again.

"It's all an emergency these days," Saint replies, playfully rolling his eyes. He catches me to him for another quick kiss, before grabbing some clothing for himself. "All hands on deck," he reports, dressing. "Apparently, the peer review results for the Alzheimer's drug trials are publishing in a matter of days. And his sources at the review board say, it's good news."

"That's huge," I blink. Wren worked on an early phase of the drug trials, and I know that Saint's family company, Ashford Pharmaceuticals, has everything riding on its success.

"Huge? It's going to change the face of modern medicine," Saint enthuses. "I mean, not just for the millions of families who won't have to watch their loved ones slip away from them, but beyond that, the roads it opens up for treating other neurological diseases..." He looks thrilled. "You know, all this time I've been pushing back so hard against my family legacy, resisting being the dutiful son and heir, but now... Now I feel proud that Ashford could be making a difference like this. Actually doing good. And, of course, making a stinking great profit, as I'm sure my father would remind me," he adds with a wry smile.

"Can't forget about that part," I agree. It's amazing news, and I wish I could be more present to celebrate with him, but a part of me is already anxiously eying the clock, counting down to my meeting with Wren.

"You want to get lunch?" he asks. "I'm sure I could sneak away long enough to toast with you."

"I, umm..." I rack my brains for an excuse, still distracted.

Saint notices. He steps closer, and tenderly cups my cheek, searching my face. "Are you OK?" he asks, concerned. "You've been quiet since the party last night. Not too overwhelming, I hope? Everyone was just teasing, talking about boring domesticity," he adds. "I promise, there'll be nothing boring about our living together."

I quickly force a laugh. "I know. I'm fine," I lie, glancing away. "There have just been a lot of big changes for me recently, I'm still catching up. Dropping out of my studies at Oxford, moving in here with you, starting full-time at the Ambrose Foundation..."

"And giving up on your quest to avenge Wren," Saint finishes softly.

I jerk a nod, feeling guiltier than ever for keeping this from him. The whole reason Wren spiraled, the whole reason I thought she'd killed herself, was because of a brutal, twisted attack that happened last year in Oxford. I swore I would find who was responsible, and Saint has been by my side every step of the way in my search for Wren's attacker. He's risked it all to investigate his friends and help me bring about justice for her death.

And now she's not dead... Everything in me wants to tell him.

But I promised her. Pinky swore.

And until I know what's going on—how this impossible situation has come to be—I owe her my loyalty, even if it's eating me up inside.

"I'll settle in soon," I tell Saint brightly, and he must be reassured by my act, because he smiles, and releases me.

"How about we go shopping this weekend?" he suggests, buttoning his shirt. "We can pick out some furniture and things for this place together."

I frown. "But it's already furnished," I say, looking around. Saint's mews house in Kensington is the height of understated luxury, full of artistic, vintage pieces and gorgeous textiles.

"I want you to feel at home," he smiles over at me. "Like it's *our* home, not just mine."

"Even if I want to paint the living room bubblegum pink, and replace your beloved record player with a pinball machine?" I manage to tease, touched by his determination to open his life to me. Saint was a wild and reckless playboy for long enough, I'm guessing he's never thought about a woman's design preferences in his life.

He laughs. "Whatever you want, darling. Chicken coop in the back garden. Sex swing in the library. Now, on second thought, that last one sounds like a must-have for us..." he adds with a smolder, and I can't help but smile.

"I love you," I say softly, even as guilt curls in my gut.

"Good," Saint says with a playful smirk.

I laugh. "Arrogant, much?" I smack him lightly on the arm as he sweeps me into a hug.

"Grateful. Very, very grateful..." Saint kisses me slowly, until my legs are jelly and my heart is beating fast. "And I plan on showing you just how much tonight," he adds with a low rasp. "Hint, it involves those silk ties I absolutely refuses to wear to the office. Because I think they'd suit you far better, tied down and spread wide on that bed like a good girl, while I make that tight pussy clench until you see God."

. . .

I SEE Saint off to the office with a final breathless kiss, and then look around the house, feeling restless. I still have hours to kill before the meeting with Wren, and I know I'll go crazy if I stay cooped up here with all my questions, so I grab my jacket and laptop, and take the Tube over to Shoreditch, where the Ambrose Foundation headquarters are based.

"Tessa, good to see you," my boss in the fundraising department, Priya, greets me with a smile as I step into the converted warehouse, buzzing with energy and chatter. "I hear we'll be seeing a lot more of you, too."

I nod. I've been working part-time, mostly remote while I juggled my studies in Oxford, but now that I'm living full-time in London with Saint, the plan was to become a full-time employee, too. "I hope that's OK."

"Of course!" Priya smiles warmly. "Your influencer campaign is shaping up so well. We're all so excited to launch it in the new year. And I have a number of other projects where I'd love your input. I'm just about to jump on a call, but how about I swing by your office later to discuss?"

"Maybe yours would work better," I reply. "Mine's a little hectic." I nod to the desk in the middle of the open-plan floor where I've been working. Except today, someone else is sitting there. I pause.

"Oh, didn't Hugh tell you?" Priya laughs. "You have your own office now."

"I do?" I gasp in excitement.

"Right this way." Priya shows me to a cool, funky room on the second floor, filled with a desk, potted plants, and a window overlooking the bustling street below. "Vik is spending the next few months in Islamabad, overseeing our education programs there," she explains. "So this is all yours. On one condition: You keep the plants alive," she adds with a grin.

"Of course!" I beam, looking around. "Thank you, this is great."

Priya checks her watch. "I'll find you later," she says, and bustles off, leaving me to take in the cool, private space. There's a comfy couch in the corner, colorful artwork on the walls, plus photos of various Ambrose Foundation staff around the world, working on their projects. I smile, pleased to be a part of the team, and hopefully contributing to our impact, too.

I settle in with my laptop, determined to focus and get some work done.

But that focus lasts all of five minutes. No matter what I do, my thoughts keep going back to Wren.

How is this even possible?

In the first days after her disappearance, my, er, *our* parents and me clung to the desperate hope that she might still be alive. She left a suicide note, which they found with her purse and shoes on the beach, along with an empty bottle of prescription pills. But even after the Coastguard searched the waters nearby, they didn't find a body.

Surely, somehow, she might have survived.

But as the days turned into weeks, our hopes faded. Nobody had seen or heard from her, not one single clue to suggest she'd made it off that beach alive. She'd been erratic and suicidal before, and it was clear the police thought she'd done it again—and was successful this time. They called off the search, closed the case file, and soon, we all accepted the heartbreaking truth.

She was gone.

Now, I sit there, trying to make sense of this new reality, the one where Wren has been alive all this time. Was she in hiding? How did she disappear so thoroughly? Why would she stay away so long?

What could have driven her to such a drastic act in the first place?

No matter how many times I turn it over in my mind, I can't make sense of it—or why she would suddenly appear in Saint's garden last night, revealing herself to me after all this time. She was scared. In trouble, somehow? But why the secrecy, the wig and disguise? And on top of it, demanding that I keep her return a secret—from Saint, in particular?

I shiver, chilled. The Wren I knew would never have put her family through this traumatic ordeal, so clearly I don't know Wren half as well as I thought I did.

What does she want from me?

"Knock, knock." There's a tap at my door, then Hugh enters. "How are you settling into your new digs?"

"Great!" I exclaim loudly, trying to shove the thoughts of Wren aside. "I love it in here. But are you sure someone else shouldn't be getting this office? Someone more important."

Hugh chuckles. "Believe me, with the way this influencer campaign of yours is shaping up, you're the VIP around here."

"Don't," I roll my eyes, blushing, but he insists.

"No, really. Priya showed me the plan for the rollout, and some of the names you have signed up to participate. It's impressive stuff," he adds. "Of course, I don't know who on earth LadyJaneLocks or BeastMode are, but I'm told they're quite the celebs with the younger crowd."

I smile, relaxing. It's so much easier to chat to Hugh now that I crossed him off the list of suspects who might have been behind Wren's attack. He was safely in Stockholm, giving a TED talk that weekend, so I don't have to keep my defenses up or view him with suspicion anymore.

"LadyJane is a hair influencer," I explain. "She has two million followers on Instagram and TikTok. And BeastMode is a gamer, he's huge on Twitch. I saw he posted a bunch about his dog, so I figured he would be a good fit for one of the animal protection campaigns."

"Twitch, Beasts... You ever feel old before your time?" Hugh asks with a grin.

I laugh. "Constantly. These influencers are still teenagers, and they have more of a platform than most big sports stars, or Beyonce." I pause. "OK, well not Beyonce."

"And since we can't sign her up to promote the Foundation projects, I'd say you're doing just fine with this list," Hugh agrees. "Coffee?"

"I'd love some."

We stroll downstairs to the kitchenette area, chatting about some of the Foundations upcoming projects. "I've been itching for us to expand," Hugh confides, as he sets the expensive espresso machine humming. "And not just in scale, but also the kind of projects we support. It may be unseemly to say, but it's easier to get people to donate money for starving orphans in some far-flung nation than it is to get them to pay attention to problems right here at home. I'm hoping in the years ahead, we can focus on issues right here in England: drug rehabilitation, food banks, the less sexy charity goals."

"And how does your father feel about that?" I ask, before I can stop myself. Hugh's father, Lionel Ambrose, is in the running to become the next British Prime Minister—and seems to have the votes sewn up, if the polls are anything to go by. "I just mean, he likes to paint a rosier picture of the country, that's all. At least, judging by his campaign speeches."

I remember meeting him at the Ashford Pharma event, seeing how he charmed and worked the room, every inch the trustworthy politician.

Hugh gives a wry smile. "My father and I have very

different priorities," he replies, thankfully not seeming offended by my comment. "But we are alike in one way, we have a vision for the future. For this country. That mission is all that matters."

I blink, surprised by his grim tone. Then he flashes a grin. "And if BeastMode and Lady Jane will make it happen, then I say, I'm all in," he adds. "Even if they make me feel about a hundred years old."

I laugh, relaxing again. "I'll get one of the interns to make you a cheat card," I suggest. "So you don't mix up your GoJo with your GoPro."

"Please do." Hugh sets the espresso to drip, then expertly adds steamed milk in a swirl. "And *voila*. If all this fails, I can always run off to Rome and become a barista," he adds with a grin.

"I'm impressed." I take a sip. "Wow, this really is good."

"Annabelle begged me to train the staff for her wedding breakfast," Hugh says, looking amused. "Apparently, she wants her and Max's initials swirled into all the foam on every cup."

I laugh. "That sounds like Annabelle."

"Did you get the itinerary?" he asks.

"Itinerary?"

"For the wedding events. They kick off next week, you know, and it's scheduled down to the minute," Hugh looks mock-serious. "I think she even put the bathroom breaks in."

"I'll have to check with Saint," I say, amused. Then I pause. "You don't really think Annabelle meant it when she said I would be a bridesmaid, do you?"

Hugh smirks. "Not only did she mean it, but I would wager you a hundred pounds she's already having the bridesmaid dress altered and is making a personalized flower crown for you. Or rather, one of her poor minions is."

"Oh dear," I laugh. "Isn't that kind of weird, me being a part of the wedding? I just met you all!"

"But you're part of the family now, aren't you?" he asks. "I mean, Saint's like a brother to us, and if he's happy... Then we are, too."

I smile back, touched. "He should be happy," I crack, and then realize that came out sounding dirtier than I meant. "I just mean, with everything going smoothly at Ashford," I add quickly, and Hugh laughs.

"Yeah, I heard some whispers about that. I'm glad. A lot of people have a lot riding on the Ashford Pharma fortunes... including the Foundation here."

"How do you mean?" I ask, puzzled.

"Our endowment is invested in the markets," Hugh explains. "I don't follow the details, but since it was all set up before I took the reins... I'm guessing a tidy sum is tied up in Ashford shares. My father likes to keep his friends close, and their profits closer."

"Oh." I blink, not sure how to process that. Just another example of how tightly all these powerful families' fates are intertwined. But before I can respond properly, my phone buzzes with an alarm. It's 1:30 already. I need to go meet Wren!

"Hot date?" Hugh asks, as I quickly rinse my coffee cup in the sink.

"I'm meeting with another influencer," I lie quickly. "Not sure if they're a good fit, so I thought I'd sit down face-to-face and check the vibe before I mentioned anything."

"Great work," Hugh grins. "Let me know if it all pans out. We're rooting for you."

. . .

I ESCAPE BACK to my office to grab my things, then head out. Shoreditch is on the East side of London, about a twenty-minute walk from the address Wren gave me, and I walk fast, my nerves twisting tighter with every step.

Why the cloak-and-dagger routine? Couldn't she just have sat down and talked last night? She was on edge. *Scared.* Acting like she could have been discovered at any moment... I wonder now if she thought she was being followed.

I walk a little faster, glancing around me, but the streets are busy and nobody is paying me any attention. My surroundings turn from the newer hipster coffee shops and boutiques to a slightly seedier side of London, the East End of disheveled diners, mini-marts, and boarded-up shops. It's definitely far from the glamorous hot spots Saint and his friends frequent. Nobody I know would expect to find me way out here.

But clearly, that's the point.

The Two Hearts pub is on the corner, a dingy local spot with faded carpet and a weary-looking barmaid on duty behind the bar. Early in the afternoon, the place is quiet, with just a few drinkers alone at the bar, or heads bent over the horse racing scores.

And Wren. Already cloistered in a booth in the back, half-hidden from the room but with a clear view of the door.

I make my way over, relieved she turned up at all. If she slipped away from me again... I would have no way of finding her. No way to even prove she'd shown her face at all.

"Wren," I greet her, smiling despite everything. Just to see her face fills me with emotion, even if it is drawn and tired, her eyes jumping nervously around the room.

"Don't call me that, not so loud," she says hurriedly, pulling me down in the seat across from her. She's nursing a soda, and has one waiting for me, too. "Did you tell anyone you were meeting me?"

"No."

"No one?" Wren demands, grabbing my hand. "Not even Saint?"

"I told you that I wouldn't." I pull my hand away. She's scaring me now, so sharp and intense, but none of this meeting makes sense. "I hated lying, but I made you a promise, and I've kept to it. Now it's your turn to keep your side of the bargain," I continue, leveling her with a stare. "Tell me what's going on. Wren... I want answers. I deserve to know the truth!"

Wren exhales. She glances around the room again, but nobody's paying us any attention. Finally, her posture relaxes. She gives me a nod. "You're right. I'm sorry for all the sneaking around, but you'll see, I'm only trying to protect you. All of it was to protect you."

I shiver. "What are you talking about? Start at the beginning," I add, needing to make sense of this. "Faking your death, the suicide note... You planned it? It was all an act? You never meant to kill yourself?"

Wren slowly nods. "I didn't see any other way. You see, a few weeks after I got back from Oxford, I started getting threatening letters."

"What kind of threats?" I ask, confused.

"They said I needed to keep quiet, that bad things would happen. Not just to me, but to Mom and Dad, and to you." Wren swallows, fear flicking across her face. "They had photos, Tessa. Surveillance of you, at that nonprofit job you were working. Out running in the mornings. They drew a bullseye on the photo."

"Oh my God," I breathe. "Who was doing it? What did they want?"

"I didn't see any other way out," Wren pleads, not answering my question. "Everything was falling apart, you were already so worried about me, and I... I was losing my grip.

I didn't know what to do. I thought if I could just disappear, then they wouldn't care about you guys anymore. You could be safe."

"Who?" I demand again. "Who were these people? What did they want with you?"

Wren swallows hard. "There's something I didn't tell you, something that happened when I was in Oxford..."

"Connected to the attack?" I ask.

She shakes her head. "Something else. Something big..."

She trails off, clearly still terrified by whatever it is she knows, that made these people come after her.

I lean forwards. "You can trust me, Wren," I promise her. "I won't let anyone hurt you again."

She gives me a faint smile, and for a moment, I see a spark of the old Wren in her eyes again. My beloved sister. My closest friend. "What are you going to do, beat them with your tennis racquet, the way you did with Marcy Littleton when she called me a stuck-up nerd at camp?" she jokes softly.

"If that's what it takes," I vow. I take her hand and squeeze it. "We're in this together now. Please, Wren, whatever's going on, you don't have to deal with it alone anymore."

She squeezes back. "I know. I hate to bring you into this, but I can't stay silent, not when you're with him now."

Him? Does she mean Saint?

"I tried to warn you to stop digging," she adds. "I sent you that note..."

"That was you? But why?"

I'm frowning at Wren in confusion when she takes a deep breath, and continues: "It was my research, at Ashford Pharma. I stumbled across something I should never have seen. It's the Alzheimer's drug, Tessa," she says, looking stricken. "The results from the trials were all faked. The drugs don't work."

"No..." I gasp, stunned.

She nods. "That's what they were threatening me about, to keep me quiet. They said..." Wren's voice breaks, but she soldiers on, urgent. "They said that if I ever revealed the truth, then they'd get to you. They would show you the inside of that cell, the way they did to me. And they wouldn't use the drugs, either. They'd make sure you remembered every single moment."

Chapter 3

Tessa

I can't believe it.

I sit in the dingy back booth, staring at Wren in disbelief. "But... I don't understand," I stammer, reeling from her revelations.

Ashford Pharma is faking their miracle Alzheimer's drug? All that work for nothing, all of Saint's excitement and hopes—

Then the other part of what she told me sinks in. That they would do the same thing to me that they did to her...

"Why would they threaten that?" I ask. "How could they even know the details about your attack, unless..."

I trail off in horror.

"Unless somehow, it was connected to what I found at the Ashford labs," Wren finishes for me. "That's what I think. I discovered the faulty data a week before it happened. I didn't realize right away what I'd found," she adds. "I thought maybe the file was corrupted, or it had been a data-entry error. The numbers just didn't make any sense. I reported it up the chain at the lab and didn't hear anything else about it. Then the attack happened, and it was the last thing on my mind. But once the threatening letters started arriving, it made me think the two things were linked. Like maybe the attack was a warning," she says, "or revenge, or to scare me into packing up and leaving my fellowship, going back to the States. It worked," she adds grimly. "I didn't want anything else to do with that place."

I sit there, trying to process it all. As my head spins, a group of people enter the pub. Younger guys, dressed in soccer shirts, already sounding rowdy.

Wren tenses. "Let's take a walk," she says, already rising to her feet.

I want to argue, but what can I say: That she's being paranoid? She's already been a victim of a brutal attack and threats against her safety.

I would be flinching at shadows, too, if I were in her shoes.

I nod, and grab my things, following her back outside to the busy street. Wren looks around. "This way," she says, and takes off, walking fast, ducking through the pedestrians and darting out suddenly to cross the street.

"Woah, hold up!" I hurry after her, rushing to catch up. "You look like you're running from someone," I tell her. "Slow down, it's OK."

Wren eases up her pace, just a little, but I can tell that she isn't happy.

We turn into a small park area with muddy grass, and a few kids kicking a ball around. We loop around the edge, as Wren keeps a watchful eye on our surroundings, and I try to think up a plan.

This is way out of my league. Falsified pharmaceutical trials, violent threats... And if this really is the reason behind Wren's attack, I feel sick just thinking about it.

"We need to tell Saint," I tell her. "He can help us."

"Are you out of your mind?" Wren whirls to face me. "He's one of them. Hell, it's his family business, his name up there above the door. Ashford Pharma. For all we know, he could be behind what happened to me."

"He's not," I vow immediately. "We can trust him!"

Wren shakes her head. "He could be dangerous, Tessa, don't you see? That's why I risked everything to come back: To warn you."

"About Saint?"

"I told myself I could never tell you the truth, that I had to stay dead forever, but then I saw photos of the two of you, on Max Lancaster's social media," Wren says. "I didn't realize you were together. That you were serious, or that you were still digging into my attack. It's not safe, Tessie," she pleads. "*He*'s not safe."

"You're wrong," I tell her calmly. Even in all this chaos and confusion, Saint is the one thing I can be certain of. "I can rely on him. He's proven that to me, repeatedly. He's been helping me," I add. "He was willing to do whatever it took to find the man who attacked you."

"And you believe him?" she demands.

"Yes." I hold her gaze. "I trust him... with my life. Whatever's happening at Ashford Pharma, it's got nothing to do with him," I add. "He wasn't even involved with the company until a few weeks ago."

Still, she shakes her head. "You can't trust them!" she says again, getting more hysterical. "I thought I knew my friends in Oxford, my colleagues, that they would never be capable of hurting me... And look what happened. I was wrong—and I've spent every minute of every day since living with the consequences!"

"Shh, it's OK," I try to soothe her, but Wren is sobbing now, in great hiccupping gulps.

"You can't tell him. Please Tessa, don't do it!"

"Alright!" I finally agree, desperate to calm her down again.

"I won't tell Saint. At least, not for now. But we need to figure out what to do, and soon."

She nods. "I'm working on it." Wren backs away, like she's about to disappear again.

"Wait!" I blurt, panicking. "Where are you staying? How can I reach you?"

She pauses, looking reluctant. "Trust goes both ways," I remind her. "Pinky promise, remember?"

She relaxes a little. "Do you have your phone?"

I pull it out. She takes it, and programs in a number. "You can reach me with this," she says, handing it back. I see that she's put the name as 'birdy,' a childhood nickname Dad used.

"Will you be safe? " I ask, feeling a pang. "If you would just come back with me, you could stay with us, we could figure this out—"

"I'll be fine," Wren interrupts. "I'll talk to you soon. But please... Be careful with Saint. What I just told you, about the drug results... That's information someone would kill to protect."

She turns on her heel and strides away before I can say another word. I watch her go, my heart aching with fear and confusion.

Will I ever see her again?

Part of me wants to follow her, and make sure she's safe, but I know I can't risk breaking the fragile trust we have now. She's made it this far; I have to believe that she knows how to take care of herself.

So, I slowly turn and begin my journey home. I walk back to the Tube station in a daze, and almost miss my stop back in Kensington. By the time I've made it down the luxurious leafy streets to Saint's house, a million miles from the noise and bustle of East London, the whole afternoon with Wren feels like a dream.

"Hello?"

I hear Saint's voice calling when I let myself in. "It's me," I call back, and follow the sound of his yell up the stairs to one of the guest bedrooms. It's up on the third floor, perched under the slanted eaves of what used to be an attic. I look around, curious. I haven't been up here, besides Saint's insistence that we fuck in every room in the house to celebrate my arrival.

"What's going on?" I ask. The bed that used to occupy most of the space is now dismantled in pieces in the corner, and there's a desk against the wall now, and a comfortable armchair in front of the window. Saint is assembling bookcases on one wall, parts and power tools spread on the floor around him.

He straightens up with a smile, his head nearly skimming the lowest part of the ceiling. "You're early," he says, greeting me with a kiss. "Ignore the mess. I wanted to surprise you."

"With what?"

"Your new office," he says proudly. "Slash library, slash kinky sex den. Whatever you want."

My heart melts. "This is for me?" I ask, looking around again. The room is cozy and sunlit, and I can just picture curling up here with my laptop or a good book.

"All yours," Saint confirms. "There's already more than enough room for guests downstairs, and I have my office, so why shouldn't you have your own space, too? We can decorate any way you like," he adds. "Bubblegum pink and all. Although, we might have a hard time getting a pinball machine up two flights of stairs," he adds with a grin, calling back to my earlier jokes about a big redesign.

I shake my head. "It's perfect as it is," I tell him, and it is. The guest room was already done up with a classic William Morris wallpaper, and now with the plush velvet chaise and a vintage standing lamp, it's the ideal reading nook. "Thank you."

"It's my pleasure," Saint says, pulling me into a kiss. I melt against him for a moment, reveling in the warmth of his embrace, but too soon, my guilt over Wren drowns out the moment.

I hate keeping secrets from him, especially something this big, that affects his life and family, too.

I pull away, and bury my face in his chest, hugging him tightly. Saint seems surprised, but he holds me, gently stroking my hair as I try to pull myself together.

"Sorry," I blurt, stepping back.

"It's OK." Saint looks at me with tenderness in his dark eyes. "I think I know what's going on."

"You do?" I pause, certain my guilt is written all over my face.

"It's Wren, isn't it?"

I look at him in panic. *How does he know?*

"What do you mean?" I gulp, wishing so much that I could just come clean. That this secret wasn't looming between us, when all I want to do is hold him tightly.

Saint brushes a lock of hair from my face, still so supportive and understanding. "I know it must be hard, to move on," he explains. "You've spent months focused on finding out who attacked her. Of course you're going to feel a little lost and disoriented, without that purpose driving you anymore."

I exhale in a whoosh. "Right," I say quietly, my guilt twisting sharper than ever. "You're right."

"It'll be OK," Saint reassures me. "I know a lot of terrible things have happened, and a part of you will always grieve that loss. But you deserve to be happy. Life is short; you have a lot to celebrate, too."

I stare at him, and realize, he's right. I do have something to celebrate: Wren is *alive*.

I've been so caught up in all the panic and fear surrounding her return, I haven't taken a moment to simply absorb that incredible fact. My sister is alive. The one thing I hoped and prayed for and would have given anything to see... It happened. It's real.

All the rest of it—the threats, and mystery, and uncertain future—it all seems to pale in comparison to that one miraculous truth.

Wren is alive, and whatever else happens, nothing can take away from that unexpected gift. We'll figure the rest of it out, in time. But right now?

I have my sister back.

I break into a wide smile and throw my arms around Saint's neck. I launch myself at him, kissing him hot and hard, needing to celebrate this incredible twist of fate. He stumbles back, laughing, before gripping me more securely.

"What's that for?" he asks, smiling.

"I'm just happy," I beam. "About... the office. Thank you."

"Wow, well just wait until I've finished assembling these built-in bookshelves," Saint gives me a smoldering grin. "Then you'll really want to thank me, all night long."

I laugh. "We should celebrate," I say, my heart pounding. "Like you said, life is short. I want to treasure every win."

And getting my sister back from the dead is about as big a win as I can dream of.

"Alright then," Saint's expression turns playful. "A special occasion, hmmm..."

I feel a shiver of anticipation. Saint's special occasions always involve some new, thrilling adventure, and I can tell from the gleam in his eye, today will be no different.

"I know just the thing," he says. "Go dress for dinner, while I make a couple of calls. And Tessa?" he adds, as I head for the door.

"Yes?"

"Wear a dress this evening," he says, the gleam turning wolfish. "Loose skirt. Shoulder straps."

My pulse kicks. "Are you going to tell me why?"

"Now, where would the fun be in that?" he smirks. "You'll find out soon enough. If you're a good girl, that is."

I bound downstairs to dress, full of excitement. Somehow being good with Saint really means being very, very bad...

And I can't wait.

Chapter 4

Tessa

After getting dressed up—and following Saint's instructions to the letter—we jump in a cab across town, to a charmingly romantic jazz club that's hidden down a flight of stairs, just off the lights and buzz of the theaters on Shaftsbury Avenue.

"I love this place," I smile, looking around the basement. It's dim and discreet, with faded leather booths and little tables set out around the stage, where a jazz trio is playing a sultry tune. "Like something out of a movie."

"They make the best martinis in town," Saint says, pulling out a chair for me and beckoning the waiter over. "Olive and a twist?"

I nod, happily taking my seat as he orders our drinks, and some French fries for the table. AKA, me. "You're a fast learner," I laugh, when he asks for the snacks. "You know I can't drink on an empty stomach."

"Well, I have big plans for us this evening," he says with a wink, and my smile grows. "Can't have you getting grumpy before the night has even begun."

"Am I going to need my stamina?" I ask, flirty.

He smirks. "Perhaps. And a head for heights."

Interesting... They quickly bring our drinks, and I settle back, letting the sound of the music wash over me. Everything with Wren seems far away, and it's a relief to set my questions and fears aside for the evening, and privately celebrate her return.

"Cheers," I say, raising my glass.

"What are we toasting to?" Saint lifts an eyebrow, looking devastatingly handsome in a crisp button-down shirt and black denim, his casual uniform of choice.

"To us," I say, meeting his eyes in a smile. "And unexpected blessings."

"I'll drink to that." Saint clinks his glass to mine and takes a swallow. "Everything about you is unexpected, Tessa Peterson."

He doesn't even know the half of it, but I just smile. "Says the man who keeps a Taylor Swift record hidden in the back of the case. Yes, I found it," I add, smirking. "You're going to have to work harder to hide your guilty pleasures, now I'm living under the same roof."

"Who's guilty?" Saint retorts, his dark eyes sparkling with mirth. "You know me, darling. I embrace all my pleasures wholeheartedly. And for the record, *folklore* is an underrated classic."

I laugh. "Power tools, pop music... I'm learning all kinds of new things about you, *professor*," I tease.

"What about you?" Saint asks, fixing me with a sizzling gaze. "What have you been hiding from me?"

Wren.

I bite back my biggest secret, and pretend to think, instead. "Hmm... You'll just have to find out for yourself, won't you? You have a pretty good track record learning all my dirty little secrets," I add, giving him a sultry look. "Sometimes, I think you can read my mind. You seem to know what I'm thinking, what I *want*, better than I even do myself."

That first party, sitting in the dark with me legs spread to him and my gaze locked on his... In the club, pinned against his body as a soft, foreign mouth slowly licked me into a frenzy... On my back in that ornamental maze, coming my brains out under the stars...

Somehow, Saint has given life to the desires I'd only ever dreamed about; taken my breathless fantasies and made them real. Made *me* more real: A woman who pursues her own pleasure, and claims it without shame; discovering more about my own thrilling, sensual needs with every passing day.

I meet his eyes across the candlelit table, reveling in the sizzle of chemistry in the air between us. "So, what am I thinking now?" I ask, flirty.

Saint's mouth curls in a wolfish grin. "Things that would get us thrown out of this place before they even bring the food."

"Correct."

He leans over, and draws me in for a slow, steamy kiss. "All in good time, darling," he tells me softly. "The night is young. And I have something for you."

I straighten in anticipation, wondering if it's some sexy, playful new toy. But Saint pulls a velvet jewelry box out of his jacket pocket, and places it on the table, nudging it over to me. "Open it," he says, and I blink.

The box looks expensive: deep blue, and discreet. "Saint..." I start, feeling self-conscious. "You've already given me so much..."

But he nudges the box again. I take it, and slowly lift the lid.

I gasp.

Inside, is nestled a gorgeous necklace: a delicate platinum

chain, with a small bird pendant, bejeweled with diamonds and emeralds. As I lift it out, the pendant swings, jewels catching in the candlelight like the bird is taking flight.

"Saint..." I whisper, overcome. "It's beautiful."

"The bird is for Wren," he says softly. "So you can carry her with you, always."

My guilt sparks again, but it's overwhelmed with affection that Saint would search out a gift that has so much meaning to me. "I love it," I swear. "I love you. Thank you."

Saint gets up, rounding the table to help me fasten the delicate clasp around my neck. The pendant nestles in my cleavage, glittering. "You see, I decided to give people *more* excuses to look at your chest," he murmurs playfully, and I laugh, glad to lighten the mood.

"They can look, but you're the only one who gets to touch tonight," I tell him, flirty. "In fact... I love the diamonds, but I'm thinking I need a pearl necklace to go with the gift."

Saint hisses a breath, his gaze drifting over me. My body tightens in response, waiting for him to say the word for us to get out of here, somewhere we can be alone. *On my knees. Mouth open, and ready for his cock...*

But when Saint holds out his hand to me, it's not to yank me from the club. "Later, darling. First... I want to dance."

"Dance?" I echo, surprised. In all the time I've spent with Saint, I can't recall seeing him anywhere near a dance floor.

"Come on."

He leads me to the little dance floor in front of the stage. It's still early, and the club is only half-full. Nobody else is dancing yet, but I couldn't care less as Saint draws me into his arms. "Keep it nice and slow, fellas," he tells the musicians with a grin, and they laugh, and oblige us, segueing into a languid track that makes me think of steamy summer nights.

I rest my head against Saint's chest, and we sway. I'm close enough to feel his heartbeat and lose myself in the warmth of his embrace. His body is taut, pressed against me, and his arms loop around my waist, fingertips resting at the base of my spine. He strokes me softly through the silky fabric of my dress, back and forth, back and forth...

Heat ignites inside me, just from that one, subtle touch.

I shift closer, my breath quickening. Saint keeps us swaying, not skipping a beat.

"I dreamed about you last night," he murmurs, his breath hot against my ear. "You were naked in that necklace, on a tropical beach somewhere..."

I shiver. "Tell me more."

He chuckles, low and seductive. "We were laying in the shade of some palm trees, and you... You were begging me to let you come."

My thighs clench. "Sounds like a fun vacation," I whisper, sounding careless even as my blood gets hotter.

"But I wouldn't let you," Saint says softly, then nips my earlobe with his teeth. "Not until you sucked my cock like a good girl and earned that orgasm. You took it so well for me, darling. Every last inch."

I stifle a moan, so turned on now it should be illegal in a public place. But of course, that only makes me hotter, being surrounded by people while Saint whispers filthy things in my ear.

"Saint," I whisper, my knees weak. "*Please...*"

"What's that, darling? Ready to go?" he asks, sounding amused, and when I lift my head to look at him, there's mischief in his eyes.

"You know I am," I smile back at him, loving the playful teasing, and how he can take me from zero to soaking wet in the space of a single slow dance.

"Then let's go."

. . .

Saint pays our tab and pulls me from the club and into a cab, but instead of directing it towards home, he sends us across the city, to a historic church sitting, unchanged, in the center of the city. By the time we climb out of the car, the sun is setting, and the place is busy. Tourists mill in the courtyard outside, and Saint leads me through the crowd and over to a small doorway in one of the tower walls.

'*No public entry*,' the sign says, but Saint pushes the door open and leads me inside.

"We can't go in," I protest, looking around at the dim, historic rooms. "It's off-limits."

"I called in a favor from a friend," Saint tells me with a wink. "I wanted to give you a private tour."

"Is that right?" I ask, relaxing. Inside, there are a series of old chambers, with the original fireplaces preserved, and displays telling the historical significance. "So what is this place, Mr. Tour Guide?"

"This is Freshfield Tower," Saint says gamely, leading me to a narrow circular staircase, and starting the climb upwards. "It's very old, built... by someone, at some point, in the distant past."

I smile, trying to keep pace. "This is a very informative tour."

"Ah, but the important part isn't what's inside," he continues, as we climb higher. "But what's waiting at the top."

After another flight, I'm out of breath, but then Saint reaches the top and opens the door for me, and I step outside—losing my breath for a different reason.

"Oh, it's beautiful," I exhale, taking it in. We're on the flat roof of the tower, with only a stone balustrade separating us from the view. And what a view... Sunset is streaking the sky over London, and from our vantage point here, at the very top of the tower, I can see the whole city spread beneath us, from Hyde Park, all the way to the river and Parliament.

"I thought you might like it."

When I turn back, Saint is watching me, standing beside a folding table and two chairs, set with an ice bucket of champagne, and a picnic basket. "Dinner," he says with a smile, plucking the champagne out, and uncorking it with a pop.

I laugh, delighted. "It's very romantic," I tell him, leaning in for a kiss. "An A-plus date idea."

"Are you grading me now?" he asks with a smirk.

"That depends..." I take a sip of champagne, straight from the bottle. Loving the way the bubbles feel on my tongue. "What will you do to secure that perfect grade?"

"Oh, I have some ideas..."

Saint takes the bottle from me and has a swig. I can't help drifting back to the balustrade, looking out at the view. Below us, the courtyard is emptying out at closing, the crowds thinning until just a few stragglers remain.

Saint moves behind me, his hands on my waist. "They say King Henry the Eighth used this tower for his private assignations," he murmurs, body warm against me.

"How scandalous," I smile.

"I'll bet he took his women up here, to enjoy the view..." Saint sweeps my hair to one side and drops a sizzling kiss on the bare curve of my neck. "And take a few other things, besides..."

Slowly, he hitches up the skirt of my dress, and teases his fingers over the front of my panties.

I gasp, excitement flaring. "It is a very impressive view," I manage to reply, gazing out over the city. His fingers skim again, teasing softly under the waistband before sliding down, hot against my bare skin.

He buries his fingers between my thighs, sounding a low

groan as he sinks into the slick, wet heat. "You're so wet, darling. You're *drenched.*"

I answer with a soft moan, sinking my head back against his shoulder as he slowly starts to play: Circling my clit in slow, sweet strokes that have me gasping. His other hand grips the stone balcony, which I realize is the perfect height to hide his sinful touching.

"All those people," I manage, breathless with pleasure. "They have no idea what you're doing to me. If they look up, we seem like two people just innocently enjoying the view."

Saint pauses. "You're right," he says. "We should do something about that."

Suddenly, he slides my dress straps down my shoulders, and tugs my bodice down too. I gasp. I'm not wearing a bra, and suddenly, I'm half-naked in nothing but the diamond pendant: my breasts bared to the cool evening air – and anyone who might look up.

"Saint—" I start to protest, instinctively moving back from the balcony, but he stands firm, pinning me in place.

"That's better," he murmurs, voice thick with lust. Then he slips a hand back under my skirt, and resumes his wicked strokes, circling my clit with a swift, sure caress that melts my resistance and leaves me panting.

Oh God.

I look down again, feeling a new, wild thrill take me over. Anyone could look up. Anyone could see...

"Saint," I gasp, thrusting eagerly against his hand.

He chuckles darkly in my ear. "God, I love this exhibitionist kink of yours," Saint growls in approval. "I can feel you clenching, just imagining their eyes on you..."

I feel it too, and when he moves his other hand to palm and play with my breasts, I stifle my moans. It feels so good, too good, already I'm cresting towards my climax, but Saint can read my body like a book now, and he knows just when to pull back.

I give a little whimper of protest.

"Hush," he scolds me, sounding amused. "Now be a good girl and lose those panties."

I do what he says, eagerly wriggling out of them, but leaving my dress rucked around my waist. I catch a flash of his expression as I do it, and the dark, hungry expression in his eyes takes my breath away.

God, I love him like this.

Sure, his tender, attentive side makes my heart sing, and the playful, teasing part of him makes everything better, but *this*?

This is the Saint who makes me weak with desire. In control. Expert. Commanding my pleasure in a way nobody else ever has. Ever could.

All mine.

He spins me around again, so I'm facing out, bent over the balcony. "Want to make a little noise for them, darling?" he chuckles, deep and sexy in my ear. Then he yanks my hips back, spreads my legs, and thrusts into me in one thick, swift stroke.

Oh my God.

I cover my mouth to keep from crying out, lost in the feel of his cock driving deep inside me, pinning me to the balustrade, *fuck, so deep.* It's incredible, and I thrust back against him, eagerly meeting his strokes as we find a dirty, rapid rhythm and the heat starts to rise—

And then he stops. When I'm panting, silently chanting for more, my body taut and my whole world contracting to just the sweet, wild drive of his cock, so close to my climax I can taste it...

He stops.

No!

I bite my lip to keep from wailing, already trying to thrust back and to keep him deep inside. But Saint grips my hips tightly, keeping me pinned there in place as he withdraws, until only the tip of his cock is nudging at my entrance, leaving me shaking and clenching to have him back inside. Filling me up, the way he belongs. The way I *need.*

"Saint, please..." I gasp with longing.

"That's right, darling," I can hear the satisfaction thick in his voice. "If you want my cock, you're going to have to beg for it."

I twist, panting, trying to look at him, but Saint just smirks and turns me firmly back to face the view. The courtyard. And the few people still bustling around below. Right now, they're oblivious to our sexy game, but if I cry out, if I raise my voice at all, they'll hear us.

They'll look up, and see...

Me.

Breasts bouncing, half-naked, bent over the balcony, being fucked senseless.

Oh God.

Excitement and panic hums through me, mingling with the desire already flooding my bloodstream. *I can't.* Not here. *Fuck.* This isn't some masked party, or the privacy of the club. This is in public, broad daylight. Well, sunset. But either way, it's wilder and more shocking than anything we've ever done before.

He can't be serious...

Can he?

"Please," I murmur softly. "Saint, please..."

"I can't hear you, baby." He runs his fingers down my back, scratching softly. Making my whole body shiver, crying out for the friction deep inside where I need it most.

"Please," I whisper again. "Please fuck me."

"Sorry, sweetheart. Not loud enough." Saint lands a teasing spank on my ass, and I yelp. "Oh fuck," he groans, sinking into me, just a little. "You like that, don't you? I can feel your pussy clench."

He spanks me again, and I try to thrust back, needing more of him. Fuck, just a few inches more. I'm so close, teetering on the edge of an epic orgasm, desperate to fall all the way.

But Saint keeps me trapped there, stone rough against my stomach, one hand heavy on my bare back; barely filling me up.

"You know what I'm waiting for," he reminds me, grinding up, just a little. Enough to make me sob. "Ask for it nicely. Ask nice and loud, and I'll give you what you need. All the way to the fucking hilt."

I moan, stranded there on the precipice of pleasure. My whole body is a live wire now, taut with need, and every tiny shift and movement of his swollen cock inside me feels magnified, dragging with a wicked friction, driving me out of my mind.

But there are still people in the courtyard below us. Still people who would hear...

Then his hand slips between my legs again and gives my clit the whisper of a caress.

I can't take it. I break.

"Please!" the word falls from my lips in a fevered cry. "Please, more!"

"Louder." Saint rubs me again, and I sob, out of my mind.

"Please! Oh God, please fuck me!"

"Louder, baby."

"Saint!" My voice rings out loudly—*fuck, too loud!*—as Saint finally grips my hips, yanks me back, and slams all the way home with a ragged groan.

Oh. My. God.

I scream, my voice echoing in pleasure over the courtyard.

Someone turns, looking up. A woman, I see, as the thrill and shame and pleasure hit me like a tidal wave, but then Saint is snapping his hips, driving into me again, deeper this time, *fuck*, and I lose my mind in the illicit rush. I squeeze my eyes shut and just surrender to the moment, not caring about anything but the thick thrust of his cock and his low groans of pleasure and the relentless rhythm that fills me up, *owns me*, drives me over the edge.

I explode, climaxing with a howl that I swear they could hear clear across London as pleasure wracks my body and blots my mind clean.

"Christ, baby..." Saint fucks me through it, his movements turning frenzied as I wail and shake in his arms. "Fucking clench my cock, just like that. Good girl. *Fuck...*"

He comes with a low roar, shuddering his climax into me, and we collapse forward together, sweaty and gasping against the balcony.

I gulp for air, finally opening my eyes again.

The courtyard is empty. The woman is gone.

Holy shit.

I let out a gasp of thrilled laughter, and feel a rumbling chuckle from Saint, too. "Oh my God," I mutter, reeling. My body is flooded with pleasure, humming and lit up. "What *was* that?"

"That was your discovery kink, darling."

Saint withdraws, and zips up before tenderly turning me to face him. He looks far too collected and smug for a man who just made me lose my mind, but I can't even hate him for it, not when he kisses me softly, as sweet now as his body was just demanding. I melt in his arms, feeling breathless.

Feeling *incredible.*

"I didn't even know that was a thing," I admit, beaming.

He laughs. "Oh yes. It's a good one. The open office door...

the people in the garden just outside... The risk of someone walking in and catching us, seeing you taking my cock."

I shiver. "I like it," I admit. My heart is pounding in my chest, and I know, it's not just because of him. The moments we're alone together are mind-blowing enough, but this...?

This was something else.

"Between that and your exhibitionist side... You're going to keep me a busy man," Saint muses, kissing my forehead. "Busy, and hard as a fucking rock."

I laugh, about to nestle into his arms, when suddenly, we hear the sound of footsteps from the stairwell.

Somebody's coming!

I panic. The risk of discovery is one thing, but actually getting busted half-naked in a public place—

"Relax," Saint orders me softly. In one swift motion, he pulls my dress back up, and then tugs me over to the picnic table, pulling me into his lap and pressing a champagne glass into my hand, so that when the aging security guard emerges onto the rooftop, panting from the climb, he finds us sitting together sharing a romantic drink.

Perfectly innocent.

"Everything alright?" Saint asks calmly, as if a minute ago he wasn't buried to the hilt, fucking me senseless.

As if my thighs weren't sticky with his come under this dress.

"Aye. I think so." The man looks around, clearly puzzled. "We had some reports about a noise. A woman screaming..."

I try not to choke on the champagne.

"Really?" Saint squeezes my hip, but he doesn't skip a beat. "We didn't hear anything, did we, darling?"

I shake my head, worried that if I open my mouth at all, I'll start giggling.

"Perhaps it was the birds?" Saint suggests. "They can make a terrible racket sometimes."

"Aye..." The guard looks around again, downcast to have missed out on some drama. "Sorry to interrupt, Mr. St. Clair."

"Perfectly alright," Saint says cheerfully. "Safety first, and all that. Have a biscuit for your troubles," he adds, offering a box from the picnic basket.

The guard brightens. "Don't mind if I do."

He takes a cookie, and then returns the way he came, leaving us alone.

I finally let out the laugh I've been holding in. "I didn't know there were guards on patrol!" I protest, hitting him playfully.

Saint grins. "Why, would that have made you hotter?"

I pause. "Probably," I admit, smirking.

"Is it the uniform, or...?"

"Saint!" I laugh again, and he raises the champagne bottle.

"Unexpected blessings, hmm?" he says, echoing my earlier toast.

I beam, snuggling against him. There's definitely nothing expected about life with Anthony St. Clair...

I just have to hope he likes surprises as much as I do.

Because I meant what I said to him when I promised not to keep secrets anymore. I touch the jeweled pendant dangling from my throat. The bird, in flight. Wren. He wanted me to keep her close, but the truth is, she's closer than he ever could imagine.

And when I tell him, I know that everything could change.

Chapter 5

Saint

I could get used to this...

I wake in bed, with Tessa sprawled naked beside me. She's sleeping soundly, perfectly at peace. I like to think I played a part in that, wearing her out so thoroughly last night with my hands, my tongue, my cock...

I smile, watching her slumber, hair spilled in a halo around her head and her breasts bared, already making my cock stir beneath the sheets. Christ, this woman... She's a whirl of contradictions and playful new discoveries, and even though I've spent my life in search of novelty and adventure, I know that I've barely scratched the surface of her delightful, sexy imagination.

And now she's here. Not just in my bed, but in my home, too. Her clothes in the closet, her books and papers mingling with mine on the shelves. Her favorite brand of American biscuits in the pantry, and her shampoo perched on the bathroom ledge. I've been half-expecting to have a moment of regret since she moved in—the natural reaction of a man who's spent his life living entirely on his own terms—but instead, the second thoughts haven't so much as crossed my mind. All I am is...

Happy.

No restless itch, no brain working overtime, just that simple contentment settling deep in my bones that I haven't felt in years. As if everything has finally clicked into place for me, and now I finally know my place in the world after a lifetime of reckless searching.

No longer the disappointing second son, the rebel heir, or wayward professor.

Just *her man.*

I finally get out of bed and go take a shower. Work at Ashford HQ is at a breakneck speed these days, and I know everyone is buzzing for the publication of the test results review, coming any day now. Finally, a treatment for Alzheimer's... I'm on top of the world just thinking about it, and the difference it's going to make, the lives it'll help. I may have spent my life resisting my family name, but now, I'm actually proud of the work they've been doing. Of course, their motive has always been profit, not progress, but this time, the end results will be the same.

I just wish my older brother, Edward, was alive to share in this moment. Fuck, he'd be so happy, knowing that the St. Clair family was making a positive mark on the world, following his selfless example and commitment to help people, and using our privilege and wealth for something good. Already, I'm thinking ahead to the ways we can use these results to direct other research in related fields, degenerative neurological diseases like Parkinson's, Huntington's...

I could spearhead it all. Come into the Ashford fold, the way my parents always wanted—but on my own terms. And with Tessa by my side, doing her own philanthropic work at the Foundation...

Maybe this can be the start of a whole new chapter for us all.

I'm still smiling when I dress, and step back into the bedroom to find Tessa awake, doing something on her phone. She sees me, and quickly tucks it away, giving me a sleepy, satisfied smile that's like a bolt to my heart.

"Good morning," she says softly.

"Yes..." I say, moving over to give her a kiss. Her body is warm, and curls against me like she was made to fit. "It is."

"I had that dream of yours," she says, stretching again.

"Which one?" I ask, distracted by the curve of her ass. Hell, this moment right now feels like a dream. The prelude to a particularly filthy one...

"The tropical beach," she says, sitting up and fixing me with a flirty look. "You and me, little drinks with umbrellas in it, wild vacation sex..."

"Oh really?" I arch an eyebrow, grinning. "Tell me, what in particular is special about vacation sex?"

"The coconuts," Tessa replies, with a playful grin.

I laugh, pulling her closer for a real kiss, the kind of slow, sensual exploration that makes her body flush and her eyes turn glassy. But before I can tip her back into the pillows and show her that I don't need tropical fruit to make her come screaming, she pulls away. "I'm too hungry to function. Ravenous," she adds, and bats her eyelashes at me.

I can take a hint, especially when it's delivered by the naked woman who has my heart in a chokehold. "Breakfast, then," I agree, smiling. Her phone buzzes again, and she checks the screen.

"I'll be right down."

I make my way to the kitchen and put some music on as I collect eggs and veggies for a simple scramble. It's a dreary, overcast day, typical for November in London, and I can't help thinking of that tropical beach somewhere... Max and Annabelle's wedding is in a week, and I wouldn't miss my old friend getting hitched for the world, but after that, there's no reason why I can't whisk Tessa away for a little sunshine. And some coconuts...

I'm just sliding some toast onto her plate when Tessa comes in, cheeks pink from the shower, dressed in comfy jeans and an oversized sweater. "*Le petit dejeuner* is served," I say, setting the plate down with a flourish. But she pauses in the doorway, biting her lip. "What is it? I promise, I fished out all the shell," I add.

She smiles, but looks reluctant. "I have something to tell you," she says softly.

"You hate my eggs?" I joke.

She shakes her head, looking more serious now. "I know I shouldn't have kept it secret," Tessa says in a rush. "But I promised, and I didn't want to spook her, not right away, and—"

Before I can ask what on earth she means, the doorbell sounds.

Tessa looks relieved. "I'll explain everything," she reassures me, before disappearing down the hall to answer it. A moment later, I hear voices, another woman talking with Tessa as they approach the kitchen.

"... Are you sure he won't be back—"

Then they're in the doorway, and the strange woman stops dead, looking at me in fear and panic. "You said he was out, that it was safe to meet here!" she cries, and Tessa immediately leaps to soothe her.

"It's OK, I promise, we can trust him—"

"Tessa, no!" She's got dirty brown hair under a ballcap, bundled up in a shapeless coat and scarf.

"Please, just calm down and listen for a moment," Tessa

implores her. "We need him if we're going to figure out how to end this. Five minutes, that's all. Please, Wren..."

Wren?

I stare at the stranger in disbelief as they bicker. Tessa showed me her sister in photos, and now, if I look closer, I can see the resemblance: the same bright, intelligent eyes and jawline, even under the ratty hair and smudged makeup.

It's her.

But how in the world...?

"Does someone want to tell me what's going on?" I finally ask, my voice coming out far calmer and more reasonable than I feel, for a man who's staring at a ghost.

A ghost whose death has been haunting Tessa every moment I've known her, driving her to unthinkable lengths.

"There's something you need to know," Tessa takes a deep breath, then turns to Wren. "Tell him," she instructs her sister firmly.

"No—" Wren tries to argue, but Tessa stares her down.

"Yes. It's time, Wren. Tell him everything you told me, about Ashford, and the drug trials. I'm not going to keep this secret from him. I love him, and he needs to know the truth."

And just like that, my whole world turns upside down.

Ten minutes later, I'm sitting at the table with Tessa and Wren, dumbstruck by the news: Wren was never really dead—and the reason for her disappearance.

"I'm so sorry," Tessa says, taking my hand. "She showed up Friday night, after the party. I wanted to tell you, but she made me promise not to."

"It's OK," I reassure her. Christ, she must have been over the moon to see Wren again. Even now in the midst of all this drama, I can tell, she can't help but look at her sister and smile. To have Wren back, after thinking she was gone forever...

I couldn't be angry, not when this means so much to Tessa.

"I didn't even know what was going on until we met again, and she explained everything," she adds.

I snap back to reality at her words. *Everything* being the massive fraud being perpetrated by my family's company... And the fact they may have kidnapped and assaulted Wren to scare her from revealing the truth.

"Faked... How?" I demand, not wanting to believe it. Our Alzheimer's drug, the future of the entire company, all nothing but a sham?

Wren sighs. She's still looking at me with suspicion, and clearly doesn't trust me, but Tessa nods, urging her on. "Explain it—to me, too. In plain English," she adds. "Not your science talk."

"The drug we were developing was designed to stop certain plaques forming on the brain. They were testing on mice, it's the stage before human trials," Wren tells us. "When I came in, they'd already finished that phase and the results were so good, they were fast-tracking the human trials."

I nod slowly. I skimmed the info packets a few weeks ago.

"But... I was running some modelling on the test results when I found anomalies," Wren continues. "The data set I was using didn't match the official results. The clinical markers were way underperforming, compared with the published results."

"The drugs didn't work?" Tessa translates.

Her sister nods. "Not the way they needed to, to continue the research. And definitely not enough to move to human trials. I thought maybe the data set was corrupted somehow, or they were outdated results, so I flagged it for my boss at the lab. And then everything happened..." she says, her face turning shadowed. "And

I knew that it wasn't a mistake. They faked the results and moved ahead with the human trials, and they needed me to keep quiet."

I get up, and start to pace, trying to make sense of it. *Christ, this is a nightmare.* All the hopeful patients and families that have been holding out for a miracle, waiting for Ashford to publish the new trial results...

I pause, struck with a sudden hope. "Even if what you're saying is true, and the animal tests were all faked, how do we know the human trials didn't work?" I ask, seizing on the gap in her story. "Those results could be genuine!"

Wren shakes her head. "If that drug protocol didn't work in mice, it *can't* have worked in humans! The results showed no improvement in the plaque development, no improvements in cognition. There's just no chance. The science doesn't work that way."

"And why would they come after her?" Tessa asks me quietly, her eyes wide. "Why would they threaten her, halfway across the world? Nobody cares what happened to a bunch of lab mice a year ago. Not unless..."

She doesn't finish. She doesn't have to.

Not unless the fraud has continued. Not unless the next set of drug trials were altered, too.

Not unless Ashford's entire future is being built on a lie.

"What I don't understand, is how they think they can get away with this." Tessa frowns. "Surely once the drug is released, people will realize it doesn't work?"

Wren shakes her head. "Even if a medication only shows, say, a 10% improvement in some patients, sometimes that's enough to justify making it available to everyone. And for a disease like Alzheimer's, that has no other proven treatment, people will leap on that chance, however small..."

"It's why Ashford has sunk so much into the research," I

agree, numb. "Whoever finds something that works—even just a little—they'll own the entire market. Zero competition. And a degenerative disease like this, it's hard to track someone's progress. They could just claim a patient would have declined even faster without the drug."

"Which is why the controlled trials are so important," Wren says tightly. "That data is the only real proof anyone will have that the drug works."

The scale of the lies is unbelievable. Rolling out a drug they know is useless to millions of people around the world...

"Something like this... The faked results. The cover-up. Who at Ashford would have known?" I ask, already sick to my stomach.

"It wouldn't need to be many," Wren shakes her head. "The edits could have been slipped in as soon as the results came in. They just forgot to scrub the original file from the data server. And my colleagues, they never would have stood for it," she adds fiercely. "You don't fake the data. It's a cardinal sin of science."

"Your boss, that you reported it to," Tessa asks. "Could he have made the changes?"

"She." Wren corrects her, and nods. "The project was her baby, Valerie had eyes on everything. Dr. DeJonge," she explains.

Tessa and I exchange a look.

"What?" Wren asks.

"Dr. DeJonge died, a couple of weeks ago. A car wreck," I answer slowly, my very bad feeling getting even worse.

Wren looks stunned. "They got to her, too."

I open my mouth to argue it was drunk driving, a tragic accident, but then I pause. Chilled to the bone.

How do I know that for sure?

I remember the conversations I overheard, snatches in his hospital room.

"My father was paying her, off the books," I tell them. "She was threatening to reveal something. I thought it was an affair, but maybe it was blackmail instead."

If Valerie was blackmailing my dad, threatening to reveal the truth about the project... She was a liability. One more obstacle in the way of Ashford's success.

Just how far would my father go to protect the company, protect the family name?

I sink down in a seat again. I can see from Tessa's troubled expression that she's thinking the same thing.

"What do we do now?" she asks, and it takes me a moment to realize, she's asking me.

"Evidence," I reply at last, pulling my shit together. "We need evidence of the trial fraud before we even think about anything else. Wren?"

She shakes her head, looking frustrated. "I don't have anything. I told you, I reported it to Valerie. My system access was revoked, right after, she said it was a tech mix-up and they'd sort it all out, and then the party happened... When I got back to work, my server access was restricted, but by then, I didn't care. I had other things on my mind," she adds grimly. Tessa reaches over and gives her arm a sympathetic squeeze. I'm reminded again of the brutal lengths somebody has been going to in order to cover up this fraud.

Assault, threats, maybe even murder...

What else are these people capable of?

"You need to stay hidden," I tell Wren. "Right now, you're the only person who can expose what's been going on. They need to think you're still dead."

She nods, still looking at me with distrust in her eyes. "You keep saying 'They,' but you're one of them, aren't you?" she challenges me. "You're a St. Clair. The heir to all of this."

"Wren—" Tessa speaks up, but I interrupt her.

"Yes, I'm one of them," I agree. "It's my family's name above the door. Which makes me your best chance of uncovering the truth."

Wren doesn't like that, I can tell, but even she can see the logic. "You can get the evidence?"

"I can try," I say grimly. "This original data, the proof you found. Would they still have it?"

"I think so," she nods. "Data like that, you wouldn't wipe it. You'd need it to keep modelling similar upgrades to results all the way down the line."

"Never mind the science," I shake my head. "Where can I find it?"

Wren pauses.

"It wouldn't be on the server in Oxford anymore, not after I stumbled over it," she says slowly, and I can see her brilliant mind at work, running over the possibilities. "Ashford headquarters, here in London," she decides finally. "The VIP labs, security is as tight as they come. I only visited a couple of times, and even then, they didn't let me out of their sight. I heard a colleague talk about the backup servers there. That's where the original trial data will be. Can you get access?" she asks.

I pause. "Probably. I've never stepped foot down in the basement before, so it might raise some eyebrows but... We'll cross that bridge when we come to it."

Wren nods. "Phillip can help," she says. "Even just point us to the right server regions."

"Phillip?" I ask.

"He worked with me on the research team," Wren replies. "He would be horrified to know they're misrepresenting the data like this. He's our way in."

"He's a good guy," Tessa agrees. "And we need him."

"I don't know," I say, reluctant. "We don't know who else we can trust."

"I'm not sure I even trust you," Wren snaps, but I hold her gaze calmly.

"I love Tessa. I'll do anything to protect her, anything she wants," I emphasize fiercely. "And she loves you. Which is why I'm letting you sit here in my house and imply that I'm involved with this whole plot. That I would support lies and fraud, and even murder."

"Saint—" Tessa tries to protest. "She doesn't mean—"

"Yes, I do." Wren narrows her eyes at me, assessing. I stare back, not flinching for a moment. And whatever she sees in my face must pass some kind of test, because finally, she exhales. "Fine. Maybe you are totally oblivious to what's been going on right under your nose."

"My, thank you," I answer dryly.

"Guys," Tessa speaks up. "We don't have time for this."

She's right. "Fine. You organize a meet with this Phillip man, and I'll work on keeping Wren hidden," I say.

I take my phone, and step outside the back door, dragging in a long breath of the chilled November air.

I need to think clearly. I'm not sure Wren and Tessa realize the stakes of what we're discussing here, but I do.

Which means I have to keep them safe.

I call my cousin, Imogen. "I need a favor," I say, as soon as she picks up the phone.

"What happened to all the pleasantries?" she teases me. "How have you been? How's work? Did your date with the man from the tennis club go well?"

"No man who plays tennis on the weekends could ever keep up with you," I reply shortly. "This is serious, Immie. I need to borrow your place in the country for a little while."

"Of course," she says, sounding surprised. "I need to be here in town for work the next few weeks, anyway."

"Good." I take another breath, thinking fast. "What's the security like?"

Imogen pauses. "Nothing fancy. I have Ring cameras, and a remote app for the alarms. Why?" she asks, and then clearly thinks the better of it. "You know what? I don't need to know. I'll email you the security codes and a link to share the videos."

"I knew you were my favorite St. Clair," I tell her gratefully.

She laughs. "There's not much competition. It's either me, or Cousin Miles, or your brother in the running."

She hangs up, but I stand there a moment longer, realizing what she said.

My brother. *Robert.* Fuck. He's been running around at Ashford, trying his best to make this rollout a success. He'll be devastated to learn the truth about what's been going on. My mother, too.

But I can't think about that right now. I have to stay focused on the most important thing: Protecting Tessa, and keeping her sister safe. I don't know who was behind Wren's attack or the threats, but they've made it clear, they're willing to hurt Tessa to get to her.

I won't let that happen. Not at long as I'm alive to draw breath.

The door opens, and Tessa steps outside. She doesn't say anything at first, just moves straight to me and wraps her arms around me, burying her face against my chest.

I hold her tightly. As much as I'm reeling right now, I can't imagine the rollercoaster of emotions she must have experienced over the past few days.

"I'm so sorry," she says finally, lifting her face.

"You're sorry?" I echo. "What do you have to be sorry for? This is my family. Our crimes. My father..."

I trail off, not able to say it out loud just yet.

Tessa's face clouds with tender sympathy. "Do you really think he's capable of being behind all of this?" she asks softly. "Falsifying the trial data is one thing, but going after Wren... Valerie's 'accident'...?"

Fraud. Violence. Murder.

The accusations hang, heavy in the air. I search my heart for excuses or explanations, but in the end, I have to give a slow, resigned nod. "He's not a criminal mastermind," I say, thinking of the man who raised me. Judgmental, sure. Absent, and single-minded, of course. But a cold-blooded killer?

No.

"The thing about my father is, he's weak," I say with a sigh. "Greedy. The Ashford reputation is everything to him, and I can see how all of this might have gotten out of control. If initial trials failed, and he tried to cover them up... Maybe he genuinely thought the human tests would be different, or maybe by then he'd already sunk too much into this one drug succeeding... I can imagine how easily the lies all mounted up."

"But what about the attack on Wren?" Tessa reminds me quietly. "And Valerie's death?"

I can't imagine my father with blood on his hands. I just can't.

"Maybe he isn't alone in the fraud," I wonder. "There are other investors with everything riding on this drug launch. Powerful people. With the connections to make bad things happen."

"Like Cyrus Lancaster," Tessa says, "Max's father. He's a big Ashford investor, isn't he?"

"Yes," I agree, chilled. "Hugh's father, too. Lionel Ambrose has staked his political reputation on Ashford Pharma, it would ruin his chances if a scandal like this got out."

Tessa gulps. "No big deal, then," she says brightly. "Our suspect list just includes the most powerful men in the country."

Powerful people who will stop at nothing to keep their secrets hidden.

"Promise me you'll be careful now?" I demand, taking hold of her shoulders. I look into her eyes, urgent. "I mean it, Tessa. Whoever these people are, they're not fucking around. Billions of pounds are on the line. And compared to that..."

"We're all expendable," Tessa finishes, looking pale.

"It's going to be alright," I promise her, drawing her into my arms again. I hold her, fueled by a new sense of purpose. Of protection.

No matter what happens next, I won't let anyone hurt her.

She's mine, and I'm going to keep her safe. Whatever the price.

Chapter 6

Tessa

"Are you sure that red SUV doesn't look familiar?" Wren asks, peering out of the car window and fretting as the driver takes us across town to meet Phillip. "I thought I saw it, parked back near Saint's place."

I check. "It wasn't there," I reassure her.

"I'm certain," Wren frowns. "It could be following us."

"The license plate reads 'MR BIG,'" I point out with a smile. "If they're trying to stay inconspicuous... That car isn't the way to do it."

Wren sits back, anxiously toying with the fraying cuff on her oversized parka. Even though she's still vibrating with tension, I can't help but smile, just looking at her.

My sister, alive again.

She sees me looking. "What?"

"Nothing, just... Admiring your new look," I say, teasing her over her disguise. "Very stylish. What is it, grunge chic? And the eyeliner, too. Bold."

Wren gives me a small smile. "I was running for my life,"

she points out, patting her ratty dyed hair. "I didn't exactly have time to go to a salon."

"No, I like it," I smile. "I hear backcombing is in this season."

"We can't all be getting spa treatments, living the life of luxury," she shoots back. "You're the regular kept woman these days."

"I am not!" I protest.

"Are too," Wren smirks. "Nice digs, your future duke has. Rich, handsome... Tell me he's got a small dick he's overcompensating for, or it really will be unfair."

I give her an airy grin. "A lady doesn't kiss and tell. But I will say... Saint is gifted. In all departments."

"Bitch," Wren laughs.

"Thank you," I beam back, feeling a rush of nostalgia and affection. How many nights did we sit up, gossiping over guys? How many times did I take that easy banter for granted, assuming she would always be around?

I'll never take it for granted again.

"You really trust Saint, don't you?" Wren asks me, looking just as nostalgic as I feel. "I can see it in the way you look at him."

I nod. "I love him," I answer. "He's had my back from the beginning, every step of the way. Even when I suspected his best friends of being behind your attack, he didn't hesitate to step up and do the right thing. It may have started as a wild fling, but... I trust him with my life now."

Wren gives me a small smile. "I don't think I've ever seen you like this over a guy," she says. "So happy and comfortable with him."

"You mean, despite the looming conspiracy and threats?" I crack dryly.

"Pesky details," she grins back, and I have to laugh.

I know that we're in the middle of something big, something dangerous, but sitting here talking like this with her... It fills my heart with joy. Somehow it feels like everything's going to be OK.

The glass divider between us and the driver slides down. "We're here," he tells us, pulling over outside a swanky apartment building, right in the heart of Spitalfields, a buzzing shopping district in a historic area, full of expensive boutiques and restaurants.

I look around as we get out, confused. This place screams money, and from what I've seen of Phillip, he's more of a worn-out tennis shoes and threadbare sweaters kind of guy.

Wren must be thinking the same thing, because she pauses on the sidewalk. "Are you sure this is the right address?"

"It's the one he texted," I reply with a shrug. I didn't tell Phillip anything about Wren in our messages, just that I needed to speak to him ASAP. So, we head inside, through the gleaming marble lobby, and hit the button for his floor.

As we swoop up, I wonder what he'll say when he sees Wren. I got the impression that he had a crush on her when they worked together, so I know he'll be overjoyed to see her again.

Joy doesn't even begin to describe it.

"What...? How...?" he gapes at her when he opens the door. Wren gives her old friend a massive hug, and then a playful shove.

"Since when do you wear designer suits?" she teases.

Phillip stays frozen in place. "This is impossible," he whispers, looking like he's just seen a ghost.

Which, technically he has.

"You're the scientist," Wren says with a grin. "So how about you let us in, and start analyzing the sensory data?" She gives his arm a pinch as Phillip stands aside, looking dazed.

Inside, I let Wren fill him in with the bare bones details of what's happened. He takes it the same was as Saint did—with wide-eyed disbelief.

"Impossible," he shakes his head. "Valerie would never compromise the research like that. It was her life's work!"

"Work that produced no successful results," Wren reminds him gently. "She was determined that this protocol was the key to everything, she staked her reputation on it. And Ashford Pharma's entire future, too. If it failed... Can't you imagine she might help cover up the real results, to buy us all more time?"

Phillip exhales slowly. "It's *possible*," he admits, looking reluctant.

"So you'll help us?" I ask eagerly. "We need someone with access to the research and data to look for the evidence that Wren saw. And now that you're head of the department, it's even better. You can check all the records."

He looks back and forth between us. "I don't know what use I can be," he says anxiously. "The research phase is long since over. All the original data will be filed away, who knows where? I'm just filling in as lead, until they find somebody else and—"

"Phillip, please." Wren leans closer and takes his hand. "We need your help on this. I need you."

She gazes at him, and Phillip seems to melt under her stare. "Of course I'll help you," he says, gazing back. "As soon as I get into work today, I'll start looking. Where do you think it'll be stored? Valerie's files are a mess," he adds. "You know what she was like when it came to organization."

While they discuss server logs and data sets, I move to the window. It's a chic, luxurious apartment full of high-tech gadgets, and a gorgeous view of the city.

"Where are my manners?" Phillip jerks to his feet suddenly. "I haven't offered you anything to drink. Tea?

Coffee? La Croix?" he adds to Wren, and she laughs, clearly over some in-joke.

"If you're offering..."

He moves to the gleaming kitchen area and opens a massive fridge, neatly organized with sparkling drinks and expensive foods.

"What happened to suffering in the name of science?" Wren teases him, clearly happy to see her old friend again.

Phillip looks bashful, handing her a soda. "It's a corporate rental, Ashford is footing the bill. They needed me down here in London in a hurry, you see, to take over as head researcher after Valerie... After, well..."

After she died. Potentially murdered.

"Will you be safe?" he asks Wren, suddenly looking concerned. "My god, if Valerie's death really wasn't accidental..."

"I'll be fine," Wren reassures him. "We're leaving London right after this, to stash me safely in the country. I'm sure I won't find any trouble lurking in Farleigh-Under-Lyme," she adds with a grin, naming the small village where Imogen's country house is located.

Phillip nods, looking relieved. "Keep me updated. I'll call you, Tessa, as soon as I have any information."

"Good." I nod. "And thank you, Phillip. I know this isn't easy, but all we're trying to do is get to the truth."

He gives a smile, even as I see the conflict in his eyes. "Anything for Wren."

Saint picks us up from Phillip's building, and we hit the road, stopping only to pick up groceries and a duffel of Wren's belongings from the dingy hostel where she was staying.

"I've never seen you travel so light," I tease, as she tosses the bag in the backseat. "What happened to your deep conditioning mask, textbooks, five different novels...?"

"I learned to keep it simple, and move fast," Wren replies. I catch a glimpse of her distant, haunted look in the rearview mirror as we pull away again. I feel a pang. She's been running all this time, always looking over her shoulder, hiding in the shadows.

And the hiding isn't over yet.

"Well, I'm sure Imogen keeps this place fully stocked," I say warmly. "She strikes me as the kind of woman who has the best of everything. In fact, I bet you ten bucks she has at least five different kinds of face masks and scrubs."

Saint lets out a snort beside me. "Ten," he offers.

"It's a bet."

We soon leave the city behind and drive out into the open countryside; the highway turning into winding two-lane roads, bumpy with mud, and the sprawl of suburban houses replaced by empty fields, woodland, and a few charming villages. After about an hour's driving, Saint turns down an even bumpier track, and finally pulls up outside a charming cottage, nestled in the trees. It's set way back from the road, hidden from view, and in the middle of nowhere.

The perfect place to hide.

We climb out of the car, and even Wren looks more relaxed as she takes a deep breath of country air. "This is great," I tell Saint with a smile. "Thank you."

"Imogen sent all the security details," he says, punching in a code for the door, and leading us inside. The house is decorated in an elegant country style, with lots of overstuffed furniture and floral prints. The rooms are small and cozy, low ceilings and historic wooden beams, but with all the modern touches I'd expect from Imogen. "There are alarms on the doors, and a couple of cameras, too," Saint explains, as we take a look around. "Although, she warned me that they'll get tripped by animals sometimes. Foxes and rabbits from the woods. So if you get an alert, don't panic."

Wren nods slowly. "I'm afraid I'm pretty much wired to panic, these days," she says with a wry smile.

"Ooh look, she's got a flatscreen TV, a nice wood-burning fireplace..." I announce brightly, wanting to lighten the mood. "You can curl up with a glass of wine and watch all the BBC Austen adaptations your heart desires. I've half a mind to stay here with you," I add, meaning it. I don't like the thought of Wren out here by herself. Or anywhere alone right now.

She's been on her own for too long.

But Wren seems to pull herself together. "You can't stay. You need to be back in London, carrying on like normal," she tells me firmly. "We don't know how closely they're keeping tabs on you, especially this close to their big announcement. Tensions will be running high."

I think of all the warnings I got to back off my investigations into Wren. She wanted me to stop digging around, but she wasn't the only one. The man who assaulted me in Oxford... The suspicious noises I heard outside Saint's flat.

The feeling like I was being watched.

"I don't know," I reply, still reluctant to leave her. "Saint can cover for me. Wouldn't I be safer here with you?"

"Annabelle's hen do is tomorrow," Saint reminds me. "You know she'll cause a fuss if you don't show up. And if you stay, then I'm not leaving either," he adds, determined.

Dammit. Saint needs to act normal more than any of us—and use his position at Ashford to uncover whatever he can.

"Fine, I'll come back to London," I agree reluctantly. "But text me every hour," I order Wren. "Every half-hour."

"Relax," she rolls her eyes. "I'm the big sister, remember? I'm supposed to be the one giving you the lectures about staying safe. And besides, I have the TV and wine. It'll be like a vacation for me. God knows I need one."

I know she's just trying to make me feel better. I pull her into a hug, emotional. "I just got you back," I tell her, muffled against her hair. "I can't lose you again."

"You won't." Wren pulls back and gives me a reassuring nod. "Nobody knows I'm here. This is the safest place for me to be. Now, you two should get back on the road," she nudges me towards the hall. "I'm going to take an hour-long shower and wash my hair."

"Then I definitely won't stand in your way," I sniffle, trying to pull it together. "Because I love you, big sister, but you need it!"

We drive back to London in comfortable silence. I'm suddenly worn out from the emotion and drama of the past few days, and Saint can clearly tell, because the moment we're back at his London house, he takes me by the hand and leads me up to the calm of the main bathroom suite.

"Sit," he tells me gently, perching me on the armchair in the corner. Then he starts the faucets running into the massive claw-foot tub, checking the temperature and adding a whole bottle of lavender bath oils, until there are bubbles billowing, and the room is filled with a fragrant steam. "Don't move," he tells me, before disappearing downstairs again.

I couldn't if I tried.

Wren's reappearance, her shocking revelations... It's been a whirlwind, and that's on top of my decision to quit Oxford and move in with Saint, taking our relationship to the next level. But sitting there, exhausted, I still feel a sense of peace deep in my heart. Despite everything, I know I'm exactly where I need to be.

With him.

Saint returns, carrying a tray of my favorite snacks, and a steaming pot of tea. "I brought supplies," he says with a warm smile.

"Angel," I smile back. "Although, you might have to carry me to the tub, I don't think I can move a muscle."

"Undressing you...? Hmm, what a chore," he teases, setting the tray down on a stool beside the tub. Then he does just that: peeling my clothes slowly from my body, until I'm naked, and sinking into the hot water with a sigh of relief.

"That feels amazing..." I say, leaning back into the bubbles.

"Good." Saint knees beside the bathtub and reaches for a soft washcloth. "You need to relax. You must have been running on pure adrenaline since Wren showed up again. The body can't keep it up without crashing," he adds, dowsing the cloth, and slowly running it across my shoulders.

I melt into his touch, feeling the stress leave my body with every slow, deliberate stroke. He massages my back and arms, running the damp cloth over my aching limbs until I'm almost liquid.

But still, I can't shake the worries in the back of my mind. "I hate all this lying and sneaking around," I confide softly. "We just got to this place where I was going to leave all that behind me for good, and start a new chapter, and now... Now it's all more complicated than ever, and you're the one who's going to have to lie, as well."

Saint gives a rueful smile. "I know, baby," he says, sitting beside the tub. "I can't say I'm looking forward to going in to work at Ashford tomorrow and looking them all in the eye. Wondering what they know. Who's behind this.... I thought that the company was finally doing good work," he adds. "Changing the world for the better. But now... It's all just a lie."

I feel an ache for him. We're talking about his family here. Flesh and blood.

"I've ruined everything for you," I whisper, feeling guilty. If I'd never turned his world upside down... If we'd never met...

"No," Saint says fiercely, cupping my cheek. "You saved me, Tessa. I was killing time, amusing myself with meaningless distractions. I thought just opting out of my family bullshit was enough, but you've showed me there's something more than that. Something real. This matters, what we're doing," he adds, eyes full of determination. "The truth matters. Doing the right thing, and making a stand, no matter what the cost."

My heart melts. I reach for him, kissing him passionately, his mouth hot and searching against mine as I run my fingers through his rumpled hair and slide my tongue deep to tangle with his.

Saint groans against my mouth, and the sound shivers through me. The sound of raw desire. I pull away, and rise to my feet, the water running off my naked body.

He gazes up at me for a moment, full of reverence, and I feel a hum of power. When he looks at me like that, I feel like the center of the universe. *Invincible.* I hold out my hand, already breathless with wanting him.

"Take me," I tell him boldly. "Saint... I need all of you tonight."

He rises to his feet, his expression turning dark and hungry now. "Is that so, darling?"

He takes my hand and helps me step out of the bath. Still naked. Still wet—and getting wetter by the moment. "How, exactly do you want me?" he murmurs, settling a towel around my shoulders, his hands skimming my damp curves. "On my knees for you, baby? Giving that sweet pussy the tongue-lashing it deserves? Or on my back, watching those magnificent tits bounce as you milk my cock dry?"

I give a moan at the filthy images, swaying into his warm hands. He slips his fingers between my legs, dragging them lightly through my drenched core. Saint sounds a hiss of satisfaction. "So wet for me, aren't you? You're going to feel like heaven... But first, I need a taste."

He withdraws his hand, and brings it to his lips, slowly licking his fingers clean as his eyes stay locked on mine.

My stomach twists. *Fuck, it's hot.* Watching him savor me, like the finest wine.

"Your turn." He moves his fingers to my mouth, and slowly pushes one inside. I shudder with an illicit thrill, tasting myself on his skin as I close my lips around him and suck.

Saint growls. "That mouth of yours is going to be the death of me. I knew it the minute you talked back in class," he adds, as I slowly swirl my tongue over the pad of his fingertip. "You were giving me a piece of your mind, and all I could think about was how beautiful you'd look on your knees with my cock in your mouth."

I moan, already light-headed and panting. God, he always knows just what to say. How to tease and provoke me, to spark that fire of lust inside.

"And this body of yours..." Saint lets the towel drop, and stands back, eyes roaming over me. "One day I'm going to tie you down and come over every inch of you. Spend the day making you scream with pleasure, and jacking off over your perfect tits, until you're painted in my cum. Marked as *mine*."

I gasp, blood rushing to my cheeks, and lower. He says it so casually, like he's suggesting a weekday pastime, but oh, his words make me blush and tremble, just picturing it.

Tied down. At his mercy. Begging him for more...

I sound a whimper, and Saint chuckles, lifting his eyes to my face again. "You love it, don't you," he says with wonder. "The parties, the clubs. Pushing the limits..." He traces over the curve of my neck, and I gasp. "Discovering just what kind of pleasure is possible."

He dips a kiss in the hollow of my throat as his hand strokes lower, curling around the curve of my breast, making my knees weak as he softly circles my aching nipple. "... Learning how far you'll go for that rush of release."

"Yes," I cry, my voice twisting with need.

Saint's grip tightens in response, and I moan at the exquisite pressure, the pinch of tender skin.

"I love it *with you*," I add, locking eyes with him. "All of it, it's *you*, Saint. You're the one who's shown me everything. You unlocked this part of me, I only ever dreamed about before. It's only you."

Lust flashes in his eyes, and then he's on me: kissing me furiously, lifting me from my feet and spinning me around, setting me in front of the vanity with my palms on the cool marble and my legs spread, bent at the waist.

"Fuck, look at you, baby," he groans, eyes meeting mine in the mirror. He runs his hands over my breasts, and I shudder, watching his hands cover me; tease me; toy with my nipples until I'm moaning. "So beautiful. So fucking perfect," he growls, then strips. I start to turn, eager to help him shed his clothes, but he captures my hands again, keeping them pinned in place. "No, darling. Stay right there. Don't move an inch."

I don't. I stay spread and naked for him, trembling with anticipation; watching his reflection as he discards his clothes behind me. His body is chiseled as marble in the dim light; his cock springing free, thick and hard.

Mine.

I clench from the memory of him thrusting deep inside me. My body already knows, there's no sweeter prize. "One of these days, I'm going to tie *you* down," I tell him breathlessly. "Keep you for my pleasure, riding you over and over again until you beg for mercy."

"Fuck, darling, be my guest." Saint locks eyes with me in the mirror again. "I'd die a happy man buried in your sweet cunt."

And then he slides his hands over my hips, notches his cock against my core, and slowly, *fuck, so slowly*, sinks inside.

Oh....

Our sighs of pleasure mingle, echoing in the bathroom as he thrusts deeper, deeper, pushing me down over the vanity until I'm bent double, impaled on his cock all the way to the hilt.

Fuck.

I'm gasping, stretched wide and shaking for him, and I can hear Saint's low curse of pleasure. "Christ, darling..." he sinks a hand into my hair, slowly pulling my head up so I'm staring into the mirror again. "Look at yourself," he growls, holding me there in place. Not moving. Filling me so perfectly, like I was made to take him. Made to be fucked.

"Look what a good girl you are, taking my cock."

I shudder, thrilled by the lewd, filthy sight of us: Saint positioned there behind me, hand wrapped in my hair like a tether as I'm bent double, gasping from the thick, delicious stretch of his cock.

And I can see it in my face, God, I can see the raw, animal need taking me over, how I'm panting, flushed, already grinding back against him, greedily searching for that extra inch.

I look filthy. Debauched. Debased.

I look *free.*

And then Saint draws back his hips, and thrusts. Deep. Deeper. *Fuck.*

I howl in pleasure, my whole body jolting into the vanity

with the force of his thrusts. "Yes!" I scream, as he buries himself to the hilt again. "Yes, Saint, *oh*!"

He scoops an arm around me, lifting my torso back against his chest. "You need it deep, don't you, darling?" He grinds up into me at a new angle, making me wail. "You need this dick so deep, you'll feel me for days. Walking the streets, thinking about the way I fuck you. Sipping your coffee, getting wet with the memories. You'll have to go excuse yourself from that important meeting, won't you?" he growls, moving his wicked fingers between my thighs, strumming my clit in time with every thick, grinding stroke. "Can't keep your hands off this pussy, not when it needs my touch. You'll hide in your office and get yourself off with a pillow over your face, trying not to make a sound. But they'll hear you, anyway. They'll all know. You can't help but scream for mercy when you remember what my cock can do."

Fuck.

I climax with a cry, shaking wildly in his arms as the pleasure drowns me, a rush of sweetness in my veins. But Saint doesn't pause for breath. He slides out and spins me around, sitting me up on the edge of the vanity, facing him now.

He parts my thighs, and kisses me deeply, and this time, when he sinks back into me, it's infinitely slow.

My God...

My body is still trembling from the force of my first orgasm, but now I'm on the edge of another all over again. Fuck, it's overwhelming, the slow drag of his cock inside me, pushing deep, as his tongue invades my mouth. A wave of sensation envelops me, every nerve in my body on fire as his body crowds in closer, chest to chest, his hips grinding pressure on my clit with every stroke, and his cock...

God, his cock is stretching me open, the sweet friction stoking a fire that curls at the base of my spine, flames racing through my bloodstream. Setting the world ablaze. There's nowhere to hide. Nothing but the two of us, and Saint, everywhere, all around me, *inside* me, taking me to heaven and back.

"Say it again," Saint demands, and when I open my eyes, I find him staring at me with a ragged desperation in his gaze. A man clinging to the edge of self-control. "Say I'm the only one."

"It's you," I cry, as he rocks into me again. *Oh. God.* "It's only you. Saint, I love you!"

"Tessa..." he chokes out my name, thrusting faster now, an animal force taking over the both of us. "Fuck, I've got you. I've got you, darling. I swear. I'll never let anyone hurt you. *Never...*"

The blaze becomes an inferno, devouring everything in its path as my climax rips through me. I come apart with a scream, and Saint answers with a roar, embedding himself deep as I spasm in pleasure, our orgasms taking us over, fusing us together as one.

But it's only as the pleasure ebbs, and I can think straight again that I realize what he was saying.

Danger is coming.

And maybe I should be more scared, but right now, locked in Saint's embrace, body wild with pleasure as we gasp for air, I've never felt safer.

Because I know this is the only place I belong. With him.

Forever.

Chapter 7

Tessa

With everything that's been happening, Annabelle's bachelorette party is the last place I want to be.

"I'm not in the mood for a spa day," I warn Saint, dressing that morning. The invitation said 'girls' day glam'... Whatever that means.

"Which is why you need it. We agreed, business as usual," he points out, as I select a matching silk set in cream, shot through with subtle gold threads—about as close to sparkly as my wardrobe gets. "And usual, in this case, business means a party. We can't let anyone know that Wren is back, or that anything is different than last week."

"I know," I sigh reluctantly. "But did you see the itinerary Annabelle's assistant sent over? It's laminated and glittery, with 'champers breaks' every half hour."

He smirks. "Sounds like fun to me. What else are you going to do, sit around the house all day alone, worrying?" he adds.

"Yes," I grumble.

He laughs. "You'll be eating cupcakes and getting

pampered, lucky bugger. Meanwhile, I have to go into the office, and pretend to care about budget breakdowns."

"Still no word from Phillip?" I ask, anxious.

Saint shakes his head. "He said it might be a few days, before he could zero in on the hidden servers. We don't want to raise suspicions at Ashford," he adds, and I nod, sighing.

"I just wish we didn't have to do any more sneaking around."

"Let me worry about that today," Saint says, dropping a kiss on my lips. "Today, your job is to have a good time."

I give him a look.

"Alright, a tolerable one," he modifies, smiling. "But at the very least, you can take comfort in the fact that there'll be excellent food."

Which is how I wound up in the middle of a luxury spa with Annabelle and a dozen of her very best friends, slathered with face masks, wrapped in matching monogrammed robes and sipping champagne.

"To 'belle!" they toast, squealing. One of many toasts—and it's only four p.m. "The future Mrs. Max Lancaster!"

"To me!" Annabelle cheers, beaming. In addition to her robe, hand-stitched with her and Max's initials in a tiny heart, she's wearing pink fluffy slippers and a glittering tiara that might possibly not even be fake. "I can't believe it's really happening. End of an era, girls!" she crows, waving her glass around.

"And not just for her," Imogen murmurs beside me. She's also berobed, with pink goo on her face, but somehow, she still manages to seem far more elegant than the rest of us, taking a sip of champagne as she gives me a knowing smile. "I dread to think what Max is doing to celebrate his final days of freedom."

"Saint says the bachelor party isn't until the weekend, right before the wedding," I report.

"Smart." Imogen smirks. "That way, he can't do too much damage. Or get too far," she adds. "Otherwise, he'll wind up on a boat in the South Pacific, floating towards freedom."

I take a bite from one of the spa snacks, an array of exotic fruit. "You think he might try and bail on the wedding?" I ask, feeling a bolt of concern for Annabelle. As much as I have my reservations about this whole marriage, I can see how excited she is, giggling wildly and posing for pictures with her friends.

"Max? Oh no, he'll be there, at the end of the aisle with bells on," Imogen says, confident. "He would never embarrass his father like that, not after all the planning and effort that's gone into it. Cyrus adores Annabelle. Or rather, he adores her title and breeding. She's the perfect mogul's wife. I'm surprised he didn't try and snap her up himself," she adds, with a scandalous sparkle in her eyes. "But then, Max is far more charming. And doesn't have hair plugs."

"Imogen!" I laugh, relaxing. I was worried about standing out, since Annabelle and the other women have known each other for years, but everybody has been so friendly and welcoming.

It's almost enough to make me forget the crisis looming outside the swanky confines of the spa: Wren, hidden away in the country, killing time while Saint walks the halls at Ashford, looking for evidence of their crimes. And here I am, playing games of 'never have I ever' and hearing all about honeymoon plans, with the whole hen do getting our feet get scrubbed in warm water for the pedicures.

I suppose Saint is right, and I should savor the distraction while I can.

The calm before the storm.

I check my phone again. There's a text from Wren, right on schedule:

'Still here, still fine! I'm baking bread, would you believe? I figure I have the time to kill.'

She sends a photo too, of her posing with a bowl of dough.

"Is my cousin worried we're leading you astray?" Imogen asks. I quickly tuck my phone away.

"What, Saint? No," I blurt quickly. "He knows what happens on a bachelorette stays there."

"Oh my god," one of the other women interrupts, a lanky blonde. "That's how I know you. You're the one who hooked Saint!"

"They're living together," Annabelle announces loudly. "He asked her to move in with him. In fact, he insisted on it!"

Everyone reacts.

"Oh my god," one woman gasps, eyes wide. "You locked him down? How did you do it?"

"Yes, tell us your secrets," another agrees. Fiona, I think her name is, with glossy brown hair and tasteful makeup. "I've been waiting simply ages for Dickie let me have so much as a drawer! I mean, God, the man has five guest bedrooms in that penthouse, but I'm still lugging my hair-straighteners in my Longchamp bag every time I spend the night!"

"I... Um..." I blink, thrown by the sudden attention. These wealthy, glamorous women are suddenly all staring at me eagerly, hanging off my every word like I'm some kind of role model. "No secret, I'm afraid," I manage to reply. "We're just in love, that's all."

"Love?" She deflates, disappointed. "That's no use to me. Dickie wouldn't know love if it walloped him over the head."

"Tessa's being modest," Annabelle says with another wink. "She has him hanging off her every word."

"The great Anthony St. Clair, brought to his knees..." The woman beside me sighs wistfully. "You love to see it!"

And I did, this morning, when he licked me senseless on

the kitchen table—and then served me a plate of pancakes. "To soak up all the booze," he said, with a smirk.

I cough, glad my blush is covered by this face mask. "They're talking like he's some kind of celebrity," I mutter to Imogen, surprised.

She smirks. "In these circles... He is. I mean, eligible future dukes are few and far between. Usually, you have to put up with a few false teeth and jealous ex-wives if you're going to bag a title. And the Ashford title..." she whistles. "That's about as old and wealthy as it gets. The land, the company, the accounts... And Saint will inherit it all."

I feel a cold shiver run down my spine.

I've been thinking about the emotional fallout of all of this for Saint: his divided loyalties with his family, the lying and sneaking around, the prospect of a messy trial or scandal when we find the evidence of the drug trial fraud.

Now, I realize that's not all we might be tearing down.

His future. His family's place in history. One of the oldest and most prestigious names in the British aristocracy.

The Ashford legacy. Saint's future legacy.

I gulp.

He's always said he didn't want any part of it. He's spent the last ten years running in the opposite direction: idling at Oxford, dabbling with academia, fine wines, and women to pass the time. But the end result was never really in doubt. In the end, it would all be his: the land, the wealth, and the title—whether he wants it or not.

The Duke of Ashford.

I THINK of the turrets and grounds at Ashford Manor, those somber family portraits lining the grand hall, all the way back for centuries. Saint was supposed to be the next of them, safeguarding their achievements for a new generation—instead of tearing them down.

What will he be left with, once we've blown the scandal at Ashford Pharma wide open? Does he even realize what he's risking here?

"You guys should see the way he looks at her," Annabelle declares, still gushing about me and Saint. "He's totally smitten. It's the cutest thing. I bet they're next down the aisle..."

Fiona snorts. "Sorry, but I just can't imagine it," she trills smugly. "You can't get a leopard to change his spots, and all that."

Before I can speak up to defend Saint, Imogen does. "You mean like Dickie?" she asks sweetly.

Fiona shoots her a sharp look before quickly covering it with a laugh. "Of course, getting them to pop the question has never been your problem, has it, Immie?" Fiona smirks. "You know this one is a runaway bride, don't you?" she adds to me. "What's it now, five broken engagements?"

"Three," Imogen replies casually, still lounging there, sipping champagne like she doesn't see the claws coming out.

I blink. Imogen has never mentioned her dating life, but I guess I shouldn't be surprised that she has men lined up to sweep her off her feet.

"We lose count, you see," Fiona continues merrily. "She just can't make up her mind. I heard poor Harold is still devastated. Harold Caruthers, Esquire. The *third*," she explains. "Fabulously loaded, such a sweet man, head over heels for her. Imogen here broke his heart."

"The man proposed after three dates," Imogen says dryly. "It'll mend. In fact, why don't you give poor Harold a call?" she adds sweetly. "It sounds as if he's closer to commitment than dear Dickie. He'll give you a drawer for your knickers, at least."

Fiona's eyes flash, but before she can say something else

catty, Annabelle speaks up. "My toes are wrinkling; I think it's time for afternoon tea! Cyrus booked us the solarium at Sketch, isn't that sweet?"

"So sweet!" the others coo, and thankfully, a catfight is avoided.

AFTER SHOWERING and changing at the spa, we reconvene for the fleet of specially hired Rolls Royces to chauffer us to the next stop on our bachelorette train. I ride with Imogen and stick by her as we take our seats in the tearoom, where we're served a dizzying array of cakes, finger sandwiches, and of course, more champagne. It's a cool, modern restaurant, and the entire room is more like an art installation, done up like a woodland glen, with real moss on the floor and branches looming overhead, laced with real blossoms and flowers. Annabelle is in heaven, and insists on a half-hour photo shoot, posing around the room.

I hang back, digging into the food. "Fiona seems to have it out for you," I murmur to Imogen, watching the other woman preen and check their reflections.

"Fifi? Oh, she's held a grudge since boarding school, when I beat her out for Lady MacBeth in the summer play." Imogen rolls her eyes. "And everyone knows Dickie is dragging her along now. He'll shape up eventually and marry her, it's not like he has any better options, but she won't forget the humiliation of having to wait."

"Sounds like a recipe for a long and happy marriage," I quip, and Imogen laughs.

"I know, it must all seem terribly mercenary from the outside. We're a few generations past pre-contracts and arranged marriages, but not everything has changed. We're still raised to marry someone from the same social circle, the right background, to continue on the family line."

"But you haven't," I point out. "Although you've clearly had the offers."

Imogen exhales. "No, I haven't. Not yet. Maybe I'm simply delaying the inevitable, but I like to hope there's a little more for me in the world than Harold Caruthers, Esquire."

"The third," I add dryly, and she smiles.

"How could I forget? No, the truth is, I'd rather build my own empire than sit back, and wait for some man to inherit his."

"Your party-planning business," I nod.

"Right. That."

I see a flash of a cryptic smile on Imogen's face, but then it's smoothed away as Annabelle joins us, hurling herself into the booth with her empty champagne glass waving in the air. "More bubbles, please!" she beams.

"It's early days yet," Imogen chides her gently. "Why not have some cake?"

"It's my party, and I'll drink if I want to!" Annabelle insists, her cheeks flushed. She already seems tipsy.

"Well, alright," Imogen tops up her glass. "But I'm not the one who's going to hold your hair back when you're puking your guts out at the end of the night."

"Tessa will, won't you?" Annabelle leans against me. "She's the best. You've been so good for Saint, do you know that?" she adds, fixing me with a wide-eyed stare. "He hasn't been fucking anyone since you, and that never happens, he's the biggest whore around. Whoops," she giggles, "I just mean..."

"It's OK," I reassure her. "I know all about his reputation."

"Apparently, his dick is miraculous," Annabelle whisper-shouts. "A miracle dick!"

I have to laugh.

"Aaaand that's my cue," Imogen rises, smiling. "Please, have fun talking about my cousin's dick."

She moves off to chat to the others, while Annabelle collapses back dramatically in the velvet booth. "You're so lucky," she sighs. "Saint would never hurt you. I bet he'd do anything for you."

I chuckle. She's tipsy, and that's undoubtedly influencing her words. But there's also something wistful in her tone.

"You and Max have fun together," I say, encouraging.

"Right. Fun," Annabelle gulps her champagne. "As long as I look the other way. If I had a pound for everything that I *haven't* seen... Well, I wouldn't have to marry Max now, would I?" she laughs, too loud, but before I can ask anything more, two of her girlfriends swoop in to show her some social media post about the party, and she's dragged away.

But I watch her for the rest of the evening. She plays the part well: The bubbly aristocrat, gushing over cupcakes and designer party favors, but I know that Annabelle is smarter than she looks.

She deserves more than a tense, anxious marriage to Max Lancaster and his wayward dick, that's for sure. But I remember what Annabelle told me, about Cyrus Lancaster investing in her father's business, giving a job to her brother. Everything's connected, the same way that Saint's family ties seem to sprawl through the aristocracy, with favors and old debts.

She couldn't back out of this wedding now, even if she wanted to. And as the night continues, and we move to a swanky nightclub for more cocktails and dancing, I know she realizes it, too.

"Keep an eye on her, maybe?" Imogen murmurs to me, nodding to where Annabelle is dancing with drunken abandon in the middle of the dance floor, eyes closed, head back, wailing along with a Kylie song. "I have to get going, early meeting, and I wouldn't trust these bitches not to leave her in the backseat of a taxi... with someone she shouldn't be with."

"I'll make sure she gets home safely," I nod, noting the hungry gazes of the guys in the club, trying to move in close.

"Thanks. See you soon." Imogen gives me a kiss on each cheek, and then politely says her goodbyes to the others before making a swift escape.

I envy her. I'd love to slip away too, and make it home for an early night with Saint, but now I'm on official babysitting duty, that's not going to happen. I send him a quick text, and then settle in, nursing a soda, and watching Annabelle and her friends get well and truly wasted. By the time midnight rolls around, I've just about hit my limit of gushing small talk about Binky's new interior design job, and Vivi's newborn.

"... And of course, we couldn't have done it without the night nurse, and the au pair, and of course, Norris's old nanny, who's stayed with him all this time..."

I look around, realizing I've lost track of Annabelle in the crowded club. "Fascinating!" I interrupt loudly. "Be right back. Ladies room!"

I make my way down from the raised VIP section, scanning the dance floor. I don't see her anywhere, and—

Over there. I catch a glimpse of blonde hair and pink fabric, and quickly cut through the crowd. Annabelle is in the narrow hallway to the bathrooms, cornered by a snooty guy in a designer suit. He's leaning in, getting too friendly, and when I get closer, I can see that her tiara is askew and she's so drunk, she can barely stand.

"C'mon, babe," the guy takes her arm, leering down the front of her dress. "Let's get out of here. We can go somewhere quiet—"

"What a great idea!" I interrupt loudly, pushing between

them. "Let's go, Annabelle. Come along," I add, when she makes a whimper. "Time to go home. Alone," I add, fixing the man with a furious glare.

He backs off, looking disappointed.

"Wanna stay..." Annabelle slurs, yawning. "Wanna dance."

"You've already danced plenty," I tell her gently, steering her away. "Time to go home, and hydrate."

She nods. "Good hydration is ver' important. For th' skin. Elasti—elasticity."

"That's right."

I collect our stuff and manage to get Annabelle's address from one of the other women, before getting her into a cab. We spend the journey with the windows wide open, and me praying she can hold her liquor for the ride, but luckily, the apartment she shares with Max is nearby. It's a luxury, modern building, and the doorman helps me steer her onto the elevator and swipe the security pass for the penthouse floor.

"Thanks," I tell him, relieved. "Just had a little too much fun celebrating, that's all!"

"Of course, miss." He bobs his head respectfully, and steps out, as we swoop upwards.

The elevator opens directly into the apartment, a stunning penthouse that takes up the entire tenth floor. It's flashy and modern, like something out of a magazine. Exactly the kind of thing I'd expect from Max. But looking around, I don't see so much as a hint of Annabelle in the stark, monochrome rooms. And definitely no pink.

"OK, let's get some water into you," I say, depositing her on a spotless white couch. I fill a glass and dig up some aspirin from my purse. "And take these, too."

"You're so *nice*," Annabelle slurs, as she obediently gulps the water. "And Saint's so *bad*. Bad can be fun, but I hope he doesn't cheat on you. They all cheat in the end, no matter how hard you try..."

I feel a pang of sympathy. "Time to get to bed."

She shakes her head stubbornly. "No. I'm hungry... You know what I want?" she beams, sinking back into the couch cushions. I have plenty of experience dealing with drunken roommates after a college rager, so I slide off her shoes, and tuck a blanket around her, as she yawns, still babbling.

"A bacon and brie baguette," she sighs dreamily. "God, I used to have them all the time at Oxford. There was this little place in town, Harry's Caff, they did the best greasy sandwiches..."

She lolls back, thinking about the perfect breakfast, but something she said itches in the back of my mind.

Harry's...

I've heard of this place before. Did Saint take me there?

"... They would toast the buns in butter, you see. And then melt everything on top, just right..."

And then it hits me. *Harry's.* That's the place that Jamie Richmond said his source used to leave him information about the Blackthorn Society. He was investigating them for a big newspaper exposé, and someone on the inside was feeding him details. He never knew the source's identity, but they used the café as a drop.

I stare at Annabelle, putting the pieces together.

"It was you," I gasp, surprised. "You fed Jamie the information. The photo of Cyrus and the others. You were trying to bring Blackthorn down."

Annabelle looks at me blankly for a moment—and then giggles. "Whoops!" she beams, clapping a hand over her mouth. "You found me!"

"But... Why?" I gape, my mind racing. Nobody would

suspect Lady Annabelle DeWessops of a secret rebellion. Even now, I can't wrap my head around it.

"'Cause it's not right..." she yawns, snuggling deeper under the blanket. "What they get away with. I thought someone could stop them... What they did to your sister..."

I go cold.

Wren.

"What do you know about that?" I demand, but Annabelle's eyes are drifting shut. "Annabelle?" I say, louder. "Do you know what happened to Wren?"

"Someone took her..." she slurs. "Was dark. Didn't see who. Sorry.... 'Swhy I invited you. Thought you could get them... But you can't," she adds softly. "Nobody can stop them. It's jus' the way things are..."

She rolls over, and drifts off, sounding a snuffling snore.

My God.

I sit back, stunned. Annabelle was my mystery clue all along. She sent me to that Midnights party when I first arrived at Oxford, on the track to find Wren's attackers. She must have seen a glimpse of Wren being taken, after the Blackthorn party, and assumed it was connected to the secret society—just like I did.

She was trying to help me find the answers, despite the risk.

I feel a wave of affection and tuck the blanket more securely around her before going to refill her water glass. The penthouse is immaculate, filled with expensive trophies: a liquor wall of the finest scotch, a Banksy graffiti on a chunk of concrete, a signed '66 soccer World Cup shirt in a display case... All of it evidence of Max's vast power and resources. There are photos of him on the wall, shaking hands with Presidents and kings... Chilling on a private jet with Saint and Hugh... Hanging out on a yacht with friends I recognize from the Blackthorn Society reunion.

They're untouchable. Just like Annabelle said.

And some of them may be behind the Ashford conspiracy.

I feel a tremor of fear. Whoever is trying to silence Wren has already proven they'll stop at nothing to eliminate anyone who stands in their way.

So what will they do, when they realize that we're closing in on the truth?

Chapter 8

Tessa

I wake with a hangover, despite barely drinking half of what Annabelle and the others downed last night.

"Oh God, what happened to me...?" I groan, shuffling into the kitchen, where Saint is already dressed and sitting, reading the newspaper with his coffee. "I used to be able to party all night, and then leap out of bed in the morning like nothing was wrong."

"Time happened," he replies, looking amused. "You're not twenty-two anymore."

"And I would never usually wish I was, but... *Owww.*" I sink into a chair, and he gives me a kiss on the forehead.

"Bacon and eggs, that's what you need. A proper English fry-up," he announces cheerfully, opening the oven to whip out the loaded plate he has warming for me. He puts it on the table, and fills my coffee cup, too. I groan. "Trust me, it soaks up the booze," he insists.

I pick up a piece of dry toast and take a tentative bite.

"Did you have fun, at least?" Saint asks, watching me with a smirk. "The photos were a treat."

"There were photos?" I gulp.

"All over Annabelle's social media. Nothing incriminating," Saint adds, reassuring. "In fact, they look like a professional shoot." He shows me on his cellphone, and I skim through them, relieved to find I'm barely a blur in the back of the beaming group frames.

Memories of Annabelle's drunken confession come back to me. She has no idea that Wren's attack wasn't an isolated frat-boy incident, that the conspiracy we're searching for stretches way beyond entitled secret society parting.

It's more dangerous by far.

I check my phone. There's already a breezy message from Annabelle:

'OMG, wild night. I don't remember A THING! Hydrate, ladies!'

There's also a 'Good morning' from Wren. I decide to Face-Time her, and place the call.

"Reporting for duty, with my morning check-in," Wren teases. Then she squints at her screen. "What's wrong with you?"

"Champagne," I mutter. "Lots of it."

She laughs. "Try those electrolyte powders. Take it from a scientist, they'll help you bounce back."

Saint looks up. "I think I have some of those."

He goes to investigate, while I chat to Wren, and give her an edited version of last night's events. She laughs when I describe the designer party favors, complete with gold name-plate necklaces and an engraved keepsake box with a framed photo of Max and Annabelle. "He has balls, I'll tell you that," Wren rolls her eyes. "Came on strong with me, and I almost fell for it, too—until I heard he already had a girlfriend."

"What are you up to?" I ask, sipping my coffee. "Everything's still quiet down there, right?"

"As a mouse," Wren reassures me. "I'm actually loving the chance to exhale. I've moved on from baking bread to a nice apple and oat cake."

She displays the cake, cooling on a rack in the charming kitchen. I applaud. "Look at you, Martha Stewart."

"Call me Nigella, please," Wren cracks, and I smile.

I can already see that she's looking better. The dark shadows under her eyes are fading with a few good nights' sleep, and there's a familiar sparkle back in her eyes. I know it won't be so simple for her to move on from the trauma of what's happened to her, but I can't help hoping; taking these small improvements as a sign that it might be possible in time. After we finish this. And with a hell of a lot of therapy.

"Anyway, I better get back to my busy schedule," Wren teases. "There's a radio play on the BBC at noon, and if the rain lets up, I might even go for a walk."

"Not too far, though," I remind her, concerned.

"Just nearby, don't worry," she reassures me. "I'll check in later. And hydrate!"

She hangs up. Saint returns with the hangover mix, but I've barely taken a gulp when my phone rings again.

"Popular," Saint smirks.

I check the screen and pause. "It's my mom," I say slowly, feeling a terrible wave of guilt sweep through me.

I meet Saint's eyes. "She doesn't know. About Wren. She still thinks she's dead."

"Shit."

We stay frozen, my handset still buzzing there on the table. Wren and I discussed it briefly, and we decided that for now, they should stay in the dark. There's far too much to explain over a phone call, and with everything still so uncertain, it doesn't make sense to shatter their hard-won stability and plunge them into shock and disbelief.

But deciding not to tell them, and seeing my mom's photo waiting on the caller ID are two entirely different things.

I let it go to voicemail, and then send a quick text. *'Busy with work! Talk soon xx.'*

"I feel terrible," I tell Saint, the guilt gnawing in the pit of my stomach.

He wraps his arms around me in a hug. "I'm so sorry."

"I can't talk to her, I wouldn't be able to bring myself to lie," I add. "What am I supposed to say? She lost her daughter and grieved her. She's still grieving! Am I supposed to just talk to her like everything is normal, knowing the truth—that she never needed to go through that pain in the first place?"

"I know, but you're just trying to protect her," Saint says softly. "The same way Wren did, staying away for so long."

I look at him, my guilt hardening into something else. The first small burn of anger.

God, I've been so caught up in relief and joy to see Wren again, I haven't even focused on the rest of it. All the unanswered questions that suddenly flare to life in my mind.

"She never needed to go through it," I repeat slowly. "None of us did. I mean God, faking her own death? Who does that?" I demand. "Wren could have come to me, explained what was going on. I would have helped her! I would have done anything for her. At the very least, she could have sent me some kind of sign that she was OK. Instead... Instead, we all had to go through hell, thinking we'd lost her forever!"

I clench my fists, remembering the awful, black grief of it. So bottomless and relentless, I could barely get out of bed some days.

"I blamed myself," I tell Saint, hotly. "I spent months wondering if I could have stopped her... Somehow, if I knew the exact signs. I hated myself that I didn't save her! How could she do that to us? What the hell was she thinking?"

Saint waits patiently for me to finish my furious rant, then he offers me a supportive hug. "She's the only one who can tell you that," he says, squeezing me tightly. "You need to talk to her, if you want answers."

I draw back. "I can't," I say, frustrated. "I'm scheduled at the Foundation for meetings today. It's supposed to be business as usual, remember?"

He shakes his head. "I'll cover for you. Drive down to Imogen's house and talk it out with Wren. I can tell Hugh you're sleeping off the bachelorette party, he'll understand."

I pause. "I can't go out there to see her all steaming mad."

"Why not?" Saint asks. "You have every right to be angry at her. And it'll do you no good to let it just fester. You need to talk. She owes you that much," he adds, and I nod.

She does.

I love my sister, and I know she was only trying to protect me, but she fucking broke my heart. And I need to know why.

I THROW some things in a bag, and hit the road in Saint's prized Aston Martin, my frustration and anger growing with every mile. By the time I make it to Farleigh-Under-Lyme, I'm boiling over with resentment for everything Wren put us through.

"Tessa!" Wren opens the door, smiling. "Perfect timing. I just put a batch of scones in the oven," she adds, as I follow her into the cottage. "I may have mixed up the baking powder with the baking soda, though, so don't get your hopes up. Somehow, I can complete a complex chemical reaction in the lab without blinking, but baked goods are like a whole new challenge."

I step into the cozy kitchen and watch as she bustles making tea. "I didn't come here for scones!" I finally blurt. "What the fuck, Wren?"

She blinks at me in surprise.

"You faked your own death!" I exclaim, my voice rising in anger. "The Coast Guard searched the lake for a week! Every morning we had to wake up wondering if today was the day when they'd find your body, and then somehow it only got *worse* from there. We had to bury an empty casket. Dad barely said two words for a month, he was drinking so much all the time. And Mom... She was *destroyed*, Wren. Totally destroyed. I didn't think she'd ever pull herself back together. Do you have any idea what you put them through?"

There's silence. The drizzle of rain taps lightly on the cottage windows, and Wren's face collapses, teary-eyed.

"I'm sorry," she says softly. "I hated knowing I was hurting them."

"Not just them!" I yell. "What about *me*? You think I didn't fall apart, too? I lost you, Wren. You were gone! And every minute of every day, my heart broke all over again thinking I'd never see you again, that I had let you down, that I should have known—"

My voice breaks, and I dissolve into loud, hiccupping sobs, wracked with the echo of that terrible guilt.

Wren moves close and puts her arms around me. I try to push her away, still mad, but she holds on tight. "I'm sorry, Tessie, I'm so, so sorry."

"Sorry doesn't take it back," I cry. "How could you do that to us? How could you do that to *me*?"

"I couldn't see any other way," Wren says, and when I look, I see that her expression is pleading. "You have to understand, I wasn't thinking straight. After the attack, I was already spiraling, and then when the threats started... I was depressed and fucked-up, scared out of my mind, and I didn't know what to do. I thought everything would just be easier if I disappeared. That you'd all be safer without me. And then once I did it, once I left that letter on the beach and walked away... I couldn't take it back. No matter how much I wanted to. But I missed you too," Wren says, crying as well. "Every day. I was alone, without my family, and all I could do was tell myself that it was worth it, to keep them from hurting you."

My anger melts. How could I stay mad at her when she's suffered so much, too? This past year was hell for her too: always keeping to the shadows, looking over her shoulder, divided from the people she loves. She's not the one who truly deserves my wrath.

No, that's better saved for the ones who are responsible for all this grief and pain.

Whoever kidnapped her. Whoever threatened me.

Whoever is trying to silence us about the Ashford Pharma trials.

I finally hug her back, cradling her slim frame. Too slim. Yet more evidence of all her stress and anxiety. "I know you thought it was for the best," I whisper tearfully. "I just hate that it happened at all."

"Me too..."

Finally, she releases me, sniffling. "Look at us," she says, wiping her cheeks with a wry grin. "Nobody would think we're fighting to expose a billion-dollar company."

"Well, they underestimate us at their peril," I crack, also trying to clean up my tears and snot. "Now, about those scones..."

Wren laughs. "They'll be done in... ten more minutes," she reports, checking the clock. "Do you want to be ambitious, and try to make some lemon curd, too?"

"That sounds like... Exactly the kind of quiet, uneventful plan we need."

. . .

I SPLASH cold water on my face, and join Wren with her sifting, stirring, and mixing. We make the curd, and take out the scones, which are only *slightly* mishappen and sunk.

"Not bad, for my first try," Wren decides.

"They taste great," I report, as we take our tea into the cozy living room and settle in by the fire. And finally, with all my anger and shock out of the way, and no more drama interrupting us, we just talk. For hours, about my investigations in Oxford trying to track down her attacker, and how she kept herself hidden during her months on the run.

"It turns out, it's easy to get a fake ID," she says, curled up on the other end of the floral couch. "I just hung out near the dorms at the University of Chicago, and pretended I needed a hookup to get into the bars. I got a whole bunch of them, too," she adds. "I'd switch out every month, staying in cheap hostels, and working for cash under the table waitressing and bartending."

"You... Tended bar?" I ask in disbelief. Wren barely stepped foot in the local watering holes during college, she was too busy studying, and pulling all-nighters at the lab.

"I know," she grins. "But I'm a fast learner. I can mix a mean martini. I kept track of you online, on social media," she adds. "And when I saw you'd gone to Oxford... Well, I had to get my hands on a fake passport, too. I knew you were doing something boneheaded, going back there."

"That's me," I reply lightly. "Stubborn and fueled with a fiery vengeance to hunt down the man who attacked you."

She gives me a smile. "Thank you," Wren says softly. "For trying, at least. It's been driving me crazy, too."

"Your memory still hasn't come back?" I ask.

She shakes her head. "I can't decide if it's a blessing or a curse. What I remember is bad enough, and I know that's not the half of it."

The windowless cell. The shackles on her wrists and ankles.

The man with what looked like a serpent crown tattoo on his thigh.

I shiver. "It was bad enough when we thought it was some random psycho attacking you for kicks, but now... Someone did it for a reason. To silence and scare you."

It was planned. Calculating.

And all to benefit Ashford Pharma's future profits and reputation.

Wren can tell what I'm thinking. "How's Saint doing?" she asks, measured, and I can see, she doesn't totally trust him yet. I understand why. He has as much to lose as the rest of his family if we succeed in exposing their crimes.

"He's trying to snoop around at Ashford, as much as he can without drawing any attention," I add. "But I know it can't be easy for him." I sigh. "He was never on good terms with his father to begin with, but there's a big difference between disagreeing with his plans for you in life and having to accept he might be behind this kind of cover-up. His older brother passed away too," I add. "Ten years ago. It's how we grew closer. He knew what I was going through, losing you."

It's no wonder Saint urged me to talk it out with Wren. He would probably give anything to have the chance to talk to Edward again.

It makes me treasure this moment even more, cozied up here together over tea and scones for what I hope is the first of many afternoons like this.

"Would you stay?" Wren asks, looking curious. "When all of this is over, I mean. Would you stay in England, with him?"

"I think so..." I can't help the smile that curls on the edge of my lips when I think about a future with Saint. "I really like my job at the Foundation, and I can picture myself building a life here. With him. Of course, that all depends on us exposing the bastards who hurt you and stopping them from going ahead and releasing the drug," I add. "Simple."

"Simple," Wren agrees with a rueful laugh. "Sometimes I can't wrap my head around it," she says, shaking her head. "I'm the nerdy scientist, and the most adventurous things you ever did were falling for toxic artist types."

"Hey," I protest, laughing.

"It's true. How did we even end up here?"

"Because you tried to do the right thing," I answer simply. "And that matters. Think of all the people who would be harmed if they move ahead with the flawed Alzheimer's drug, all that hope for something that can't ever help them."

"And it's not just the people holding out for a miracle now who would be harmed," Wren says, her forehead creasing in a frown. "It's the future of the whole field. Scientists and other drug companies would all switch to working from the same assumptions, the same protocols as Valerie proved. Or pretended to prove. It would set back finding a real treatment for years. Decades, even."

We fall silent, reflecting on the high stakes. But while Wren is thinking about the medicine, I'm thinking about her. How to keep her safe and protected from these monsters. For now, she may be safe, cloistered away here in the country, but she can't keep hidden forever.

One day, she'll need to officially come back to life again.

"More tea?" she asks, getting up as my phone starts to buzz on the coffee table. It's Saint calling to check in.

"I think I'm just about full of Earl Grey," I smile. "How about we switch to wine?"

"I thought you weren't ever drinking again," she teases, clearing our plates.

"A sip or two won't hurt. Hair of the dog," I protest, picking up Saint's call. "Hi baby," I answer, and Wren gives a laugh.

"Hi, baby," she echoes, sing-song.

"Shut up!" I give her a playful shove, and follow her to the kitchen, chatting to Saint as I go.

"It sounds like things are going well down there," he says warmly.

"They are. Thank you for making me come," I add. "We had a great talk. I feel much better about everything."

"Good," he replies. "Should I expect you back tonight, or do you want to stay down there?"

I look around. It's dark outside the windows, and the wind whistles through the woods. "I think I'll stay," I decide. "I don't really want to drive in this weather. God forbid I put a scratch on your precious car."

Wren gives me a thumbs up. "There are plenty of groceries," she says, smiling. "I can make my famous mac and cheese."

"Your famously gross mac and cheese," I joke.

"Not fair!"

Saint chuckles down the line. "I'm glad you're getting the chance to spend some time together. Not that I won't miss you in my bed tonight..."

"I'll make it up to you," I promise, and he makes a noise of approval.

"I can't wait."

Suddenly, a high-pitched alarm sounds, blaring through the piece of the cottage. Wren startles, dropping a dish in the farmhouse sink. It cracks against the porcelain, smashing loudly.

"What's going on?" Saint demands.

"I'm not sure," I look around, my heart racing at the noise. "The alarm just went off."

Wren meets my eyes, looking terrified.

"It's probably just a fox," I tell her—and myself. "Imogen said they trip the alarm sometimes, didn't she?"

"Go check the cameras," Saint instructs me. "She has the feed set up on her main TV. Tell me what you see."

I hurry back to the living room, with Wren trailing behind. My hand shakes as I grab the remote, the alarm still wailing, too loud.

"Found it," I report, as I bring up the security app. There are four camera views, positioned around the cottage. "They all look clear. I can't see anything."

Saint exhales in audible relief. "False alarm," he says. "Damn foxes."

I hit a few buttons, and the alarm stops. "Phew, drama," I give Wren a comforting smile. Then her face goes slack with fear.

"Tessa..."

She point at the screen again. I turn—in time to see a shadowed figure rear up towards one of the cameras. He has a ski-mask over his face, dressed in camo fatigues. For a moment, he's frozen there, reaching for the camera. Then suddenly, it cuts to static.

The rest of the cameras all go black.

"What's going on?" Saint's voice rings out, but I can't answer. Wren and I look at each other, frozen in silent panic.

Someone's found her. They're here.

Then the sound of smashing glass comes from down the hall, and Wren lets out a terrified scream.

Chapter 9

Tessa

I panic. Wren's scream breaks through my shock: This is really happening.

Someone's come for her.

"What's happening?" Saint's voice demands in my ear. "Tessa? Tessa!"

"Intruder!" I manage to blurt, looking wildly around. The sound of the break-in came from the front of the house. The main door. What the hell to we do now?

Saint curses. "Get out!" he yells, as the sound of heavy footsteps come in the hall.

Wren grabs my hand, and drags me in the other direction, racing up the narrow staircase. I stumble on the wooden treads, dropping my phone as I reach to grab the railing. *Fuck.* It skitters down the stairs, out of reach, and I pause, wanting to dive after it—

BANG!

Plaster explodes by my head. I turn, and to my horror, I see the masked man at the end of the hallway—with a gun in his hand. He raises it again—

Wren hauls me up. "Go!" she screams, as another bullet flies, the gunshot cracking like thunder in silence of the cottage.

Oh God.

I bomb up the stairs after her, and into a bedroom. I look wildly around. "The cabinet!" I blurt, pointing to the tall display case by the door, filled with cute China curios. Wren gets what I mean right away, and together, we shove and drag, toppling it to block the door.

A moment later, the man hurls himself against the door with a THUD. The cabinet shakes, but it doesn't give—at least, not yet, but I don't know how long it'll hold. I search around the room for something, anything to use as a weapon, but there's only a rustic bed with floral linens, and vintage décor.

"We have to get out of here," I panic, my heart pounding.

BANG!

A bullet splinters through the wooden doorway, flying past our heads and smashing into a lamp. Wren stifles a scream.

I rush to the window. It's a fifteen-foot drop down to the dark yard below, with nothing to break the fall, but we don't have a choice.

"Over here!"

I fling open the shutter-style panes and scramble out into the cold night air. Vaguely, I remember a safety talk from the fire department, back in elementary school. *Don't jump, drop.* I lower myself out until I'm hanging by my fingertips, then let go.

THUMP.

The ground rears up fast, but I manage to fall and roll to one side on the damp grass. Wren's right behind me, climbing out onto the ledge. "Hurry!" I call up, hearing the loud thuds as the intruder tries to break the door down. Wren dangles there a moment, clearly terrified. Then she drops.

"Oww..." She lets out a cry of pain, landing hard and crumpling to the ground. "My ankle!"

"We have to go!" I try to drag her up, but she cries out again, finding it hard to stand.

BANG!

Another gunshot sounds, too close. The intruder's in one of the other bedrooms now, leaning out of the window, firing directly at us.

"Go!" I scream at Wren and haul her to her feet. We take off towards the dark woods. Wren whimpers in agony, limping on her damaged ankle, but I put an arm around her shoulders and manage to support her weight as we half-jog, half-stumble away from the lights of the house, and into the dark.

"That way," I pant, pointing to the looming shadows ahead: the woods that border the cottage. "We can't outrun him. We have to hide!"

Another gunshot sounds. Wren clenches her jaw and keeps moving, but I can tell that every step hurts like hell. We stagger across the back field, and finally reach the tree line, diving into the cover of the undergrowth. Here, leaves and mud are thick underfoot, and the trees quickly block any light from view, leaving us shrouded in darkness.

It's creepy as hell, and we don't even have a torch or cell-phone to light the way. But that's a good thing, I remind myself, that just means we'll be harder to find. Because I don't doubt for a second that he's coming after us.

That man was shooting to kill.

I try to keep my terror under control and think straight.

"I think the main road is that way," I gesture to the left, wracking my brains to remember. "The village is a couple of miles away. If we can reach someone, call for help..."

Wren nods, tears in her eyes.

"Come on," I say, already listening for the sound of pursuit. "We have a head start, but he'll be coming after us, and fast."

We keep moving, staggering blindly through the dark trees,

until the forest swallows us up, and there's no sound at except our own ragged breathing, and the muffled shuffle of our footsteps dragging through the mud, and my heartbeat pounding in my ears so loudly, I have to fight to stay alert for any other noise.

It's torture. Every step, I'm wondering if it'll be our last. Waiting for another gunshot to sound, and rip through the silence of the forest.

Is this how it ends?

I bite back a sob. *It's too soon!* I only just got Wren back. I only just found Saint. My whole life is waiting, full of possibility, but instead, I'm consumed with terror, stumbling in the dark trying to outrun a killer.

Still, I force myself on. One foot in front of another, deeper into the dark. But Wren's leaning more heavily on my shoulder now, and soon, I'm exhausted from the weight.

"Tessa..." Wren whimpers slowing. "Please, it hurts. I need to rest."

"No." I tug her onwards. "We have to keep going. He'll find us."

"I *can't*." Wren crumples, falling into the dirt and almost pulling me down with her. She stays there on the ground, sobbing with pain. "I can't take another step. I'm sorry. You need to on without me."

"What? No!" I haul her to her feet again, but she tries to pull away.

"I won't make it, not with my ankle hurting like this. I'll only slow you down."

"I'm not leaving you," I grind out.

"You can get help," she argues. "Run to the village. I'll hide, you can come back for me—"

"I said 'No.'" I fight to keep my voice down, shaking with anger and fear. "I already lost you once already, Wren. I'm not leaving you behind now. We survive this together, or we don't survive at all."

"But Tessa—"

"Shh!" I hiss at her suddenly, whirling around. A noise comes from somewhere behind us. "Did you hear that?" I whisper.

The noise comes again. A shuffling sound that could be an animal... Until a voice comes through the trees, muttering a curse.

Fuck.

Wren's eyes widen in terror, and I panic too. I look around desperately, and spot a fallen tree, up against some bushes. I point, and the two of us creep over, as quietly as we can.

I clamber over to behind the tree trunk, then crawl into the middle of the bushes, not caring as twigs and branches scratch at my skin. Wren crawls after me, until we're both hidden in the thick undergrowth, out of sight.

Slowly, the noise of our pursuer gets closer, and then a faint beam of light comes. The torch on a cellphone, sweeping through the trees.

Searching.

Oh God.

I silently press a finger to my lips. Wren nods, and we wait there in terrified silence.

He wanders closer. I can hear him more clearly now, crunching through leaves and twigs, not trying to stay quiet. The beam of light bobs, then pauses focused on the ground.

He's trying to track our footprints.

Every instinct tells me to creep back and to bury myself even further in the bushes; to bolt, and run for my life, but I can't risk making a sound. *I can't leave Wren.*

She silently finds my hand and clutches it tightly. I squeeze back, my heart racing wildly as the man moves closer... Closer...

... And passes us by.

Wren and I stay frozen. We barely even breathe, we just wait there, terrified, as the gunman keeps moving, picking up his pace now. The light bobs, heading deeper into the woods, until it's out of sight.

He's gone.

Wren exhales, half breathing, half sobbing in relief.

"Shh," I whisper quickly. "It's not safe yet."

She clamps a hand over her mouth, muffling the sound of her ragged breathing, as I crouch there, listening hard. There's no sound of our pursuer, just the eerie rustles and whispers of the woods, but I don't believe it.

"Tessa..." she finally speaks up, softly. "I think he's gone."

"It could be a trap," I whisper back. "He could be doubling back. Or have reinforcements coming. We don't know anything."

Like who the man with the gun is, or how he found us.

I think of my cellphone, sitting useless at the bottom of the stairs, and curse. If only we could send a message, or call someone right now. I'm sure Saint is going out of his mind with worry, after hearing the gunshots.

Saint.

I think of him, and somehow, the terror eases its icy grip on my heart. He'll be coming for me. I know he will.

The only question is, will he make it down here in time?

WE WAIT.

There's nothing else but stay huddled there together, under the cover of darkness, listening for danger in the dark woods. I shift into a seated position, starting to feel the chill of the damp, cold night. I fled the house in jeans and a comfy hooded sweat-shirt, but they're no match for the weather, so we shift in closer to share body heat. Wren is wearing an old-fashioned wristwatch, and we watch the minutes tick past, infinitely slow.

I want to be anywhere in the world but here. That tropical beach that Saint dreamed about, lazing in the shade by the shallows, warm and dry, and not in fear for my life... I drift off into a daydream, until Wren tugs my sleeve.

"It's been an hour," she whispers. "I don't think he's coming back."

I take a deep breath, thinking fast. We can't stay here forever, and if we're going to make a break for it, we should do it before the cold and tiredness makes us too sluggish. If we can make it to the village, or somewhere with a phone...

"How's your ankle?" I ask her softly. "Do you think you can walk?"

Wren extends it, massaging slowly. "It's not broken, just sprained. Now that it's rested... I think I can manage."

Slowly, I craw back out of the bushes. It's terrifying, and part of me is expecting to find the gunman waiting for us, ready to strike, but when I emerge into the clearing, there's nobody there.

"It's safe," I whisper to Wren. "Come on."

She crawls out after me, and slowly gets to her feet, testing her ankle. "It's a little better," she says, face lightening with relief. "I can walk."

Thank God.

"The man with the gun went that way," I say, checking out the woods around us. "And the house is back there..."

"Then let's go this way," Wren says, pointing in a different direction. "Maybe we'll strike it lucky and find the main road. God, what I wouldn't give for a compass right now..."

"Or a map. Or some water. Or a cellphone," I agree. "There's a reason I never got my outward-bound badge in the Girl Scouts."

"Really? I thought it was because you were too scared to make it through the overnight camping, freaked out over a racoon, and had to call mom to pick you up." Wren gives me a smirk of a grin.

She's pretending not to be scared, we both are.

"At least I tried," I reply softly, taking her arm to help her balance. "You were too busy cataloging rock types to even glance outside. Nerd."

"Dork."

"Idiot."

We start walking, as fast as Wren can manage on her injured ankle. "I think I see a trail," she reports, as we move deeper in the trees. "Look."

She's right. A bare track is just about visible in the undergrowth, winding through the woods. My heart leaps. "Should we follow it?"

"It has to lead somewhere, right—"

BANG!

A gunshot whistles from behind us, exploding a tree trunk nearby. BANG!

He's back.

"Run!" Wren screams, grabbing my hand. We bomb down the trail, fleeing as more gunshots follow, and the sound of fast pursuit. *Oh God.* I gasp in panic, skidding over the wet leaves and tree trunks, clinging to Wren's hand for dear life. We're not even trying to be quiet now, all that matters is getting away.

"He's right behind us!" Wren cries, shooting a terrified glance behind her. Another bullet comes whistling past, as we zig-zag and veer across the trail.

"Up ahead!" I yell, as the trees thin out and I spot the smooth blacktop of the road. "Go! Go!"

Headlights approach, moving fast, as we race out of the

woods. I slow for a split second, already wondering if the car is friend or foe. What if he has an accomplice? What if we don't—

BANG!

A burning sensation rips across my shoulder, but there's no time to stop, or even think. I power ahead, pulling Wren behind me as I scramble up the bank and hurl myself onto the road in front of the oncoming car—

"Stop!" I scream, throwing up my hands against the blinding glare of the headlights. For a terrible moment, I think I'm too late, and the car won't stop in time, but then the brakes screech in protest, and the car fishtails to a stop.

The driver leaps out. It's Saint.

Oh, thank God.

"Tess!" He rushes over to us, grabbing Wren before she falls. "What happened? Are you alright—"

"There's no time, he's coming!" I blurt, "He's got a gun!"

Saint's face changes. "Get in the car," he orders, and then I see, he's got one too: A small black handgun that he pulls from his waistband. "Now!"

BANG! Another bullet whistles past us, and I see the dark shadow of the masked man emerge from the tree line.

Saint fires back, a burst of bullets that sends the gunman diving back behind the cover of the trees. He backs towards the car, still firing. "Come on!"

Wren piles into the backseat, and I grab shotgun position, as Saint lets out a final ricochet of shots. Then he hurls himself behind the wheel and guns the engine. "Are you hurt?" he demands, as we drive away, tires screeching. "Tessa, are you hurt?"

"I'm fine," I answer automatically, my heart still pounding. I look over at him, overwhelmed with love. "I knew you'd come. I knew if we could just hold on long enough..."

His face changes. "You're bleeding."

"What?" I look down and see blood soaking my sweatshirt arm.

"Tessa, did he hit you? Were you shot?" Saint's voice echoes louder, wild with panic. He reaches over, the car swerving dangerously as he tries to check me.

"Saint!" Wren yells, leaning forward. "You're going to kill us all. Eyes on the road. I'll take care of her."

Saint curses, driving fast down the winding country lanes as Wren helps me take off my sweatshirt. "It doesn't hurt much," I report.

"That's the adrenaline talking, you'll feel it soon enough." Wren checks the wound, blotting the blood away. "It's just a graze," she reports back. "The bullet barely touched her. Some bandages and antiseptic, and she'll be fine. Everything's OK."

Everything's OK...

I sit there in the passenger seat, shaking with relief and shock. I grip Wren's hand tightly; I can't believe I came so close to losing her again.

To losing everything—including my life.

Chapter 10

Saint

I'm so furious, I can barely see straight. I speed back to London with my knuckles white against the steering wheel, and then carry Tessa into the house—despite her futile protests.

"I can walk fine! Wren's the one who needs help—"

"—I don't," her sister speaks up, as I deposit Tessa on the couch, then immediately go to arm the security system. Alarms, cameras... Fuck, where's a surface-to-air ground launcher missile when you need one?

I could have lost her.

If I'd driven down a hair slower, if the bullet had been two inches to the right...

"I'm OK, Saint," Tessa insists, when I rejoin them, and press a first aid kit into Wren's hands. Her sister sets to work cleaning her wound—her fucking gunshot wound—and then bandaging it up, while Tessa huffs and sighs. She's still pale and shaking from their escape, with dirt on her face and twigs in her hair, but she's still her usual stubborn self all the same. "See?" she crows, showing me her shoulder. "It's just a scratch!"

"A scratch?!" My voice roars, deafening in the late-night hush.

Wren looks back and forth between us. "OK!" she says brightly. "I'm beat. All that desperate fleeing can really take it out of you. Where's the guest room?" she asks me.

I nod down the hall.

"Great! So I'm going to go take a sleeping pill, and put my noise-canceling headphones on, and go to bed while you two... Do whatever!"

Wren makes herself scarce, leaving Tessa and me alone. "You need to go to the hospital, to get checked out properly," I order her.

"What I need is a hot shower and a good night's sleep. Why don't you put the kettle on, and make us some tea?" she adds, before moving past me, and heading upstairs.

Tea. *Tea?!*

I try to keep it together. I know she's been through a lot tonight, but the casual way she's brushing it off makes my blood boil. Doesn't she understand the danger she was in? When I think of the two them, alone and frightened in those woods, with some psycho stalking them...

A psycho with a gun.

Ashford isn't fucking around.

I charge upstairs after her. "Do you realize what just happened tonight?" I demand, finding her in the bathroom.

"I'm fine," she insists again, and I just about blow my last remaining fuse.

"Stop saying that!" I yell. "Nothing about this is fine! When I heard those gunshots on the phone, and then you were gone... I thought you were dead! I could have lost you!""

"But you didn't." In an instant, Tessa has her arms wrapped tightly around me. Soothing me with the warm press of her body, and her soft, urgent smile. "I'm right here."

"I can't lose you, baby," I hold on like a drowning man, panic and relief and sheer desperation pounding in my bloodstream. "Fuck, I can't let you go."

"You don't have to," Tessa reassures me. She tilts her face up to me, eyes shining brightly, filled with tears. "You know, I was scared tonight too. I was so, so terrified. But the one thing that kept me sane, was knowing you would come for me. I knew you'd come, Saint. And that belief, it got me through."

I exhale a ragged breath. "Tessa... My love..."

"I'm not going anywhere, I promise. I'm staying right here, with you."

Tessa comes up on her tiptoes, searching for a kiss. And fuck, I could never deny her. My mouth crashes down on hers, all the stress and fear of the night giving way to a desperate hunger.

I need her.

Always.

"Saint..." Tessa whimpers against me, as I claim her lush mouth, tongue plunging deep. I try to be gentle, knowing she must be shaken after everything she's been through, but Tessa's kiss is hungry and wild. She grips at my shoulders, arching her body against me, demanding more.

Fuck. I give it to her.

I'll always give her everything. Until the day that I'm empty and broken, and even then, I'll give her my last breath.

Because this woman... This woman is everything to me. I knew it in my bones already, but coming so close to losing her tonight has made it crystal clear.

Nothing is ever going to part us again.

After a long, heated moment, Tessa pulls back, breathless. "I'm a mess," she says ruefully. "I've got half the forest in my hair, and the other half..." she looks down at her mud-smeared clothes and winces.

"You're beautiful." I swear.

Tessa turns on the shower, quickly filling the bathroom with steam. "Will you help me...?" she asks, gesturing at her clothing.

As if I ever needed any excuse to strip her naked.

I carefully help her out of her tank top and jeans, and then peel off her underwear, too, until she's naked. Glorious even in her muddy, tattered state.

"Your turn," Tessa says with a smile, beckoning as she steps under the spray.

I shake my head, even as my body hardens at the sight of her; hot water flowing over her luscious curves...

Christ, what I wouldn't give to sink into that sweetness, and feel her body clench and moan. But I grip my fists at my side, and don't move a fucking inch. "Not tonight, baby," I tell her gently. "You've been through so much."

"And I survived." Tessa looks at me, stubborn and perfect. "I survived, Saint. I'm alive. We both are. Against all odds. I'm not wasting a single precious moment, and nothing makes me feel more alive than when you're touching me—when you're fucking me, Saint."

She puts her hands on her hips. Naked. Wet. Her breasts jutting out, water running in rivulets over her pert, stiff nipples—

Fuck it.

I reach for her with a fevered groan, stepping straight under the shower spray.

"What is it with you getting all your clothes wet?" Tessa teases, as I push her back against the wall and kiss her so deeply, I never want to come up for air.

She moans.

Fuck, the way that sound makes me hard... My hands are already sliding over her body, exploring every wet, slick curve. I palm her breasts, dragging my mouth from hers to lick and suckle at her taut nipples.

"Saint…!" Tessa's head falls back in pleasure, and she presses eagerly against my mouth.

Christ, it's a drug, the taste of her. And I'm only getting started.

I take the shower soap and squeeze a handful into my palm. Then I stroke every inch of her, lathering the suds over her skin, and letting the flow of hot water wash away every smudge and mark from tonight.

Almost everything.

"Your bandages," I realize. "They're getting wet."

Tessa looks at me, already flushed and gasping. "So we'll put new ones on."

I have to laugh. "How did I find such a horny, stubborn woman?" I tease, and she gives me a smirk.

"Luck."

She pulls me into another kiss, her fingers fumbling with my soaked clothing. Then I press one hand between her thighs, my fingers searching, teasing at her clit, and she shudders, distracted.

"That's right…" I growl with satisfaction, feeling her body sway and melt. I stroke again, a slow, precise rhythm I know drives her crazy, every time. "That's how my baby likes it."

"Yes," she gasps, eyes bright. Mouth open. Panting for more. "Yes, Saint, *please…*"

Watching her come undone for me, she's a goddamn work of art.

"You don't understand, baby," I find myself groaning, as I sink one finger, then another into her wet, clenching heat. "I can't lose you, because I'm *addicted.* I'll always find you. I'll always keep you safe. Because this sweet pussy, there's nothing like it in the world."

I drop to my knees, and spread her legs wider, and bury my face between her thighs.

Tessa screams my name as I lick against her, rasping my tongue against her clit over and over, until her legs give way and she's flailing against the marble tile. But that doesn't slow me, not for a second, I just lift her with my shoulders, pinning her there in place as I lap greedily at her slick elixir.

Mine, all mine.

Fuck, there's nothing like it. I'm hard as a rock, and I could come right now, just from the taste of her, and the wild pleasure of her cries.

"Saint..." she's sobbing now, as I thrust my fingers inside her tight cunt again, *fuck, so tight,* I'm on the brink of losing all control and fucking her senseless, but even in my haze of animal lust, the only thing that matters is her pleasure. Feeling the wild shake of her release.

I angle my fingers, and begin to pump, rubbing up inside her just right, in time with my ravenous tongue.

"Oh God!" Tessa cries, her whole body shaking now. Trembling with need. "Fuck, don't stop! Right there. *Oh*!"

She's gripping my hair tightly, holding on for dear life as I gorge on her pussy. Swirling. Lapping. Batting her clit with my tongue. I flex my fingers inside her, filling her up, loving the way she wails for me, body shaking like she's losing all control.

Her sister better have used those headphones, because fuck, my baby's screaming the house down tonight.

"Yes! Yes!" Tessa's thighs are so tight around my neck she could choke me out, but who needs oxygen at a time like this?

I close my lips around her swollen clit and suck. Hard.

She climaxes with a scream, her whole body spasming as the pleasure takes her over.

In one move, I rock back onto my heels, letting gravity and my firm grip bring her down into my lap. I part her legs wider, line up, and thrust into her still-clenching pussy, impaling her on my dick.

Fuuuuck.

Tessa sounds another scream of pleasure, clenching hard around my cock as I fuck her through her first orgasm. And it's only her first, because I'm damn sure, the way this pussy feels going off, I won't ever stop.

"Saint..." she clings to me, glassy-eyed as I thrust up inside her. "Oh *fuck*."

"That's it, every last inch." I urge her on, shifting her weight so she's straddling me properly. "Ride me, darling. Be a good girl and make those pretty tits bounce."

Her cheeks flush at my filthy instructions, eyes bright as she does what I say: Tessa grips my shoulders tightly and starts to move.

It's fucking heaven.

The way this woman knows just how to work me: lifting her hips and sinking down to take every inch of my straining cock inside her; clenching me with her tight inner walls, and grinding just right. Her head is tipped back in pleasure, her breasts shudder and bounce.

Dear Lord, just the sight of her makes my balls tighten, eager for release. I groan, gripping her tighter. Urging her on.

And then Tessa lifts her head. She holds my gaze, slowing her wild pace, leaning closer, so I can feel the rustle of her warm breath against my lips with every gasp and moan.

"The way you feel inside me..." she whispers, sinking down to take me deep inside her again. "God, Saint, it's perfect. *You're* perfect."

I bite back a howl. *Fuck*. I know she's wrong, I'm far from perfect, my whole life I've been the black sheep. *The disappointment.* But when she's looking at me like this, loving me like this, fusing our bodies together and sobbing my name like a prayer...

It feels like I could be, with her love.

I'm drowning now, swept under the waves of her passion; my body already coiling tight, fuck, straining for release. But I can't let go, not without bringing her with me. Ragged, I reach between us to circle her clit as her body writhes and jerks. She's close. So fucking close—

And I know exactly what will send my baby over the edge.

I tilt her chin up, look her directly in the eyes, and order her: "Be my good girl, and come."

Her body breaks with a cry of pleasure, and fuck, the tight, heavenly clench is my undoing. I come, exploding inside her with a howl.

Chapter 11

Tessa

"How did they find us?"

We gather around the kitchen table in the morning with coffee, toast, and a hundred unanswered questions. I'm feeling much better, thanks to my night in Saint's arms—and his shower. My bullet graze only throbs a little under a fresh bandage and antiseptic cream, but now that the initial panic and terror is behind us, it's time to face the terrifying reality of what happened.

Someone came to kill Wren. They knew where we were hiding her.

But how?

"Did someone follow me down from London, do you think?" I ask, reflecting back over the past couple of days. "Your car isn't exactly inconspicuous," I add to Saint. "If they'd been watching this place, they could have trailed me down, straight to the cottage..."

"It was Phillip," Saint announces grimly, getting up to pour more coffee.

Wren gasps. "What? No!"

"He's her friend," I argue.

"I would trust him with my life," Wren swears.

"You already did," Saint says. "And look how that turned out. Take the evidence: Outside the people sitting in this room, Phillip is the only person who even knows you're still alive."

I see Wren's expression slip.

"Plus, he's been promoted at Ashford..." I say slowly, realizing how much it makes sense. "He's replaced Valerie as head of the whole project now. That's not a small role; you saw the penthouse. I'm guessing there's a huge pay package to match."

"Stock options, bonuses for taking the drug through to launch..." Saint agrees. "Ashford likes to make sure everyone is invested in their success. Which means he's got a lot to lose if we manage to expose the fraud."

"And you told him where we were hiding you!" I exclaim, chilled. "Remember, you made that joke about Farleigh-Under-Lyme? I'm betting the minute we left his place, he reported everything to his boss at Ashford."

"Oh my God." Wren pauses, looking stricken. "You're right. But that wasn't Phillip in the woods," she adds, frowning. "The man with the gun was broader, and more athletic. Phillip couldn't run a mile to save his life, and he's never even touched a gun."

"Ashford wouldn't send their prized scientist for a job like this." Saint shakes his head. "They'd send someone they trust. Someone used to getting his hands dirty."

I notice that Saint keeps saying 'Ashford' is behind all this, instead of naming Alexander St. Clair. Maybe it makes it easier for him to think of the company, and not his own father planning Wren's murder like this.

In cold blood.

"The question is, what do we do now?" I ask slowly.

"You mean, besides taking Phillip apart for nearly getting

the two of you killed?" Saint asks, and I can tell by the spark of fury in his eyes, he's not even kidding.

"We shouldn't do anything," Wren says suddenly. When I look over in surprise, I see her expression is focused now, thinking fast.

"But he betrayed you!" I protest.

"Exactly. We know now that he's reporting every move up to his bosses at Ashford. So, let's use that," she proposes. "When he gets in touch again, we act like we still trust him."

"We could even give him false info to pass back to them," I suggest. "Say we're quitting the whole plan. Maybe if Ashford think we're dropping it, they'll ease up."

"What do you think?" Wren asks Saint, who's been sitting there silently with his coffee.

"I think Ashford isn't easing anything, not as long as you're still a walking liability. But it might buy us some time," he adds with a nod. "Stop them from sending any more armed heavies."

"Text him now," Wren tells me. "Say we need to meet ASAP."

"But don't think I'm letting you out of my sight," Saint says fiercely.

"You can't come," I try to argue. "It'll spook Phillip. He's already intimidated enough by you, you're the boss, remember?"

Saint clenches his jaw stubbornly. "Fine, I won't meet him, but I'll be there, watching. I'll have your backs."

I stifle a smile. Is it weird to be turned on by this protective streak? I know we've all been through a lot in the past twenty-four hours, but seeing Saint so determined to keep me safe makes my heart melt a little.

And other places, too.

I send Phillip the message, and quickly get a response. "He

can meet at lunchtime, today. He suggested a café, near the river."

Saint knows the spot, and nods. "It's crowded, with lots of tourists around. Nobody would try coming after you there."

"OK..." I text back, confirming, then look over at Wren. I can tell she's still trying to wrap her head around Phillip's betrayal. "Will you manage to act like you're still friends?" I ask, worried. "If he thinks we're onto him..."

"I'll manage," Wren replies tightly. "Even if I want to rip his fingernails out for putting us in danger."

"You'll have to get in line," Saint mutters darkly. "And his fingernails aren't the only thing getting ripped from that fucker's body."

I look between them: furious and deadly. They have more in common than they thought. "As long as we're all on the same page," I say, with a wry smile. "Lunch should be fun!"

We take the Tube across town to the Southbank area of the Thames. Wren is still paranoid about being followed, and after what happened in the countryside, now I am too. So, we stick together: Wren hidden under a ballcap and dark glasses, with Saint trailing twenty feet behind us, watching for anything suspicious.

The café Phillip suggested is connected to the National Film Theater, a big complex with movie screenings and lecture theaters. There are tons of people around, and I breathe a small sigh of relief, seeing the security guards posted around the place. Nobody would be stupid enough to try and come after Wren in a place like this.

And even if they did, I'm reassured by a glimpse of Saint, taking up position at a table across the room. He hides behind a newspaper, but I know, he's watching everything.

Protecting us.

"Ready to meet your BFF?" I ask Wren. A part of me is worried she won't be able to keep up the act, but when Phillip waves, and comes over with a tray of drinks, Wren is all smiles.

"So, how does it feel, being the big shot in charge?" she asks, teasing.

"Stressful," he replies, taking a seat. "Mostly it's just mountains of paperwork."

"Your favorite. Heavy is the head that wears the crown," Wren grins.

"Were you able to take a look around the servers?" I ask, leaning forward confidentially. I don't expect for a minute that Phillip will give us any useful information, but I pretend like I do.

Sure enough, Phillip nods. "I did. I checked everything," he tells Wren. "Double-checked, even. All the human trial data, right from the start. I looked for the inconsistencies you told me about, but I didn't find anything. It's all clean."

"Oh." Wren pretends to look disappointed.

"What does that mean?" I ask, playing dumb. "There was only a problem with the first trials with the mice, but these ones are OK?"

Phillip nods. "Whatever was going on before, Valerie must have learned from the mistakes, and made sure everything ran properly with the main trial. It's all aboveboard."

"That's great news," I exclaim, pretending to be relieved. "Isn't it great, Wren?"

"Uh huh." She's looking at Phillip with tension in her gaze, and I can tell that she thinks he's lying through his teeth.

"I know you were worried the trials were compromised," Phillip adds. "But it's alright. The drug works."

"What a relief!" I exclaim. Wren still doesn't say anything. *Shit.* I kick her under the table, and she jolts.

"A big relief," she agrees. "I just wanted to make sure the science backed it up. So many people are counting on this research, you see."

"Right." Phillip coughs, looking flustered.

Looking guilty.

"But if the trials are all genuine, then we don't have to worry anymore!" I add loudly. "We can forget all about the other data and move on with our lives."

"That's good." Phillip says quickly. "Moving on is good."

"Isn't it?" Wren gives him a tight smile. "I'm so proud of you, you know. Taking over the project, running the whole team. It must feel amazing, knowing you're going to be changing the face of medicine."

"Uh, yes. It's... a big thrill," Phillip replies, swallowing hard.

Wren's smile widens. "I have to admit, I'm jealous. I miss lab life," she says, with a wistful tone. "And the new Ashford HQ! That's a step up from our Oxford digs, huh? No more getting lost in the storage closet every time we need a new petri dish," she adds with a grin.

Phillip seems to relax a little. "It's crazy," he says. "The tech they've got there... There's a new liquid chromatograph that makes my heart skip a beat."

"No!" Wren laughs. "How long were we begging for one?"

"Too long." He smiles.

"So are you all squeezed in together, the way we were?" she asks innocently, taking a sip of her coffee. "It's the basement levels, right?"

"Right. I thought I'd miss natural light, but we have a bunch of SAD lamps, and to be honest, it's easier for the sterile environment."

"Some experiments are affected by light," Wren explains to me.

"Oh, wow," I make a general murmur of interest. I'm not

sure where Wren's going with the chitchat, but I know she's got an agenda here.

"The setup is incredible," Phillip continues. "I wish you could see it. A whole floor of micromanipulators and centrifuges, then the meeting rooms... I even have my own office now, right beside the server room," he adds proudly. "With a mini fridge."

"So no more catfights when Mickey steals your lunch," Wren says with a grin.

"Exactly." Phillip smiles back. "So, what will you do now that you're dropping all this?" he asks. "You are dropping it now, aren't you?"

"Of course," Wren smiles. "After all, there's nothing to expose. You've put my mind completely at ease. So... I don't know what the future holds."

"Maybe you should go back to America," Phillip says, looking anxious. "To be near your family, I mean. You must have missed them a lot."

"You're so sweet, looking out for me." Wren reaches across and squeezes his hand. "I'm so glad we had this chance to reconnect. You've been such a big help," she adds, and I know she's privately twisting the knife. "It means the world to me that I can trust you like this."

Phillip gulps, looking seriously uneasy. "Of course," he stammers. "You can always trust me."

Bastard.

He pulls away and checks his watch in a big, exaggerated gesture. "Look at the time!" he blurts, already bolting to his feet. "I need to get back."

"Of course," Wren coos. "I'm sure they can't get anything done there without you."

"It was great seeing you," I tell him, just as upbeat. "Let us know if you want to hang out again, before Wren goes back to the States. We could all have dinner, take it easy. No more investigations and drama," I add, with a little laugh, like the whole thing was a game.

Phillip laughs along nervously. "Sounds good. I'll, umm, let you know!"

He hurries away, disappearing into the crowd.

"I bet you a hundred bucks, I never hear from him again," Wren says, scowling after him.

"So much for friendship."

WE LINGER a little longer at the café, then take a meandering route back to Saint's place, stopping at a few stores to pick up more clothes and essentials for Wren, and to make sure we're not being followed. I don't see Saint, but I can feel his watchful eyes on us, and the reassurance of his presence nearby.

"I can't believe he looked in my eyes and lied like that," I mutter, still fuming when we all rendezvous back at the safety of Saint's house. "He's a traitor. Not just to you, but the whole of modern medicine!"

"If it helps, I don't think he knows anything about them sending that man to kill you," Wren offers. "I can't believe he'd want me dead."

"Some consolation." I roll my eyes. "He's still willing to perpetrate a massive fraud against Alzheimer's patients and their families, and for what?"

"Fame, vast wealth, fast cars," Saint speaks up, joining us in the living room. He collapses on the couch next to me, taking my hand and bringing it to his lips. "People have done far worse, for far less."

"Well, we're not going to let them get away with it," I say, determined. "Are we?"

There's a pause, and something uncertain skitters across Wren's face. "I could just leave," she says quietly.

My head snaps up. "What do you mean?"

"If we drop this now, you could be safe," she tells me. "I only came back because I thought you were in danger, with him," she nods to Saint. "I had no idea it would set off this domino chain of disaster. Ashford have already proven they'd rather kill than let the truth come out. But what if we just let it go, the way we told Phillip. You could have your life back."

"But... If we let them release this drug, it's going to harm thousands of people. Millions, even!" I protest. I can't believe this. "Whatever happened to 'do no harm'?"

"I'm not a doctor," Wren reminds me. "And what happened last night... I never imagined they would try to kill us. Is this really worth your life?"

Her question sits, uneasy. Then Saint squeezes my hand.

"I'm afraid the moment to decide that came and went," he speaks up. "Even if you walked away, Wren, they wouldn't stop coming after you. Or Tessa. We have to see this through and expose them, it's the only way for you both to be safe again."

Wren sighs, giving a resigned nod. "Not all of us are St. Clairs, and indispensable," she says, clearly trying to make light of it.

"Hey, there's still one more brother to play heir. I'm not so hard to replace," Saint replies with a smirk.

"Yes, you are," I tell him, and he smiles, and leans in to drop a kiss on my lips.

Wren clears her throat loudly. "Snack, anyone?"

She exits to the kitchen, leaving Saint to kiss me more deeply. I melt against him, savoring the rush of heat that flares between us, no matter what else is going on in the messy, chaotic world.

With him, I always find peace.

Finally, he draws back, and tenderly brushes hair from my eyes. "How are you feeling? Is the wound OK?" he asks.

I nod. "It just stings a little, that's all. The graze wasn't even that deep. Wren says it may not even leave a scar."

"Not on you, at least," Saint says, softly tracing my bandage. "Seeing you bleeding like that took at least ten years off my life."

"Then we'll just have to make the most of what's left," I murmur, and kiss him again, until Wren loudly rejoins us. Then I reluctantly release him and try to get my head back in the game.

"If Phillip won't help provide us with the evidence of Ashford's fraud, we're going to have to get it ourselves," I announce.

Saint nods. "That's what I'm thinking, too. What is it exactly you would need to confirm the drug trials were a fraud?"

"The raw datasets," Wren replies, pacing restlessly. "Trials like this produce a massive quantity of data. Test subjects get checked for a hundred different things, sometimes weekly, to track their progress. We don't just measure the effect of the drugs on their cognitive function, but blood, organs, cell structures, to make sure there aren't damaging side effects," she explains. "That raw test data gets analyzed and modeled a million different ways. No matter what miraculous results they presented for review, those original datasets will be on the system somewhere. We just have to find them."

"Just," I echo lightly.

Wren smiles. "Well, Phillip *did* help," she reports with a smirk. "He told us exactly where his office is: on the second basement level, next to the server room."

"So that's what you were fishing for!" I exclaim. "I wondered why you cared about all that small talk."

"He couldn't help bragging about his swanky new office," she nods. "Now we know *where* we can access the data, I just need to get in there and download it from his workstation. He's the boss. If anyone will have full access, it's him."

"You'll go?" I echo, and Saint immediately backs me up.

"No. No chance. Absolutely not." He stands.

"Do you know how to read the raw data?" Wren counters.

"Do you want to walk in the doors of a building where everybody thinks that you're dead, and the ones who don't would like to make you that way, and soon?" Saint shoots back.

They face off, both just as determined at the other.

"Saint's right." I stand, moving between them. "Wren, come on. You can't go near Ashford Pharma. Just one glimpse of you on the security cameras will cause an emergency, but he can walk right in without anyone thinking twice. It's his name above the door!"

"I'll copy everything to a hard drive, and bring it straight back for you to analyze," Saint promises.

Wren looks frustrated, but she knows she can't disagree. Saint has access beyond even the regular employees, and sure, they might be surprised to see him snooping around the laboratories, but I'm sure he can wing it.

Saint's phone sounds. He checks the message. "It's time," he says, nodding to Wren.

"Time for what?" I ask, confused, as Wren retrieves her bag, and the things we bought today. "Where are you going?"

My panic must show, because Saint places a reassuring hand on my arm. "She's just going to go stay at Sebastian and Avery's place."

"What? Why?" I demand.

"I've got a target on my back," Wren speaks up. "I'm not spending another night under the same roof as you, Tessa. I won't put you in danger like that again."

"Tough. That's not your choice to make," I say angrily, moving to block her.

"Hey." Saint plants himself in front of me. He takes me by the shoulders, looking down at me reassuringly. "This is to protect Wren. To protect the both of you."

"It's safe here," I insist.

"But Seb's place is safer. It's a fortress," Saint explains. "Bullet-proof windows, gated driveway, 24/7 guards. He's used to people gunning for him. It's built to keep the bad guys out."

"It's OK, Tessie." Wren nods. "It's smarter this way, splitting up. They won't know where to find me."

"And even if they do, they have a fat chance of getting past Seb's high-tech system," Saint agrees. "It's just for the night. We'll all meet back tomorrow."

I exhale. It doesn't look like I've got a choice here, so even though I hate the idea of being parted from Wren, I slowly nod.

Soon, the door sounds. It's a burly security guard, sent to collect Wren. "See?" she jokes, giving me a hug. "No offense to your guy, but I want someone like this standing between me and a bullet."

I muster a smile. "Text every hour."

"I will... If I'm not luxuriating," Wren jokes. "Apparently, this Sebastian guy is even richer than Saint. You know how to pick your friends," she adds with a wink, before heading to the SUV waiting outside.

As they leave, I catch a glimpse of the guard's shoulder holster. He's armed.

Good.

"I know you don't want to be away from her again," Saint says, as they drive away. "But we have to play it smart now. Ashford is scared, and scared animals are the most dangerous. They're capable of anything."

There it is again: *Ashford.*

"Do you think your father is planning all of this?" I can't help but ask.

Saint's expression tightens. "I don't know. But either way, they won't be for long. We need to finish this soon, before they have a chance to regroup, or come after you again."

Inside, I track Wren's journey on my phone app, before she FaceTimes to show she's arrived safely at Sebastian's home. "Seb and Avery out of town, but they have *staff*," Wren whispers, from what looks like a palatial modern bedroom suite. "Some guy asked me how I like my steak cooked, and my coffee in the morning. And another woman whisked all my bags away to launder and press my clothes."

"You hear that?" I call to Saint, wandering upstairs. "You're going to have to up your game."

I enter the bedroom and stop. He's changing clothes, into a crisp button-down shirt and designer tailored suit. The kind of clothing he wears to the office.

The kind of outfit he'd choose if he was going to snoop around Ashford Pharma without raising suspicion.

"Sleep tight," I tell Wren quickly. "I'll talk to you in the morning."

"Love you!"

I hang up, and watch Saint button his shirt. "Going out?" I ask slowly.

He looks over. "I told you, we're running out of time. I need to go to Ashford tonight and download the data, before they decide to cover their tracks."

"OK then." I nod—and move to the closet, too. I flip through the racks of brand-new outfits, before picking a red plunging dress, and strappy heels. "Do you think this will work?"

Saint pauses, frowning. "Work for what?"

"Our break-in. Because I'm coming too."

Chapter 12

Tessa

"Out of the question."

Saint doesn't even think about it, he just stalks out of the dressing room, leaving me to scramble into my showstopper of a dress. Really, it's a costume to match his as we stroll past the Ashford Pharma guards, because there's no way I'm staying home tonight.

I squeeze into the tight red silk, and struggle to zip up the back. I can't reach. "Can you please get this?" I ask, emerging into the bedroom and presenting my bare back to Saint.

"Take it off."

His voice is curt, and when I turn to face him, I see that his handsome face is marred with a frown. "I thought you said that there was no time to waste," I reply with a smirk. "But if you want to squeeze in a quick workout before we leave..."

"Don't be cute. You know what I mean," Saint warns me, pulling on his jacket.

"I'm afraid cute is just a natural state for me," I reply, still teasing. "Fine. I'll zip it up myself."

I reach, wriggling, until I finally manage to yank it up.

"There. Do you think I look like a future duke's trophy girlfriend?" I ask, fluffing out my hair.

"Tessa..." Saint's voice is like steel. "You're not coming."

I arch my eyebrow. "Well, that would be a first with you."

"Tessa!" he exclaims, frustrated. "This isn't a game!"

"You think I don't know that?" I put my hands on my hips and glare. "I'm the one who was stalked through the woods last night, shot at, and barely escaped with my life."

"Which is why you're not coming anywhere near Ashford!" Saint yells, his voice ringing out with frustration. "I'm not putting you in harm's way again!"

I pause. Clearly, I'm going to need a different tactic.

"You want to leave me here alone?" I ask. "You just said it wasn't safe enough for Wren to stay."

Saint frowns deeper. "That's not what I meant."

"But it's true," I move closer, and run my hands up his lapels. "The safest place in the world for me is right by your side."

I kiss his neck, running my lips softly over his skin; feeling his body tense, his cock hardening against me.

"What was that rule you made?" Saint sighs, but he's already sliding his hands around my waist and drawing me closer. "About not using sex as a weapon..."

I smile. "If I remember right, you broke that rule *all* the time."

Saint makes a noise of lustful frustration. He kisses me, hard enough to make my knees weak and my head spin, then draws back. "If we're doing this, we do this my way," he warns me. "You do exactly what I say, there's no room for error, or arguing once we're in that building. Understand?"

I nod eagerly. "Understood."

"I mean it, Tessa." Saint keeps hold of me. "You know what

they did to Valerie. What they nearly did to you and Wren last night. If we make one wrong move..."

"I understand, Saint," I promise. "We get in, copy the drive, and get out."

"And if I tell you to walk away, you get the hell out of there," he adds. "As fast as you can."

"Which, in these shoes..." I give him a smirk, and he flicks his eyes to the heavens in a rueful plea.

"Did I say this was taking ten years off my life? Make it fifteen."

We wait until after ten p.m., when Saint says the offices will be pretty much empty, then take a cab over the Ashford HQ. My nerves twists tighter with every mile. I know I was making light of it back at the house, but I know how important the next few hours are: They're everything. Without proof of Ashford's wrongdoing and fraud, there's nothing we can do to stop the drug launch and all the damage it will do.

And if we don't expose them... Ashford will keep coming after Wren to silence her. We got away at the cottage last night out of sheer luck—but how long will that luck hold?

I don't want to find out. Which means we have to get into the laboratories tonight to download those original datasets.

We pull up outside the building and get out of the car. I take a deep breath. The huge marble lobby lies silent, the lights of the city glittering outside the vast glass frontage.

"Ready?" Saint asks, looking determined.

"Ready." I nod.

He slings an arm around my shoulder, and we head for the main doors.

"Evening, Sayeed," Saint calls to the guard on duty, as we

stroll in. I make a show of tottering on my heels, clinging to Saint's arm in my skintight dress like a wide-eyed date.

"Mr. St. Clair," the guard looks surprised to see him here so late. "Burning the midnight oil?"

"Something like that. I promised this one a tour of the CEO's office," Saint gives me a meaningful look, and I giggle.

"Can you really see Buckingham Palace from your window?" I coo.

"You'll be seeing a whole lot more, darling." Saint squeezes my ass, every inch the bachelor playboy.

Saint swipes his security pass and steers me through—just as a pizza delivery guy barges in, half-hidden behind a stack of boxes. "Order for Moussad?"

The guard frowns. "That's me, but I didn't call for any pizza."

"Moussad, Ashford Pharma, a dozen pepperoni, says right here." The pizza guy deposits them on the lobby desk. "That's a hundred and forty-four quid, plus tip."

"But I didn't order anything."

"Your name's on the order."

"I'm a bloody vegan!"

They start to bicker over the mystery order, as Saint and I approach the elevators. When we're sure that the guard is distracted by our little pizza delivery ploy, we veer off, diving into the stairwell instead.

The door swings shut behind us.

I hurry down the stairs, but Saint catches my hand. "Slow down," he says, pulling me into a kiss on the first landing. "We're on a romantic tour, remember?"

I force myself to take a breath, whispering there together like a pair of young lovers. There are cameras everywhere, and since we have no way of avoiding them or shutting them off, we have to pull this off in full view of the security team.

"Once everyone is packed up and gone for the night, the guards just hang out, playing video games and watching for anyone out of place," Saint murmurs, still nuzzling at me. "They're not going to come after the CEO for taking a little after-hours tour of the place."

"OK..." I nod, steeling myself. Then I back away, giving Saint a big flirty beckoning gesture. "Why don't you show me your equipment, hot stuff?"

He grins. "My laboratories get you hot, hmmm?"

"So hot." We descend another level, hand-in-hand, and then I nod to the door. "Here. Phillip said his office was on Level Two."

We push open the stairwell door, and into a long, sterile-looking hallway. Fluorescent lights shine brightly overhead, and doors lead off on each side. "It's near the server room," I remember.

"This way, I think." Saint leads me through an open area, filled with workstations and science-y looking equipment. We're halfway across the room, when suddenly, voices sound nearby.

Fuck.

Saint and I exchange a look of panic. Then Saint dives behind the nearest desk, pulling me after him. We crouch there together, my heart pounding, as a lab door swings open, and two women in white coats emerge.

"... No, see everyone thinks the song is about Joe, but it's really about Karlie, after their road trip to Big Sur..."

They settle back at their workstations, still chatting—and oblivious to the two of us hiding here nearby.

For now.

"I don't believe it. Wouldn't we have seen photos of them together?"

"Umm, hello? That *Vogue* shoot, they were writing hearts

with their names in it! And Christian Siriano made her a rainbow dress to come out for Pride years ago, but then that got delayed, and—"

Saint tugs my hand. I glance over; he nods at a door behind us, about twenty feet away. Without waiting for my response, he begins to creep towards it, bent double to stay out of sight.

I don't have a choice, I follow, trying my best to make a sound. Luckily, the two women are talking loudly, and don't look over. Saint eases the door open, and we both slip inside.

It's dark and cramped, some kind of storage closet. Saint silently closes the door behind us, and we squeeze in close together, trying to stay silent.

"How long do you think they'll stay?" I whisper, my heartbeat pounding at the near miss.

"Hopefully, not all night." He peers through the crack in the closet the door. The women are still chatting, their voices carrying in a low hum. "We'll just have to wait here until they leave."

I look around, my eyes adjusting a little to the dim light. The closet is lined with narrow shelves and packed with boxes and cleaning supplies. I shift, finding the back wall, and Saint follows, wrapping his arms around me; trying not to knock anything down.

I catch my breath, pressed up against the solid planes of his chest, feeling both of our heartbeats race.

"So, how's your life as a charming criminal turning out?" I whisper to Saint, joking to distract myself. "Tempted to pull a Thomas Crown, and start planning wild heists?"

He gives a low chuckle. "Let's see how this one turns out, before we make any big career plans."

"I don't know, maybe Ashford is just the start," I muse, wriggling to get comfy in his arms. "We could travel the world, exposing corporate crimes, righting wrongs..."

"Or how about this is the last danger you ever see, and once this is over, we never do anything that sends my blood pressure through the roof?" Saint murmurs, his lips brushing my forehead.

"Nothing?" I tease. "But getting your blood pressure up can be so much fun..."

I shift even closer, until our bodies are molded together. Saint hisses a breath, sliding his hands over my hips. My pulse kicks—and it has nothing to do with the danger of the situation.

He just has this effect on me.

I focus on my breathing, trying to stay calm even as I'm painfully aware of every shift or movement Saint makes.

"Don't..." he murmurs softly in my ear.

"Don't what?"

"Don't tempt me."

I shiver. His palm is hot through the silk of my dress, his fingers stroking softly. "You're the one doing the tempting," I whisper, and I can't help imagining him peeling the fabric away from my body and letting it fall to the—

"... Call it a night." The women's voices sound again, muffled through the door.

Saint and I both startle out of our lustful reverie. I lean in closer to hear.

"Me too," the other woman says. "Wait a minute, I'll walk you out."

There's the noise of chairs being pushed, and footsteps receding, then a door closes.

Silence.

We wait a moment longer, my heart pounding again. Then Saint eases the closet door open and peers out. "All clear."

We creep out into the lab. It's eerie now, all the lights still on, but nobody around. Every surface is white and chrome, sterile. "I don't care how many SAD lamps they have, this place gives me the creeps," I say with a shiver.

"So, let's get this information downloaded and get the hell out," Saint agrees, looking determined.

We start to methodically search the doorways and closets leading off the main lab. I find the server room, full of high-tech equipment, and then next door, a large office. There's the usual desk and computer, but also a row of action figures lined up on a shelf, along with some framed diplomas.

Phillip McAlister.

Bingo.

"Over here," I whisper-call to Saint. He moves straight to the computer. The screen prompts a log-on. "Wren says Phillip is terrible with passwords, he always picks something too complicated, and forgets it."

"And since the new Ashford protocol is for everyone to update their password weekly..."

"He'll probably have written it down, somewhere," I finish.

We start to search the room. Saint checks the desk drawers in turn, while I scan the shelving and file cabinets. Then I spot Phillip's precious mini fridge in the corner and get a stroke of inspiration.

Inside, I find a row of La Croix sodas... and a Post-it stuck to one reading '1trueRing1Sauron!_Baggins.'

"Got it!"

I snatch the slip of paper and rush back to the computer, where Saint grabs it, and painstakingly types it in.

Access granted.

"We're in."

We share an excited look, before Saint starts clicking. "Wren isn't sure where the original datasets would be stored, so she said we should copy everything that looks related to the project."

He pulls up Phillip's file directory and zeroes in on everything with the word ARCHEMEDES in the titles. The Ashford code-word for the project. Then Saint pulls a slim portable hard drive, and plugs it in. He highlights the files and drags them over to the external drive icon.

Copying... 1...2...3%

He sits back, exhaling. My heart is racing, too. I can't believe we're doing this.

"What will you do with the information, if it really is the proof we need?" I ask Saint, as the data copies, and the completed percentage rises.

He pauses, looking troubled. "I have no choice. If they faked the trials, we have to expose them. I can't let them bring the drug to market, knowing it doesn't work."

I can't even imagine the fallout of a scandal like this. There'll be a media frenzy, that's for sure. Criminal charges, massive investigations, maybe even jail time—and that's not counting the little matter of attempted murder, either.

But still, the thought gives me no pleasure. Not when I know the price Saint will pay.

"This is your family we're talking about," I say softly. "The Ashford name."

He gives me a pained nod. "I know."

We're silent a moment, watching the progress bar creep along. The numbers tick up slowly, and it's just past 80 percent—almost home free—when I hear something, in the lab outside.

"What was that?" I freeze, my pulse racing.

"I didn't hear anything," Saint replies, but then the noise comes again, loud enough to make him stop, too.

Footsteps.

Coming closer.

Shit.

Chapter 13

Tessa

I panic. "It's not done copying yet!"

Saint and I look at each other in horror. So much for the VIP tour cover story; if someone walks in and finds us here with a hard drive plugged in and the download in progress, they'll catch us red-handed.

Goodbye, proof of fraud and corruption. Hello, trespassing and theft charges—if we're lucky.

And if we're not...

Saint curses under his breath, as I creep to the door. "Tessa," he whispers sharply. "Get away from there!"

But I crack the door open an inch, and peer out to see who's coming. Maybe we'll strike it lucky, and it's just one of the lab workers from before, here to grab something from her desk and then head out again. Maybe—

The footsteps come closer, and my hopes are cut short.

It's a security guard. A stern old-timer, with his radio in one hand, and the other resting on his holster. He's looking around, peering into every doorway and corner.

"... You sure it was down here?" he's saying into his radio. "Yeah, I'll do a full sweep. Every door."

Fuck.

I watch as the guard checks the nearest office, stepping inside, and flipping the lights on. Saint joins me, quickly assessing the situation. "What are we going to do?" I whisper. "There's no other way out, and we have to get the files. We have nothing without them. No proof at all."

He nods, looking grim. "Stay here," he orders me.

"What?" I blink. "Where are you going? Saint—"

He steps out of Phillip's office before I can stop him, leaving me stranded there, hiding behind the door watching with my heart in my throat as he makes his way across the lab.

The guard emerges from another office, and stops, startled to see him.

"Evening," Saint greets him casually, and I almost stop breathing.

What the hell is he doing?

"Who are you?" the guard demands, placing a hand on his holster. "This is a restricted area. I'm going to need to see your security pass."

"My pass?" Saint echoes, his voice amused. "Well, I suppose, if I must..." he reaches into his jacket and pulls out his wallet, flipping through. "Which would you prefer: My membership to the Century club? The keycard to my family's private suite at the Savoy? The onyx Amex, that one's a beauty, eh? Only ten in the entire country, at least since the sanctions kicked in and those Ruskies fled for greener pastures," he adds, in the rich, droll tones of a wealthy jackass.

I gulp a breath. He's bluffing it, playing up the Ashford heir angle. I cross my fingers and pray the act works.

The guard looks at him, unimpressed. "I meant, your pass for this laboratory. If you're trespassing..."

"My good man," Saint gives a chortle of laughter, "How could I be trespassing, when my family owns the damn building? Now, what was your name?"

"Uh, Richards, sir," the man says, looking flustered now.

"Richards. Fine name. Thing is, I'm down here on official business. Top secret, above your pay grade." Saint pats his shoulder and turns him back the way he came. "So it would be best if you just run along now the way you came, and forget you even saw me."

He guides him another few steps towards the door, and Richards almost goes too... But at the last minute, he stops and folds his arms. "I'm sorry, sir, but I was told to run a full sweep of the floor. If you don't mind waiting, I'll call up to the main office, and see about this project of yours."

"That won't be necessary," Saint says quickly, his casual act slipping.

"Best to be on the safe side, eh Mr. St. Clair? We'll just get this all straightened out—"

Fuck.

I look around wildly. The files are still downloading. 92%. We're so close!

Thinking fast, I quickly push my dress off one shoulder, revealing my black lacy bra. Mussing up my hair, I exit Phillip's office, calling out, "Baby? Where did you go—whoops," I beam, pretending to see Saint and the guard for the first time. "Hello Mister Security Guard," I coo. "Are we in trouble? Have you been a naughty boy?" I add, moving to Saint, and sliding my hand up his arm.

Right away, he plays along. "I'm always naughty," he smirks back at me, grabbing my ass. "I'm going to need a good spanking to behave."

"Miow!" I trill with laughter, rubbing up against him. "You're so bad!"

"But you love it, don't you, baby?" Saint says, giving me a long, steamy kiss. I wrap my arms around him, practically climbing him like a tree to really sell the bimbo act. And it works: When we finally come up for air, the guard isn't looking suspicious anymore, just seriously uncomfortable at our PDA.

"I'm sorry, Mr. St. Clair, but this area really is off-limits."

"Dammit." Saint makes a show of sighing. "I suppose we'll just have to play scientist and the sexy lab assistant some other time."

"Boo..." I pout. "I was looking forward to wearing one of those cute white coats. And nothing else," I add, winking at the guard.

He coughs, flustered. "If you'll just follow me back upstairs..."

Shit. The drive.

"I just need to grab my purse!" I exclaim, and sashay back towards Phillip's office, while Saint tries to distract him.

"I never thought the sight of some petri dishes would turn a woman on, but what can I say? Turns out she has a thing for science dorks."

I duck into the office and check the drive.

Download complete.

Yes!

I stash it, and collect my tiny evening bag, before emerging from the office again. "Now, tell me about that uniform of yours..." I fix the guard with a flirty look. "Does it come with handcuffs?"

He blushes. "I'm afraid I'm going to have to check your bag, madam."

"Madam?" I give a big gasp. "Since when did I stop being a 'Miss?' You sure know how to wound a girl," I add with a smile, slipping my arm through Saint's, and heading for the door.

But Richards stands firm. "Your bag," he says, holding out his hand.

I feel Saint tense beside me, but I squeeze his hand. "This old thing? Go ahead."

I hand it over and watch him rifle through the tiny pouch. Lip balm, aspirin, a hair tie... Saint is practically vibrating out of his designer suit, expecting us to get busted. I can't tell him that there's nothing out of the ordinary there...

Because the drive is shoved in my bra.

Richards shuts it and passes it back to me. "My apologies," he says.

"I should hope so," I pout. "We were in the middle of something before you ruined all the fun." I give a big sigh, and tug on Saint's hand. "Babe, I'm *hungry.*"

"Then we'll go get you something to eat."

"But it needs to be gluten-free, and organic," I keep up the act, as we walk back through the lab, the guard's eyes on us every step of the way. "And you know how my tummy doesn't like anything that's even *touched* a processed grain!"

SOMEHOW, we manage to act causal—and horny—all the way back to the lobby, sending a casual wave to Sayeed at the front desk, before piling into a cab outside. It's not until we're safely back at Saint's house again, alone, that I finally can exhale the wild tension that's been knotted tightly all night.

"Oh my God," I blurt, adrenaline coursing through my body. "I can't believe we just did that. And it worked!"

Saint slams the door behind us, and sinks back against it, panting hard. "Christ... When you came out of that office looking like I'd just fucked you senseless... I didn't know whether to kill you or kiss you."

"It worked, didn't it?" I beam. "He bought the whole sexy sneaking around act."

Saint chuckles, dragging a hand through his hair. "And then he searched your purse, I nearly lost it. Where did you hide the drive?"

I smirk. "Where do you think?" I hold out my arms and turn a slow circle. "Any guesses?"

Saint's expression turns wolfish. "Looks like you need a strip search."

"Yes, officer," I coo, grinning. "I've been a bad, bad girl."

"Now who's the one who needs a spanking?" Saint laughs, yanking me closer and feeling his way across my body.

"Getting warmer... Warmer..." I tease, until finally, he strokes over my breasts, and plucks the drive from where it's nestled, hidden just beneath my cleavage. "Bingo."

"I always knew, I loved your breasts," Saint says with a smirk.

I laugh. I can't help it. I feel giddy, riding high on the thrill of our narrow escape. "We make a pretty good team," I tell him, beaming.

"The best," he agrees, looking just as amped up.

There's a beat, our eyes locking in the hallway...

... Then we're reaching for each other, and fuck, it's on.

I throw myself at him, and Saint grabs me, hard, our mouths clashing together in a hot, wild kiss. We stumble back, knocking into shelving and consoles, sending God knows what crashing to the ground as he tears at my dress, and I rip his shirt open, hungrily running my hands over his bare chest.

I want him, fuck, I want him with a fiery passion that could burn down a whole city, clinging to him as he grips my hips, wrapping my legs around his waist. Saint slams me back against the wall, and I moan in pleasure, feeling his cock hard pressing between my thighs as he yanks my bra down and devours my breasts, licking and sucking in a frenzy. "Yes," I gasp eagerly, already thrusting against the hard ridge of him, loving the sweet rasp of friction even through the layers of our clothing. "Saint!"

My hands go to his belt, impatiently yanking open his zipper and freeing his cock. It's already straining for me, and I feel a rush of heat in my core as I grip him tightly and pump.

Saint sounds a raw, animal groan. He captures my wrists in one hand, pinning them above my head as he rocks against me harder, grinding me to the wall with his cock. "That's right, darling," he smirks, as I buck and gasp against him, wild for the feel of his swollen cockhead nudging up against my panties. "You know what's coming, don't you? You can't wait for this cock to fill you all the way up."

I moan with delight, loving the pressure against my clit but hating the damp fabric, now the only thing keeping him from thrusting deep. "Please," I gasp, struggling against his iron grip. "Take them off!"

Saint licks up the side of my neck and nips at my earlobe. Just as unhinged as I feel. "Are you going to be a good girl for me, baby?" he demands, panting. "Going to take every inch?"

I shudder at his filthy endearments. "Fuck. *Yes.*"

"Then *take it.*"

He hikes my dress up, rips my panties aside, and fucks into me in one brutal thrust.

I howl.

Saint thrusts deeper, pinning me to the wall as I go wild over the delicious stretch of his cock, *so thick,* and oh, the incredible friction. "Yes!" I cry, my voice echoing in pleasure, clenching tight around him. "Fuck, yes!"

"Christ, you're so wet," Saint groans, sinking deep. He releases my wrists, letting me wrap them tight around his neck as he grabs my hips and starts to thrust, hips snapping in a frenzied rhythm that makes me see stars.

God, it's too good. How can it feel this good, like I'm about to lose my mind?

"Don't stop!" I gasp, arching to meet him as the tension starts to coil. Oh God, I can feel it already, the electricity sparking deep in my spine, making my toes curl. "Don't stop!"

"Never," Saint vows, grinding deep. He slams into me, over and over, not breaking pace for a moment, not even when I'm shaking, and mewling, and writhing on his dick; chanting his name as the tension rises. Close, I'm so close....

"Oh God," I cry, shuddering in his arms as he grinds up into me again, applying pressure against my clit as his cock drives deep. "Right there, don't stop!"

"That's my filthy girl," he growls, eyes glittering wildly, pinning me in place. "Time to feel this pussy shake."

He lands a sharp slap on my ass, thrusting deep again, and God, I come apart, shattering with a high-pitched howl of pleasure that echoes through the night.

"Louder, baby," Saint hauls me off the wall; waves of release still consuming me. "We're not done yet."

He carries me through to the living room. We send another lamp crashing to the ground, but I don't care. I don't care about anything but the hot drive of his cock inside me, and the grip of his hands, and his mouth, demanding, as he claims another kiss, our tongues battling in a wild, sensual dance. We fall back onto the couch, Saint pinning me to the cushions and driving deep inside even as I'm still shaking from my last release. "Knees up, darling," he orders me with a growl, gripping my thighs and pressing them back against my chest. "I told you; you're taking every inch tonight."

He sinks into me again, and the new angle, *fuck*, it's deeper than ever. "Oh *God...*" I shake, my eyes practically rolling back in bliss as he buries his cock all the way to the hilt.

Saint groans with pleasure as I flex. "Christ, baby..." he

curses, braced there above me with his dark hair in a mess and his handsome face a picture of wild pleasure. "This pussy's going to ruin me," he swears, panting. "Every day, every fucking night, all I need in the world is to be buried right here."

"*Good.*"

I arch back, sounding a wild moan as he pins me down and fucks me senseless, so deep I lose track of where he ends and I begin; there's nothing but heat, and friction, and fuck, the incredible weight of him, pressing me into the couch, making my body quake. We're in this together, our bodies in perfect communication. Every thrust, every gasp, we don't even need words, we're past them now, careening towards the edge of release. Saint bites down on my shoulder, and I rake my nails down his back, demanding, as his body drives me higher, and the world melts away.

Nothing matters but us, right here. *Together*. And when my climax hits me, it takes him over the edge too, both of our voices echoing in pleasure as the release slams through us like a supernova, like the end of the world and the beginning, all in one.

Oh. My. God.

"Christ, woman," Saint sounds an exhausted chuckle, lifting his head from the floor. "I thought we agreed to keep my blood pressure down?"

"I thought we agreed, that wouldn't be much fun?" I retort, exhausted but grinning ear-to-ear. Somehow, we're sprawled on the antique rug. The room is in shambles around us.

And I feel *incredible*.

"Breaking and entering, corporate theft, fucking my brains out..." Saint pulls me into his arms, and we lay there together, gasping for air. "I don't know which one is going to be the death of me first."

"Definitely the fucking." I turn to kiss him, sweaty and glowing with pleasure. "Because those other things were one-offs, but we've got the rest of our lives to kill each other with sex."

"Is that so?" Saint arches an eyebrow at me, playful, and I wonder if I've said too much. Talking about the future like that when I only just moved in?

When we're still in the middle of a massive conspiracy, with danger looming at every turn...

But he just smiles at me, and drops a tender kiss on my lips, before collapsing back to the floor again. "Five minutes," he says, stretching out. "No, make it ten. Ten minutes, and a little snack, and we can put that theory of yours to the test."

"Or...." I pause. We promised not to look at the stolen Ashford info until we were together with Wren again, but I can't help feeling an itch of curiosity. What is it that we just risked everything to find? "Or... We could check the drive."

There's a beat, and then Saint is on his feet. "You get my laptop, I'll get the connectors," he says, not even pausing to pull on his briefs before disappearing down the hall.

I laugh, my body still humming with victory—and pleasure. We did it. We pulled off the heist and secured the proof that's going to change everything.

I scramble up, finally discarding my dress in favor of a blanket, and discovering a massive rip down the side. I smile, collecting the drive, and a bottle of water, before I meet Saint back in the living room.

"You owe me another dress," I tease him, as he connects the drive, and taps a few buttons to access it. "You ruined this one."

"Well, you ruined me for all other women," Saint replies with a smirk, pulling me down beside him. "So we're even."

My heart beats a little faster, as I watch him open the downloaded folders. "Which one do you think it is?"

"Only one way to find out," Saint says, sharing my excited smile. "We should check them all."

He clicks on the first file and opens it. But instead of a regular spreadsheet, the screen is covered in gibberish: just random letters and symbols, no matter how far he scrolls.

"What is that?" I ask, confused. He clicks out of the file and tries another. And another. But no matter what file we try to open, the result is the same stream of nonsense.

Saint curses, and I feel a wave of disappointment. "Did we copy the wrong thing?" I ask, my heart falling. We nearly risked discovery, sneaking into Ashford like that, and now we're still empty-handed?

Saint shakes his head, looking grim. "We got the files, but we can't read them. The whole drive is encrypted. And we don't have the key."

Chapter 14

Tessa

"Well… It looks like you had a big night," Wren notes, when we rendezvous at Sebastian's home the next morning.

"What? Why?" I blurt, flushing. I shoot a look at Saint as we enter the house.

Big mistake. He's smirking like he's replaying our wild sex marathon in full, Technicolor detail.

"I just meant, the stress of the break-in. You don't look like you got much sleep," Wren says, looking confused.

"Right. That!" I blurt, hiding my own grin. "Yeah, the adrenaline was wild. I was wired all night long. Barely slept a wink."

Screaming myself hoarse as Saint showed me exactly what a pair of security handcuffs could really do…

"I'm sorry," Wren frowns, giving me a hug. She's dressed in cozy cashmere sweats, but she's still looking far too tired and delicate for my liking. "I can't imagine how scared you must have been. But everything went smoothly, right?"

"Aside from the fact we can't get into the drive," I say, still frustrated.

"Well, hopefully Avery's mysterious friend can help with that," Wren says. "She just got here."

Wren shows us to a sunny conservatory at the back of the house, filled with orange trees and stunning art. There's a woman perched at a breakfast table in the corner, devouring a towering stack of pancakes, as the hulking butler looks on.

"Oh my God, these are amazing!" she greets us, barely pausing for breath. "And the syrup..."

"A warm maple blueberry compote," the butler announces, in a thick Cockney accent. "I must say, the chef has outdone himself today."

"He seriously has. Can I please get some more bacon?"

"Of course, ma'am."

I take her in curiously. *This* is the genius hacker sent to help us out? She looks like a beaming librarian, with square-rimmed glasses and her brown hair in a neat braid, wearing an orange knit cardigan over a dress printed with... Are those woodland animals?

"I'm Charlie," she introduces herself, as we join her at the table. "Avery said you had a nasty little encryption problem?"

"Uh, yes." Saint hands over the drive, looking just as dubious as I feel.

Charlie smirks, looking back and forth between us. "Don't worry, this isn't my usual getup," she says, whipping a laptop out of a tote bag. "I'm doing some undercover work right now, hence the friendly nanny vibe."

"Oh, OK." I feel relieved—and curious. "I thought you were a hacker?"

"Among other things..." Charlie frowns in concentration, clicking away. She falls silent, ignoring us.

"So... How long will this take?" Saint asks.

She doesn't look up. "As long as it takes."

OK.

I exchange a shrug with him, as Leon returns with a fresh stack of pancakes. "How would you like your coffee, ma'am?" he asks me. "And would you prefer grapefruit or orange juice? Freshly squeezed, of course."

My stomach rumbles. If we're going to be stuck waiting around, it would be rude to ignore the incredible spread. "Black coffee, please, and OJ," I say, reaching to fill a plate. Saint follows suit.

"Thank you, Leon," Wren smiles at him, and he retreats with a nod. "He looks scary, but he's a sweetheart, really," she confides. "He made me hot cocoa at two a.m. when I woke up screaming in the night."

"You're having nightmares?" I ask, concerned.

"It's fine!" she insists quickly, but her smile doesn't reach her eyes.

"Wren..."

"Really," she reassures me. "That's what I get for gorging on stinky cheeses too late."

I let the subject drop, but still, I don't like it. Wren is still a shadow of her former self, and even though she's not flinching half as much now that we're safely behind the bulletproof walls of Sebastian Wolfe's palatial home, I know she can't stay here forever.

I want my big sister back, the girl who would belly-laugh so loud it would set me off, too, giggling in hysterics over some dumb joke or meme online.

But that's why we're doing all of this, I remind myself. So Wren can be safe, and never have to look over her shoulder again.

"I have good news and bad news," Charlie finally announces, looking up from her screen.

"Bad news first," I decide.

"This encryption is serious business," Charlie says, giving an apologetic look. "I can't break it. At least, not without a few weeks, and a hell of a lot more equipment."

My heart falls. "We don't have weeks, and we need to get into the drive!"

"I know, and that's where the good news comes in. I recognize the setup here," she explains. "It takes a 14-digit key to unlock the data, but that looks like the only protection on the drive. Find the key, and it's open sesame."

"That's the good news?" I mutter, downcast.

But Saint takes my hand. "No, it is. Remember, Phillip couldn't keep his passwords straight, so he had them written down. My dad's the exact way. He'll never remember a key like that, it'll be written down somewhere. Somewhere close to him."

I blink. He's finally acknowledging out loud that it's his father running the show with the trial fraud. I search his face, concerned, but see only determination there.

"Then my work here is done." Charlie snaps her screen closed and stands.

"Thank you, for helping us out," I tell her gratefully.

She smiles. "I don't know how much help I've really been, but it was worth it for the pancakes." She pauses. "Do you think the chef would give me the recipe for that syrup?"

"Of course," Saint speaks up. "I'll take you to the kitchens on our way out."

He guides Charlie from the room, leaving me and Wren alone.

"Another obstacle," Wren sighs, looking downcast. "And now you guys have to take the risk to look for this key, while I sit around here. Useless."

"You're not useless!" I protest, frowning. "You're the reason we're all here!"

"Exactly." Wren levels me with a stare. "It's my fault you're in danger all the time."

"No, that's on Ashford," I correct her firmly. "They're the ones trying to cover up their crimes. They're the ones to blame, for everything!"

"But still, if I hadn't come back..." she looks down, fidgeting with her sweater. "If I'd just stayed hidden, stayed dead..."

"Wren, no!"

I get up and circle the table to her. "Having you back means everything to me," I insist, taking her hands tightly. "We're doing the right thing here. We can't let them get away with it, what they've done to you..."

"But it's all spiraling," Wren looks at me, miserable. "First it was just me at risk, now you're getting shot, and breaking into Ashford, and Saint's searching for clues from his own father... You were happy before I came back, you were building your life together."

"And we will again, when this is done," I promise her. "But we were building it on quicksand, Wren, not knowing what was really going on. Ashford Pharma is corrupt and evil. It's always better to know the truth."

"I sometimes wonder if that's true," Wren says softly, shadows in her eyes. "If I could go back, and just ignore that original trial data... If I'd closed the spreadsheet and gone for lunch with the rest of the crew, none of this would have happened." Her voice is wistful, and I can see that she's grieving for the life she could have had if she hadn't stumbled over the wrong thing, at the wrong time. "I would have finished up my fellowship, and got a great job; traveled, maybe. Fallen in love. I would have been normal, Tessa," she says, her eyes filling with tears. "It would have saved me so much grief."

I can't answer her. It's true, she's suffered more than anyone. The attack, the aftermath, running for her life, leaving everyone behind... It makes me want to weep for her—and rip Alexander St. Clair and his cronies apart. They decided their success was worth any cost.

My poor sister is the one who's paid the price.

But not anymore.

"We're going to make this right, Wren." I squeeze her hand, a vow. "I promise you, we're going to expose everything, and make them pay for what they've done."

She gives a nod, but she doesn't look convinced.

Saint rejoins us. "I called my father, and wrangled us a dinner invitation for tonight," he reports. "Since it's been so long since we all sat down together."

"You think the encryption key will be at their house?" I ask, thinking one step ahead.

Saint nods. "My father's been working from home since his heart attack. He stops by the Ashford Pharma headquarters for meetings and to check up on things, but most of his day-to-day operations are still from the house in Hampstead. If this key is anywhere, it'll be there."

"Family dinner night... Sounds like fun." I wince, thinking of his mother's icy reception every other time we've crossed paths. "And I don't know how I'll be able to sit across from your father, knowing everything he's done."

Fraud, corruption, sending a man to murder my sister and me in cold blood... It's not exactly happy family small talk.

"You shouldn't come then," Saint says immediately, but I shake my head.

"No," I say. "You're going to need someone to distract them, while you go search for the encryption key."

I turn to Wren. She's sitting there, not saying a word. "So, if everything goes smoothly, we'll have the key tonight," I say brightly.

"I'll be here," she says with a pale smile. "Where else am I going to be?"

"I'm worried about Wren," I tell Saint, when we leave the house. He's heading to work at Ashford HQ, and Annabelle's been blowing up my phone about a bridal party brunch, so we're strolling through the busy streets of London, hand-in-hand. "She's feeling guilty, she says she wishes she'd never found the issues with the drug trials."

I suggested spending the day together, but Wren just said she needed to take a nap.

"She's been through a lot," Saint says, sympathetic. "When all this is over, we'll get her all the help she needs. The best counsellors, treatment... Whatever she needs to get back to normal. She won't be alone."

I nod, but now I'm feeling like the guilty one. "I spent all this time trying to avenge her death, and catch the person who attacked her, when all along, she was out there... On her own... Scared half to death. I wasn't helping anyone by digging up the past. If anything, I made life even more dangerous for her!"

"Hey," Saint stops, and takes me by the shoulders. "There's plenty of blame to go around here. How about me? All this has been going on under my nose. With my father calling the shots." His eyes darken. "You think I'm sleeping easy at night?"

"Saint, you couldn't possibly have known!" I protest.

"And neither could you," he points out. "Or Wren. All this was set in motion before we ever knew, by people with their own agenda, operating by their own rules."

I nod. "It just doesn't seem fair," I say, sighing. "That somehow we're the ones who have to clear up this mess."

Saint pauses, and I see the memories on his face. "My brother, Edward, used to have this saying: 'The only thing that matters in the world is when you're faced with a choice: Do you do what's easy, or what's right?'"

"He sounds like a real buzzkill," I tease to break the mood, and Saint grins.

"The worst."

Doing what's easy, versus doing what's right...

The words resonate deep inside. I can see how Saint's taken them to heart, too. From the start, he's stood by me, no matter what. Because despite the fear, and drama, and pain, I have to believe we're doing the right thing here.

Somebody has to.

"So, dinner with your parents tonight," I say, feeling a new determination. "Can I show up in ripped fishnets and leather, and give your mom a heart attack, too?"

Saint grins. "Why not? We are aiming to distract them, after all."

I smile. "That would be some distraction."

My phone buzzes insistently in my pocket, and I pull it out. "Annabelle. Again."

With everything that's been going on, the wedding has been the last thing on my mind, but now it's just a matter of days away. "I'm late for the champagne brunch and Botox," I report, amused. "I'm guessing Max doesn't have quite the same schedule of events."

"Uh, nope," Saint smiles. "In fact, Cyrus pulled the plug on the bachelor party. We were all going to go hunting in Poland, but he figured that was a recipe for disaster."

"Or dismemberment," I say with a wince.

We're approaching Ashford Pharma now. It looks different in the daylight, with people in business suits bustling through the doors. "Do you think there'll be any fallout from last night?" I ask, nervous.

"You mean, from the wayward son being his usual scandalous self?" Saint smirks. "It's nothing they haven't seen before." He seems to realize what he's said. "Sorry, I just meant—"

"That the fact you were a total man-whore before we met makes a great alibi." I smile, not concerned. "It's a good thing, too. I always knew your *experience* would come in useful..."

He draws me closer for a goodbye kiss. "I told you when we met, there's a few tricks in the old dog yet."

Tricks... I'd call it a gift. Like the way he turns me liquid with just the briefest touch of his lips on mine—

"Mr. St. Clair?" A voice interrupts us. It's an older man, in his sixties, maybe, dressed smartly with a look of desperation in his eyes. "It's you! I thought it was you."

"Yes," Saint gives a polite nod.

"Please, sir, I've been trying to get an appointment," the man pleads. "It's about my Margaret. I heard there were trials, for your new drug. I'm trying to get her a place!"

Oh God.

My heart aches as the man practically begs Saint to help his wife be a part of the Alzheimer's trial.

"I heard the drug's working. Please, we just need a chance. My Margaret, she won't have much longer. She has good days but... We're running out of time. Please!" His weathered face creases with emotion, clinging to Saint's arm now.

"I'm sorry, but the trials have closed," Saint tells him gently. "I can help connect you to some information, though. Services that might help your wife."

The man shakes his head, despondent. "Nothing can help her. Nothing but a miracle. Your drug, it's the only thing. Please—"

Security arrives. "Mr. St. Clair?"

"It's alright," Saint says quickly. "There's no trouble here." He squeezes the man's hand. "I'm so sorry, but there's nothing I can do for you."

"Liar!" The man's angry cry echoes, as security steers him away. "You can help. Please!"

I watch him go, sick to my stomach. And from the shaken expression on Saint's face, he feels the same way.

"This is what they're doing," he says, low and angry. "Giving good people false hope. Exploiting their misery, just to get even richer and more powerful, while they set the whole field back. It's disgusting."

"And we're going to stop them." I give him a firm nod.

Whatever happens now, we're already in too deep to ever go back. His brother was right. There's no walking away from doing the right thing.

I just hope it doesn't cost us everything.

Chapter 15

Saint

"You know, I've been thinking..." Tessa says on the drive over to my parents' place for dinner, the lights of London glittering outside the windscreen. "We should take a vacation."

"Now?" I ask, confused. We're all set to search for the encryption key tonight, and it's the final piece of the puzzle standing in our way before we can expose Ashford for the lying, criminal bastards they really are.

"Sure," she smiles over at me from the passenger seat. "I mean, what else do we have going on? I've been feeling pretty bored," she adds with a smirk. "Life's been so dull and uneventful recently."

I laugh, relaxing. "You're right," I agree, reaching over to take her hand. "It's all the same old, same old. I'm sure nobody would miss us if we just jetted off to a beach somewhere."

"Ah, yes, that beach of yours..." Tessa gives a longing sigh. "Talk vacation to me, baby."

"I promise, once this is all over, we can jet anywhere you choose," I tell her, bringing her hand to my lips and pressing a kiss to her knuckles. "Jamaica, Fiji, Tahiti... Take your pick. Just you, me, and those coconuts," I add with a wolfish grin.

I know that it's easier said than done, and we have a mountain of challenges facing us, even if we do manage to secure the proof of Ashford's wrongdoing.

My father's crimes, I correct myself, feeling a chill.

But still, the thought that this will all be over soon gives me hope. One day, life really will be as simple as Tessa is joking. She'll be safe, and happy again, with no life-or-death choices to make—aside from what kind of cocktail to order to our beachfront cabana.

I hold onto that vision—and the idea of Tessa in a string bikini—as we arrive at my parents' house in Hampstead, north of the city.

She gets out of the car and whistles, looking up at the spacious house, half-hidden behind the garden walls. "I know I should stop being surprised by all your real estate, but seriously. This place is gorgeous."

"I suppose crime really does pay," I mutter darkly. I used to enjoy the trappings of our fortune, too: the houses and first-class travel, and exclusive access to every VIP event around. It helped to make up for the responsibilities of the Ashford legacy, the one pressing down on my shoulders with every passing day.

Now, I just look around and wonder what kind of corruption my ancestors were guilty of, to build our empire in the first place. How many people they lied to and exploited, like that poor man outside Ashford today, desperate for a cure.

"Balzac knew what he was talking about," Tessa quips, and I turn to her, recognizing the reference.

"*Behind every great fortune is an even greater crime*," I quote, and she smiles.

"This crime, they won't get away with. Ready?" she asks, holding her hand out to me.

"Ah, yes." I take it. "Lies, family drama, and a little light thieving. What could be better?"

We make our way up the path to the front door. A maid answers and takes our coats, before showing us to the formal sitting room, where I'm surprised to see my brother, Robert, pouring drinks.

"They roped you into this, too?" I greet him, pleased to see another friendly face. And hopefully, someone else to keep the conversation going while I go search for this encryption key.

Robert clears his throat, pushing back his shock of blonde hair. "Ah, yes. Tessa," he nods, looking weirdly nervous to see her. Clearly, my parents have already been complaining about my choice of partners.

"Good to see you," she smiles brightly, smoothing down her conservative navy dress. In the end, she decided not to rile my mother up with her choice in outfits: She looks perfectly demure, with her hair pulled back in a low bun, and simple makeup.

I'm the only one who knows she's wearing a sinful scarlet lingerie set under that dress.

"I'll take a scotch, if you're pouring," I tell Robert. "It's not like mother to leave her guests waiting."

"She's off seeing about the food," he reports.

"And by that, he means nitpicking with the chef," I translate to Tessa. Robert hands me a drink, and I slap his shoulder in thanks.

He flinches, looking pained.

"Are you alright there?" I ask, noticing a bandage peeking up from under the collar of his shirt.

"Fine," he replies quickly. "Just buggered up my shoulder, playing some rugby with the lads."

"Tough break," I say, sympathetic.

"My own fault," he says, with another nervous laugh. "Charging around like that. I forget I'm not eighteen anymore."

"Rubbish. You can take any of those youngsters. Robert here is the athlete of the family," I tell Tessa. "Ruby, polo, cross country... He does it all. Left me in the dust, every time."

"Really? Maybe you should work out more," Tessa gives me an innocent smile. "Try to get that stamina up."

"There's nothing wrong with my stamina," I smirk, trying to keep a straight face.

At least, not when it comes to making Tessa moan for mercy, clenching around my cock...

"Anthony, so good of you to join us."

My mother sweeps in, and just like that, all thoughts of wild passion go fleeing from my mind. The proverbial cold shower, as always.

"Mother." I press a polite kiss to her cheek. "We're right on time. Early, even."

"My, we're honored," she says dryly. "What's the occasion?"

Investigating dad's crimes.

"I heard you have a new chef," I reply instead. "One who doesn't char everything to a crisp. I couldn't miss the chance at an edible meal here, for a change."

"It's lovely to see you again, Lillian," Tessa speaks up, and I can see her fix a bright smile on her face, despite my mother's coolness.

"Indeed." My mother's eyes drift over her. "It's... nice to see you, too. We're so lucky you could tear yourself away from your studies at Oxford to join us tonight."

"Oh, haven't you heard?" Tessa replies, completely unfazed by the icy reception. "I'm no longer a student there. You see, Saint invited me to drop out and move in with him, and he wouldn't take 'No' for an answer, would you, muffin?" She moves to my side, slipping her hand possessively through my arm, and batting her eyelashes at me.

Muffin?

I try not to laugh. "That's right, pumpkin," I reply, seeing the amusement sparkling in her eyes. "I just couldn't stand to be away from her."

"You're... living together?" My mother repeats, sounding horrified.

"Yup!" Tessa beams. "Shacked up. Living in sin. My poor granny would be rolling in her grave. She always said, men never buy the cow if they can get the milk for free!"

"Oh." My mother looks like she might faint. Luckily, my father strolls in, and greets the two of us with at least a little more warmth.

"Tessa, I hear you're going from strength to strength at the Ambrose Foundation," he says, shaking her hand enthusiastically. "Hugh was singing your praises just the other day. I've half a mind to poach you, bring you in-house at Ashford. You know, we have our own philanthropic department, funding drug research and vaccine access in developing countries. We spent a hundred million last year on charitable efforts, and hope to double it, soon enough."

"That's... Wonderful," Tessa replies, and only I could tell that her enthusiasm is strained. "What amazing work you do there. Making a difference. Leading by example."

"Well, we try!" My father gives a chuckle.

I watch him pour Tessa a drink and try to reconcile the man in front of me with everything I've learned over the past week. Could he really have ordered the murder of Dr DeJonge, and the violent cover-up of Ashford's fraud? Sent a man to stalk and kill Tessa and her sister—and then stand in front of her tonight, making polite conversation and handing her a gin and tonic like nothing has even happened?

I feel a chill, unable to wrap my head around the duplicity it would take to do those things. It's downright sociopathic.

"Tell me about this social media business you have going on there," my father asks Tessa, as they take a seat. "I have to say, I can't be done with it myself."

"Isn't it all terribly vulgar?" my mother asks, "People braying for attention on their mobile phones all day."

"Mother," Robert chides her. "Don't be rude."

"I wasn't calling Tessa vulgar," Lillian protests, although the way she's looking at her betrays her true feelings. "Merely that I don't understand this constant need for the spotlight. It's so... American."

Tessa smirks. "Is that so? I heard that *Big Brother* was invented here in England. So really, you're all to blame for reality television."

As they start debating the ills of social media, I realize it's the perfect moment to slip away.

"Be right back," I say quietly, edging towards the door. "Just need to check on some things, with Harold in accounts."

My mother barely nods, still focused on attacking Tessa—politely, of course. I don't worry, Tessa can more than hold her own. She gives me a private nod, as I slip out of the room.

Go get 'em.

I stride quickly down the hallway, towards my father's study at the back of the house. It's a wood-paneled room lined with old bookcases, my father's antique desk positioned in front of the window with stacks of papers, and his laptop sitting right there beside them.

If this encryption key is anywhere, it'll be close by.

I begin to methodically search the room, starting with the

desk drawers, rifling through the contents in turn. A part of me hopes that I don't find the damn thing. I know that we need it to unlock the information on the hard drive, but if I find it here, it confirms my worst suspicions. There's still a part of me holding out that perhaps, it could be someone else in the company who's behind all this. Perhaps another executive, or board member—

And then I see it: A yellow notecard propped against the desk lamp, right in front of me.

14 random letters and numbers, scrawled in my father's handwriting.

Dammit.

My father's arrogance is breathtaking, to just leave it laying around out in the open. But why wouldn't he feel safe here, in his own home? Wren and Tessa told Phillip that they were giving up and letting the whole matter rest. My father doesn't know that we have the files copied, or that we're even coming after the proof to expose all his lies.

He doesn't know that his own son is still working to bring about his downfall.

I quickly pull out my phone, and snap photos of the passcode—and email them to myself for good measure. Then I tidy up and leave nothing out of place, before strolling back to rejoin the others.

"Ah, there you are," my mother says, looking up. Nobody is suspicious. I've barely been gone a few minutes, after all. "Dinner is ready to be served."

"Great," I say blandly, joining Tessa. She shoots me an expectant look, as the others file out towards the dining room, and I wait until they're ahead of us, before giving her a nod.

"You got it?" she whispers excitedly.

"I think so. Yes."

She squeezes my hand, pleased, but it feels like I have a lead weight in my stomach as we take our seats for dinner, and even the sight of a perfectly cooked rib roast isn't appetizing to me.

How could you do it? I wonder, staring at my father across the table, as he makes a show of carving the meat, all smiles and jovial laughter.

How could you betray Edward's memory, by turning into everything he'd hate?

Chapter 16

Tessa

I barely sleep a wink, and by the time dawn breaks, we're already back with Wren at Sebastian's guarded fortress, nervously watching as Wren enters the sequence that Saint found in his father's office.

This could be it: Everything we've been searching for, so we can expose the truth. All my hopes are resting on that one tiny string of numbers and symbols that Wren is slowly typing into the prompt.

There's a pause, and I clutch Saint's hand tighter. Then Wren gives a nod. "It's the key. We're in."

I exhale in a whoosh—thrilled, but even more concerned about Saint now. He's been quiet ever since we returned from dinner with his parents, and I know he's still trying to come to terms with his father's guilt in all of this.

"Do you see the datasets?" I ask, leaning closer.

"Give me a minute," she protests. "There's a ton of information here. It's like looking in a haystack."

"Oh. OK."

I wait, biting my fingernails with anxiety as Saint paces

back and forth. He's wired with tension, and I wish I could tell him to relax, but I know that's impossible. How would I relax, if I was in his shoes, wrestling with my father's massive betrayal?

Wren clicks around in the drive, my nerves tangling tighter as the minutes tick past. Then, finally, she sounds a bitter laugh.

"There. I knew it. I fucking knew it."

"You got it?" I demand.

Saint crowds in, as Wren turns the screen around to face us. "Whoever changed the original results, they hid it well. But those are the human trial results they sent for official review," she says, pointing to one set of spreadsheets, filled with complex numbers and equations. "And that's the ghost file, hidden on the sub-server. It's identical—except for these key markers in cognitive response."

"Plain English," I remind her.

"They didn't change much," Wren translates. "No wild claims, saying it's a miracle cure. They just tweaked one number a tiny bit, making it seem like there were enough small improvements to add up to a promising result. Enough to get approval, and clearance for general sale."

"And massive global profits," Saint adds, looking stunned. I realize that up until this very moment, he was probably holding out hope that we would be wrong about the whole thing.

Now, with the evidence right in front of us, it's impossible to deny any longer.

"We did it," I blink, feeling a wave of triumph. "We've got what we need to expose them!"

I turn to Wren, beaming, but she doesn't meet my eyes.

"*You* do," she says quietly, and gets up from the laptop.

I pause. "What do you mean?"

"You will expose them. You and Saint, together."

I begin to get a very bad feeling. Even more when Wren

tugs a duffel bag into view and takes a passport from the front pocket.

"Wren...?"

She gives me a tired smile. "This is where I leave you. I confirmed the data, I've highlighted everything incriminating in that file. You don't need me anymore."

"Of course we need you!" I cry. "Tell her, Saint," I turn to him, only to find Saint doesn't seem surprised by this development at all.

"I can't stay trapped here, waiting for this to go away," Wren explains. "I feel like I'm stuck in a prison."

"A prison with a personal chef!" I exclaim.

"I can't take it," Wren says quietly. "I can't sleep, I can hardly eat. I'm just waiting for them to find me again. Or even worse, come after you. I need to be far, far away from Ashford. Being on the run before was bad, but at least I could sleep at night, knowing that nobody was looking for me."

Saint places a hand on my arm. "Just listen to her, Tessa. She'll be somewhere safe, I've arranged everything."

"You knew about this?" I wrench away, furious. "Have you been planning it behind my back?"

"Tessie, please." Wren interrupts me. "This is my choice. I asked Saint to help get me out of here, and back into hiding again. I'll use my old fake identity, and go off the grid again, at least for a little while. Once you manage to expose Ashford, then things will be different. But for now... It's for the best. It's the only way I'm going to feel safe, if nobody knows where I am. Not even you," she adds.

"Wren..." I stare at her, tears already stinging in the corner of my eyes. I can't lose her, not again.

"You won't lose her," Saint say, knowing exactly what I'm thinking. "She'll take a burner phone, and check in all the time. Now we have the proof, it won't be long until this is over."

"But... I'll miss you," I say tearfully.

Wren pulls me into a hug. "I'll miss you, too. This is just temporary. Please try to understand."

I hold her tightly. I can't understand. I grieved her for so long, and now she's saying she wants to disappear, again? "We're so close to the end," I try to reason with her. "We could take this evidence to the authorities tomorrow! What if you get on a plane, and in a couple of days, it's all over?"

"Then I'll get on another plane, and come right back," Wren reassures me. "But this isn't my fight anymore. It was never supposed to be, but I've played my part. You've always been the strong one, Tess, not me. You can finish this. I'll just be in the way."

"That's not true." I sniff, my heart aching.

"It is. And I'm OK with that," Wren gives me a pale smile. "Because I know you'll give 'em hell."

I hold her for as long as I can, until she finally releases me. "Where are you going?" I ask, as she checks her things.

Wren shakes her head. "It's safer if you don't know."

"Will you at least let us take you to the airport?" I ask.

She smiles. "I'm counting on the ride. And help picking my snacks. The fridge here is better than the concession stand!"

We help Wren pack up her things, and then Saint drives us to the airport; Wren still anxiously watching out behind is for anyone following. I hold her hand tightly the whole way, hoping she'll change her mind, but when we pull up outside Departures, I can see, Wren's already thinking two steps ahead. She seems calmer suddenly, more focused. After all that time spent in hiding, alone, it's clear that's how she feels most comfortable.

Being cooped up, waiting for Ashford to strike, has only

trapped her with her demons. Now, I hope she can find some space to breathe again.

"You promise you'll call?" I demand, standing with her on the curb. She's got a baseball cap pulled low over her eyes, bundled up in a nondescript green parka and boots.

"As soon as I get settled, and find a way to do it safely," she nods, then gives me an affectionate smile. "I'm proud of you, you know. Going after these guys, fighting to do the right thing... I'm lucky to have you as my sister."

"Now you're going to make me cry again," I sniffle, pulling her in for another quick hug. "OK, go, before I throw you in the trunk and take you back to Sebastian's myself. Travel safe."

"I will. I love you."

"Love you, too."

I watch her disappear in the crowd, heading for the check-in hall. Then I force myself to get in the car with Saint again, wiping my eyes. "Let's go," I tell him quickly, not wanting to wait for Wren to leave.

He pulls into the flow of traffic, and then hits the brakes as a white van cuts in front of us, pulling up to the curb. Saint sounds the horn, as some burly guys leap out of the van, ignoring us.

"Guess someone's about to miss their flight," he says, pulling around them, and hitting the road again.

I sit quietly in the passenger seat for the rest of the drive back to Saint's place, missing Wren already.

"You'll talk all the time," he reminds me, as we arrive at the house. "And she's right. She's safer the further away she is from all of this. If Ashford found her..."

"I know." I swallow. "That doesn't mean I have to be happy about it."

He smiles. "Do you want to sulk for the rest of the day?"

"Yes." I fold my arms, wishing it could all be different. But I can't act naïve. I know that the only way out of this for anyone is directly through the flames.

And now we have the evidence, we have the spark to light the fire.

I follow Saint inside, watching as he carefully rearms the alarm behind us. Then we settle in the kitchen with a fresh pot of tea, and biscuits, the English cure for all ills.

Except this one.

I place the hard drive on the table, and we both stare at it. For something that looks so simple and small, it has the potential to bring down one of the most prestigious families in all of England. And a whole lot more people besides.

"So... What do we do now?" I ask. "We could turn it over to the authorities, or leak it to the press. A story like this would blow up in a heartbeat."

Saint nods slowly, looking thoughtful. "I want to wait."

My head snaps up. "What? Why?"

"Not for long," he says. "But think we should talk to my father first."

I blink, surprised. "Saint... You realize he's guilty by now."

"I do," he nods. "But it's not just him. He had to have been working with accomplices. Maybe they forced him into it, or he got in over his head, but either way, there are other people involved here, I just know it. Getting rid of Valerie?" he reminds me. "Having Wren attacked? That guy who came to kill you both? That's not my father. He may have fixed the trial data and covered everything up, but I've known that man my entire life. I can't believe he's capable of murder."

I pause, not so sure about this. "If we warn him, they have a chance to hide everything again," I point out.

"I don't want to warn him," Saint reassures me. "I want to get him to flip on the others. Come clean and tell the whole truth. We want to catch the people who did this—*all* of them. If my father will inform on the rest of them, then we'll have all the information we need. And we can force him to withdraw the drug and set things right at Ashford Pharma."

I think it through. "Having your father on our side would make us more credible," I agree. "They wouldn't be able to deny what's been going on."

"And it keeps Wren's name out of things," Saint adds, getting up.

"What do you mean?" I ask, frowning.

"She'll need to be named," he says, fetching ice cream from the freezer and setting it down in front of me, along with two spoons. Coffee flavor. My favorite. "Wren's the whistleblower," he continues. "She'll need to give statements to the authorities, answer questions. And if the media get hold of her name, well... It's a blockbuster story. Faking her death, disappearing like that... It's the stuff headlines and true crime documentaries are made of."

Shit. He's right.

And I already know that Wren doesn't want the spotlight. She's barely been holding it together with the stress of what's going on. When I imagine her photo being splashed all over the newspapers, reporters stalking her every move. And my parents...?

I wince. "You think they'd leave her alone if we can get your father to come clean?" I ask.

Saint nods. "We wouldn't even need to mention her."

"Well, I like that part of the plan." I sigh, digging into the ice cream. "But Saint... Do you really think your father would confess so easily? The lengths he's gone to already to cover this thing up. Even if you believe other people are behind the violence," I add. "He's still got everything riding on this launch. The stock price, the entire Ashford name!"

Saint pauses for a long moment. "I have to give him the chance," he says finally. "The chance to do the right thing."

"And not the easy thing," I say softly. He nods. "But he if denies it, or stonewalls—"

"Then we'll go straight to the press and expose everything." Saint agrees immediately. "Look, tomorrow is Max and Annabelle's big wedding. Everyone will be there, including my family, and every journalist around. I'll find a moment to confront him, and if it doesn't work, we can pull someone aside, and slip them a copy of the hard drive. March straight over to the Met headquarters and tell them everything."

"Tomorrow," I repeat slowly, feeling a shiver of nerves—and excitement, too. After everything, I can't wait for it all to be out in the open. No more sneaking and secrets. Just the truth, for everyone to see.

"Between that and the five million bridal events Annabelle needs me for, it's going to be a big day." I sigh, licking ice cream from my spoon. "Do we really have to go to this thing?" I ask playfully. "I mean, you've only known Max half your life. He won't miss you, will he?"

Saint chuckles. "Sure, we can bail. One of Annabelle's bridesmaids will have to walk herself up the aisle, but I'm sure nobody will notice."

"Right. It's just a small affair. Thrown together, last minute," I smirk.

"Practically an elopement," Saint grins back at me. He's clearly just as relieved to have the finish line in sight.

I eat another spoonful of ice cream, and Saint's gaze lingers on my mouth. "What?" I ask, smiling.

"I'm always astonished by your ability to distract me from... Everything," he says, leaning in and licking a drop from the edge of my lip. His tongue rasps against my skin, sensual.

Heat suffuses me.

"And I'm always astonished by your ability to turn me on," I murmur, sliding into his lap, and wrapping my arms around his neck.

"Is that so?" Saint kisses me properly, long and slow and smoldering, until my whole body feels sharp and hot with desire.

"Very so," I murmur, wriggling against him. "You know, it's our last night," I add, breathing softly into his ear. "Before things get... Crazy."

"You're right." Saint's grip tightens on my hips. "It feels like we should mark the occasion somehow..."

"Is that how it feels?" I whisper, shifting in his lap again, rubbing against him.

Saint exhales. Then he gives me a slow, wicked grin.

"Ooh, I like that smile," I say, tracing it softly. "Usually very, very good things happen when you smile like that."

"Then we better make sure tonight measures up."

Saint nods to the bureau where he keeps the mail. "Second drawer down," he says. "Go get it."

I arch my eyebrows at the order. "Yes, professor," I smirk, and sashay over. There's an elegant cream envelope nestled in the drawer. I lift it out. "This?"

He nods. I bring it back, and perch on his lap again, as Saint opens the envelope, and slides out a thick, gold-leafed invitation.

You are cordially invited...

Masks required. Discretion presumed.

Midnight.

I feel a spark of recognition. "It's like the invitation for the first party," I exclaim. "The one where we..."

"... First became acquainted," Saint finishes for me, with a wolfish grin.

I shiver with anticipation, remembering the lavish event:

the masked crowd, the performers, the sensual, wild adventures.

Saint getting sucked off by another woman, while I watched the two of them, touching myself in a frenzy.

"This is tonight?" I ask, already breathless at the idea.

Saint smiles. "I thought with everything that's going on, it wasn't the right moment for us to attend. But perhaps it's exactly what we need."

Chapter 17

Tessa

The invitation says that the dress code tonight is *Glamorous Games,* so I pick the raciest of my new outfits: an ultra-short silk swing dress that moves loosely around my body, the hemline flirting at the very tops of my thighs. I pair it with hot pink lingerie, some glittering black strappy sandals, and sweep my hair into a messy bun on the top of my head.

"It seems a shame to hide you away behind a mask..." Saint says, his eyes devouring me approvingly as our driver collects us. Still, he produces a silk bandana-style mask for me, and slips one on to hide his own face, too. In his perfectly fitting designer suit and black shirt, dark hair falling, rumpled over the mask, he looks like a modern highwayman, out to steal some hearts tonight.

Or just out to steal my breath away.

I kiss him in the back of the car, anticipation already sparkling in my veins. He's right: An adventure is exactly what I need. A way to forget all the drama and anxiousness of the past few days and to lose myself in the thrill of discovery; give myself over to pleasure, and all its games.

I wonder what limits he'll explore tonight...

After about a half-hour's drive, the car pulls over. "This is it?" I ask, looking around in confusion. The other party was at a grand country estate, every inch decorated with lush flowers and atmospheric candles: romantic and extravagant.

But as I climb out of the car, I find we're in a deserted warehouse district near the water, with empty storage sheds and industrial equipment sitting around.

Saint gives a grin. "Every Midnights Party is different," he explains, taking my hand, and leading me in the direction of the low thump of music, echoing through the night. "No two events have the same theme, or atmosphere. There's always something new to discover. And nobody knows who's hosting them, either," he adds. "It's as much of a mystery as where and when the next event will be."

"It seems like a fun job," I say, wondering how someone would even get a position as 'wild sex party planner..

Saint chuckles. "Fun, and profitable. I know people willing to pay a hundred grand, just to get their hands on one ticket. But the guest list is always a surprise. You never know if you're going to get an invite."

"You don't seem to have a problem getting on the list," I note. "Clearly, they know your reputation for having a good time."

My pulse kicks as we approach a nondescript warehouse. It looks just like the others, abandoned and grim—except for the sound of dance music emerging from inside, and the line of foreboding security guards, all masked and stationed out front.

Saint presents our invitation and trades his phone for a small identifying token. Then the guard opens the door for us, steps aside, and ushers us into the dark.

My heart beats faster, as we venture into the gloom. There's a long hallway, lit with eerie neon lights, and then we emerge in the middle of the party, and my jaw drops.

Talk about glamour and games...

The warehouse is shot through with dazzling spotlights, illuminating the industrial setting for a pulsing rave. Steel beams and brick serve the backdrop for a riotous display of circus performers, acrobats, and even fire-breathers, all dressed in glittering neon, making flashes of color in the dark. There are hundreds of people dancing to the pounding music, dressed to the nines, their masks shot through with UV stripes that seem to bob and float on the dance floor.

It's spectacular.

My grip on Saint's hand tightens with excitement as we head deeper into the party. Now that my eyes are adjusting to the scene, I can see a neon-lit bar set up along the back wall, with bottles stacked so high to the ceiling that the bartenders climb ladders and swing like acrobats to fetch them. There are dim hallways leading off the main party, with UV stripes like landing signs on the concrete floor marking the way to more private rooms, and in every corner, there's something new to look at: contortionists, or dancers, or aerialists suspended in long swathes of neon silk; all of them masked and mysterious.

For now, it looks like any other extravagant party, but I know it won't be long until all that changes.

"What time is it?" I ask Saint eagerly.

He points to a massive digital screen suspended over the party, counting down. Just a few minutes until midnight. "Not long now," he says, with a seductive smirk beneath the mask. "Would you like a drink?"

I nod, following him through the crowd to the bar. He orders himself a scotch, and a martini for me, and we pause there a moment, sipping and taking in the scene.

There's a pulse of excitement in the air, everybody glancing to the clock. Counting down.

And then the display resets. Ten seconds. Nine... Eight... Seven...

Saint moves closer, his hands skimming over the silk of my dress as he draws me into his arms.

The crowd stills. A hush falls. The music cuts out as the clock strikes midnight...

And then the *real* party begins.

The performers move in unison to the center of the vast dance floor, moving and weaving in a hypnotic pattern to the pulsing music. They shed clothing, stripping each other naked, revealing bodies painted with more neon and UV paint that glows under the lights, like animal markings, as they fan out into the crowd, bringing the guests into their seductive dance.

All around us, people begin to move with a new, sensual abandon; moving off in pairs and groups, shedding clothing and their inhibitions, as if the stroke of midnight cast some kind of spell, and released people from the polite confines of their everyday lives.

It's intoxicating.

I watch, breathless, as the spotlights swoop, illuminating flashes of debauchery at every turn. A couple dancing a fevered tango in the middle of the dance floor, slowly stripping each other's clothing away... The man already on his knees in a corner, lavishing his attention between the thighs of two naked women kissing above him... The woman splayed on the bar; eager hands unbuttoning her dress until she's laying there naked, pouring liquor onto her naked breasts for strangers' mouths to lick from her skin...

I shiver with desire, my blood running hotter with every filthy, tempting image. I can't look away. The tequila-soaked woman is just a few feet away from us, and as I watch them taste and play with her breasts, another man climbs onto the bar, and crawls between her thighs. He peels her panties away, and buries his face against her pussy, licking her hungrily, making her moan and arch in pleasure, right there in front of us.

Oh God.

I feel a shudder of lust, transfixed. I can see his mouth moving against her; hear the filthy sound of her wetness, and the way she whimpers for more.

"Getting jealous?" Saint's chuckle comes, low in my ear.

I flush, already too hot. "Maybe...

He smiles against me. "I love watching you watch them..." he murmurs, hands roaming over my silk-clad skin. "Seeing the way your breathing gets shallow... These sweet nipples getting stiff... I bet you're already wet, aren't you, darling? Watching her come undone with his tongue in her cunt."

He's right.

I moan, sinking back into his hands as Saint slowly, teasingly palms my breasts, squeezing softly. My thighs clench, just imagining how it would feel to be touched like that. Lavished with attention, right there under all these lights...

Saint turns me to face him, his eyes glittering darkly behind his mask. "So, what are you in the mood for tonight, darling? Say the word, and it's yours."

My mind reels with possibilities.

"Let's explore," I decide, taking his hand. "And you tell me, if you're feeling *inspired*."

We slowly circulate the party, taking in the debauchery at every turn. I want to surprise Saint, too; to pleasure *him*, so I keep a curious watch for where his gaze lands. The pile of naked bodies, writhing... The teasing strip show underway... Then we follow one of the neon painted trails away from the main party, and into a smaller room, and I know we've found it.

Saint's eyes flash. His grip on my hand tightens.

Jackpot.

It's another bare industrial space, this one with a raised bed in the middle of the room. There are low couches and tables scattered around it, with people lounging, kissing, *watching* the trio on display. Two men, with a woman between them. She's on her hands and knees, dress hiked up, sucking one of them off while the other fucks her from behind. But it's not cheap and frenzied, like a porn scene would be; no, this seems slow and languid. Even sensual. The men run their hands over her body, drawing moans and gasps of pleasure as she teases the cock in her mouth. The man behind her slowly sinks his cock into her, pleasure clear on his masked face as he finds a leisurely pace, savoring every thrust.

And so does she.

That's what's most hypnotic about the scene in front of us; what makes my breath turn shallow and my body tighten with desire. It's the illicit, desperate sound of her—gasping, moaning, whimpering as she grinds back on his cock, trying to take him deeper. But the men tease her, keeping her pinned there between them, softly caressing her back and breasts until she's shaking, begging for more.

"Please..." Her whimpers of pleasure echo in the hush of the room. "*Please...*"

God.

My own body is shivering, as if I'm the one being tormented by their soft caresses. And when Saint slides his hands over my breasts and stomach, I can't help but moan.

He pulls us over to one of the benches, sitting so that we're facing them, with me perched in his lap.

"Look at her..." he mutters, breath hot on my neck. "Look at how well she's taking them. Two thick cocks, baby, is that what you need tonight? Filling you all the way up?"

I whimper, my head falling back against his shoulder as Saint finds my nipples, and pinches through my dress. The burst of sensation makes me gasp. *Makes me wetter.*

"Or maybe it's the spotlight you crave..." he muses, as in front of us, the men pick up their pace, moving faster now. Pistoning deeper into her mouth and cunt. Making her body shake and moan with every thrust, as we all look on. *Watching.* "So you can show everyone how much you need me. How you beg so nicely for my cock."

I gasp as Saint slides one hand between my trembling legs. I part them eagerly, and he teases at the hem of my skirt, fingertips barely brushing the tops of my thighs. He's already hard against me, the thick outline of his erection pressing into my ass. "Is that what you dream about, darling?" he demands stroking me through my dress. "Being naked. On display. The whole world watching you be such a good girl for me, taking this dick any way I choose."

Yes. *Fuck.*

I clench, and Saint makes a low noise of approval, his fingers tracing my clit through the silk. Rubbing me softly, making me shake in his lap. "That's right. You're going to show them all just how sweet this pussy is. And who knows? Maybe if you're very good, I'll even share."

In front of us, the woman orgasms with a cry, the sound of her pleasure drowning out my own moans. She shakes and writhes, as the men pull out, and explode their climaxes all over her body, pumping and groaning as the ribbons of their pleasure coat her dress and skin. I can hear the mutters of ecstasy around us, but everything fades away, as the men gently carry her from the bed to a dark corner, and Saint leads me to take their place.

My heart pounds.

He sits me back on the bed and kisses me softly on the lips.

"Just say the word, baby," he reassures me, sliding my dress up, over my head and tossing it aside. Without a bra, I'm suddenly bared to the room, my breasts naked, and my hot pink panties leaving nothing to the imagination.

I feel a flush of self-conscious pleasure. The last time I was on display like this, we were at the club, and Saint blindfolded me. Now, there's nothing hidden: I can see the couples and groups sprawled lazily around the room, engrossed in their own filthy pleasures.

Eyes sliding over me. Curious. *Tempted.*

"Which word is that?" I ask, feeling a new boldness blossom inside me. I recline so I'm propped on my elbows, then inch my knees apart, and give him a flirty look. "'Please? Harder? *More?*'"

"All of the above." Saint's eyes flash with lust, and suddenly, he's ripping my panties away and diving between my thighs, gripping tightly to hold me in place.

Oh God.

Saint's tongue slides over my clit, and I can't help but moan.

Heads turn.

Fuck.

It's like electricity sparkling in my bloodstream. He licks me again, tongue swirling over my tender bud, and I sink back, feeling the attention settle over me like a blanket of pleasure.

Is it wrong to be so turned on like this? I don't even care. All that matters is the heat rising in my body, and the sharp ache between my thighs, and Saint's wicked, wonderful mouth lavishing me with pressure in all the right places as my moans grow louder, wild in the hush of the room. It's incredible. I can feel their eyes on me, their own hands wandering as Saint sends my body hurtling closer to the brink in record time. Closer... *Closer...*

I'm poised on the edge of my climax, panting, when Saint lifts his head. "Almost there, baby?" he asks, with a smug grin.

"God, yes," I moan, writhing.

"Good."

He lands a light slap on my pussy that makes me yelp in surprise. Then he's kneeling on the bed beside me, tearing open his pants, and freeing his thick, straining cock. "Time to show them just how well you take this dick," he demands, spreading my legs wider.

"And darling? Make it loud."

He thrusts into me, hard, and *fuck*, I cry out at the feel of him—stretching me, invading.

God.

Saint buries himself deep, grinding all the way to the hilt. I sob, trying to adjust to him, clenching wildly as the pleasure begins to build. "That's right, darling," he groans approvingly, snapping his hips back, and fucking me into the mattress.

Deep. So deep. *Fuck.*

"Clench it for me, night and tight. *Fuck*, you feel incredible... They know it, too," he adds in a low growl, just for me. "Every man in this room wishes he was balls-deep in this heaven right now."

Oh.

In a rush, it all comes back to me. The party. This room. *All those people.* The tight drag of Saint's cock inside me made everything else disappear, but now, awareness prickles my skin in a hot flood of thrilling pleasure. I gasp, turning my head to look, as Saint thrusts into me again.

They're all watching now.

Eyes, masked in the dark. Naked bodies. Hands, gripping cocks. Slid between open thighs. Mouths parted. Getting themselves off to the sight of him fucking me.

I come with a howl; I can't help it. The orgasm crashes through me, swift and sweet, and God, not nearly enough.

The pleasure is still rippling through my body when Saint rolls onto his back, pulling me to straddle his lap. "Let's give them all a better view," he smirks, like he knows just how much this is driving me wild. "Ride my cock for them, baby. Make those pretty tits bounce."

He lands a slap on my ass that echoes, filthy in the dim room. My cheeks are burning up with a breathless flush, utterly exposed here above him, but I do as he says: lifting myself off his cock almost to the head, then sinking down fast. Taking him deep.

I throw my head back and moan, loving the thick pressure of him, and the way his girth rubs up against my inner walls. I do it again, finding a slow, grinding rhythm, my breasts swaying with every stroke.

"Fuck, you're a masterpiece," Saint groans, gazing up at me. He takes my breasts in his hands, squeezing and plucking at my nipples as I grind, making me mewl with pleasure. "Every person in this room should thank God they have the privilege of watching you fuck."

But I'm the lucky one.

Riding him with total abandon, my eyes drifting around the room. I can see the fevered gazes, fixed on me, and it only makes me hotter. Watching a man jerk himself off in frenzied strokes, eyes locked on mine... The woman bent over an armchair, moaning as a man rails her from behind. Both of them watching me. Both of them gasping for more.

"They see you," Saint groans, sitting up to thrust even deeper up inside of me, matching my every stroke. He grips my hair, pulling back to lick up my neck and nip my earlobe in passion. "They see how much you love it. How hungry you are for my cock. My magnificent, dirty girl."

I shudder in bliss. It's filthy and forbidden, and so fucking hot I can't take it.

Saint grips my jaw and turns my head to look at him. "Now, show them something they'll never get to feel," he demands, his breath labored. He's close too, I can feel it, his gorgeous body tense and straining as I sink down and swivel my hips, making him curse with need. "Show them what it's like for a man to die from pleasure."

"Ask nicely."

The order falls from my lips before I can stop it, and Saint's expression flares with surprise—and a new dark excitement. Power hums in my bloodstream, and I slowly circle my hips again.

"If you want to come... Ask nicely," I tease, panting there above him.

Saint sounds a desperate groan. "Baby... *Please.*"

I'm on fire. The way he's looking at me, it's like I'm the sole flame in a dark tundra; the only star in a clouded sky.

The way they're all looking at me.

Waiting. For my permission. My gift of release.

"Louder," I command him, rising up then pausing there, barely holding his swollen cockhead.

I clench, and he curses with need.

"Fuck me, baby," Saint begs, a roar of pure need. "Use my cock. Take it, take everything. I'm yours!"

I slam down hard, taking every inch and grinding deep, over and over.

Saint explodes with a howl, coming apart, and fuck, watching him lose control is all I need to hurtle over the edge. My orgasm hits me like a tidal wave, all consuming. I throw my head back and scream as the pleasure takes me over, swelling through my body in waves of pure pleasure that leave me gasping in his arms.

We lock eyes, lost to the sensation, adrift together in the storm.

And even though I'm surrounded by dozens of people, he's the only one I see.

The only one I'll ever need.

Mine.

Chapter 18

Tessa

The day of the big wedding dawns bright and blue skied, as if even the dull London weather is no match for Annabelle's plans.

"Are you sure I don't look like an ostrich?" I ask Saint, as we're driven to the church; half the backseat filled by my enormous, feathered skirt. Annabelle had the dress messengered over to me this week, a vast fringed affair in shades of blush pink and gold, and even though I'm not an official bridesmaid, I feel like I have to play along.

"No..." Saint replies, but I can tell from the twitch of his full mouth that he's trying not to laugh.

"I knew it!" I wail, swatting his shoulder with my tiny evening purse. Also feathered. Also pink. "You get to look all dashing and dapper in full formal dress, but I'm waddling around like Big Bird at a bridal shower, here!"

"If it helps, you're the sexiest ostrich I've ever seen," Saint grins, flicking one of the feathers on my bust, and I have to laugh.

"If this is what the guests are wearing, I can't wait to see her dress," I say, as the car slows to a stop. "It's going to be unforgettable, I'm sure."

And so will today be, but for far more nerve-wracking reasons. Saint and I decided that he's going to approach his father during the wedding festivities and see if he can get Alexander St. Clair to turn on his coconspirators. With his confession, it will be easy to unravel the mess of fraud and threats at Ashford Pharma, so I can only hope that Saint's instincts are right, and his father can be convinced to do the right thing.

Saint opens the door for me, and me—and my feathers—climb out. Then my jaw drops.

"They're getting married *here*?"

We're standing on the wide white steps of St. Paul's Cathedral, the elaborate columns and stonework rising high above us, all the way to the looming dome. It's magnificent and imposing, especially with a special royal-blue carpet leading up the stairs, and uniformed staff lining the walkway.

"You know Annabelle," Saint says with a smirk. "She's the queen of understatement."

I laugh, gripping his hand tightly as we join the procession of guests making their way into the building. Inside, the exquisitely painted ceilings tower above us, covered with religious friezes and elaborate art; the place is as big as a football field, with cathedral pews lined up facing the vast, imposing alter at the far end. Everything is adorned with gold and pale pink, from the ribbons trailing tastefully from every column and pew, to the massive bouquets of lush hothouse roses and peonies billowing at every turn, a fairytale brought to life.

I blink, stunned at the extravagance. "Well... It's one way to get married, I guess."

"Not your style?" Saint asks, as an usher offers us gilt-rimmed glasses of sparkling mocktails, with rose petals floating in the top.

"Um, nope!" I laugh.

"So how would you choose to tie the knot?" he asks, a questioning smile playing on his lips.

"Without the crowds, and signature cocktails, for one thing," I reply, taking a sip. "I don't know... I've always pictured something private," I confide, feeling self-conscious. "Exchanging my vows with my partner, somewhere in nature maybe, just the two of us. The party could come later, but I like to think the wedding would be just for us. Making our promises to each other—that's all that really matters."

I pause. I never gave much thought to it before, but now I realize, Saint is the person I imagine in the scene with me. Slipping a ring on my finger, promising to love me until the very end.

I blush, glancing over at him. "Seems cheesy, I know," I blurt, feeling embarrassed.

"Not at all." Saint is gazing down at me, with a new intention in his eyes. "Let's do it."

I laugh. "Sure, why not?"

"I mean it."

I look twice, but sure enough, even though he's smiling, there's nothing joking about his expression. "Saint..." I protest, although what I'm protesting, I'm not quite sure.

"Tessa, it's you," Saint says softly, his blue eyes fixed on mine. "You're the one I want to spend my life with. Nothing else could ever compare."

I catch my breath, I'm so overwhelmed. My heart beats faster, already pounding out the answer that's on the tip of my tongue.

Yes. Yes. A thousand times, yes.

"Not now," I blurt, flustered.

Saint grins. "Well, yes. I'm not sure Max or Annabelle would approve of us hijacking their big day."

I laugh. "You know what I mean. I can't think straight, not with everything else going on. But... We'll talk about it."

"Is that a promise?" Saint asks, arching his eyebrow.

I blush deeper. "Yes. Talk," I add, but he's smiling like I just said 'I do.'

Which, maybe I did, in my way.

Saint draws me closer for a kiss, and I sigh happily, sliding my hand down his back—

I stop, feeling a hard outline of something beneath his formal frock coat. And it's not the dirty kind. "Saint?" I murmur softly. I feel the bulge in the back of his waistband again, and gasp.

He brought his *gun*.

"Relax," Saint tells me, under his breath.

"How can I relax, when you're armed!" I hiss.

"It's just as a precaution."

"But Saint—"

"No." He cuts me off firmly. "We don't know who these people are, or what they're capable of. Or when they might strike. So, yes, I'm prepared. I'm not letting anyone hurt you again."

His face is set with determination. *Protective.* And damnit, I can't help but melt, just a little. Fierce Saint can do that to me, every time.

"Bride or groom?" one of the ushers interrupts us, wearing an embroidered satin waistcoat that I already know was hand-sewn by nuns in Tuscany.

"We're with both. St. Clair," Saint gives his name, and the usher checks his tablet.

"Ah, yes. The bridal party is gathered in Chapter House," he informs us. "And the groom has the use of our Darlington

Suite." He snaps his fingers, and two more staff materialize to show us.

"That's alright, I can show them the way." Hugh joins us, looking dapper in a coat and tails, with his usually rumpled blonde hair combed neatly back against his head. "I've already gotten lost twice," he adds, grinning. "Barged in on two nuns praying, if you'd believe it."

"Now, that sounds like the start of one of your dirty jokes," Saint jokes, and Hugh laughs.

"I wish!" He kisses me on the cheek in greeting, and slaps Saint on the shoulder. "Looking fancy, the both of you. The lads and I have a running bet that nobody could look good in those feathered monstrosities, but you might just prove us all wrong, Tessa."

"You're too kind," I remark dryly.

"We were trying to decide, is it more ostrich or emu?" Saint asks, slipping an arm around my shoulders. We follow Hugh down a side hallway, again bedecked with fresh flowers and gorgeous fabrics.

"No comment," Hugh grins. "And if the bride herself should ask, I'm stunned into silence by the beauty of the occasion."

"Smart man." Saint chuckles. "How's Max doing?"

"Oh, the usual cold feet. He's threatening to climb out a window and abscond on one of the carriage horses."

I gasp. "Really?"

"Nothing to worry about," Hugh reassures me. "A couple of stiff drinks, and he'll be right as rain. I'll be the voice of reason, Saint, if you tell him life as a perpetual bachelor is severely overrated."

"It is," Saint says, giving me a satisfied smile.

Hugh groans. "Don't tell me you've got wedding bells ringing in your ears, too. Soon, I'll be the only sad, lonely fellow propping up the bar."

"If it's any consolation, I think there are a couple of single bridesmaids looking to mingle," I tell him, thinking back to the bachelorette party.

"That does help, thank you." Hugh points down a flight of stairs. "The girls are that way. Give my best to 'Belle!"

"I'll see you soon," Saint says, dropping a kiss on my lips.

"And your father..." I venture quietly, glancing at where Hugh is checking his phone.

Saint nods. "My parents will be arriving soon. I'll find a moment to talk to him. And don't worry," he adds with a smile. "Everything's going to be alright."

Hugh looks up. "Chop chop. Before Max takes that tumble out of the cathedral window."

He whisks Saint away, and I go in search of the bridal party. The peals of laughter greeting me at the bottom of the staircase tell me I'm in the right place.

"Tessa!" Annabelle greets me with a squeal, wearing nothing but a jeweled corset, hair rollers, and a hoop petticoat over luxurious cream silk lingerie. "You're here!"

"I'm here," I agree, smiling. The lavish suite is filled with flowers, bridesmaids, and a harried glam squad touching up the party. "Everything looks gorgeous upstairs."

"Doesn't it?" she beams. "Like a fairytale. And it's all thanks to Imogen!"

I turn to where the elegant blonde is perched on a chaise, strapped into her own feathered dress, barking orders over a Bluetooth headset. "No, we've cleared it with the Met. It's one-way traffic only on the approach, they'll have to bring the trucks around the back."

"I thought you swore not to get involved," I remark, when she clicks off the call.

Imogen flicks her eyes skyward. "I did, but her planner was an idiot, and Annabelle begged me at the last minute."

"I wept buckets," Annabelle says cheerfully, as a bottle of champagne gets popped to great applause. "Shameless waterworks to get her to agree. But it was worth it. You're a genius." She plants a kiss on Imogen's cheek, then giggles at the print. "Whoops, Maurice!" she calls to the makeup artist. "Touch-up over here!"

I settle in with Imogen, sipping a sparkling drink as the bridesmaids all primp and preen.

"Good plan," Imogen remarks, plucking a glass of champagne from a nearby tray. "It's going to be a *long* day."

"I think it's sweet," I say, watching Annabelle flit around the room with excitement. All her misgivings seem forgotten as her mom and sisters fuss over her makeup and jewels, and it takes three strapping wardrobe assistants to lift her wedding gown over her head; the massive skirts billowing out like a meringue.

An utterly adorable, pink-cheeked meringue.

It's almost enough to distract me from Saint's task, talking his father into coming clean about the drug trial fraud. I feel a flutter of nerves. Whoever his partners are in this, they're dangerous people, willing to do whatever it takes to silence any whistleblowers.

Will Saint be able to convince Alexander to betray those shadowy forces and do the right thing?

I can only hope.

Because if he isn't willing to tell the truth about what's happened at Ashford... Then we'll have to take him down with the rest of them. I clutch my feathered evening bag tighter, thinking of the small USB drive inside. We copied all the important files from the hard drive and left it under lock and key at Sebastian's place for safekeeping. But the information I have hidden in my purse is more than enough to bring down the Ashford empire and destroy one of the biggest companies in the country.

And it's only a matter of time before the whole world knows it, too.

"She's putting on *such* a brave face." One of the bridesmaids, Fiona, flops down beside us. She's the bitch from the bachelorette, I remember, the one who was constantly making nasty comments. It looks like she's still keeping it up, as she looks across the room at Annabelle, tutting with faux sympathy. "Everyone knows they had to *drag* Max to the church today. Apparently, he's still trashed from the stag do."

"I thought his father canceled it," I reply, levelling her with a glare.

"He did, but naughty Max went AWOL last night in Amsterdam. Hugh had to fly out on his jet and scrape him off some brothel floor this morning," Fiona adds, with a smug grin. "They just landed at Farnborough an hour ago. It's even bets whether Max will be able to stand at the altar, let alone say his 'I do's.'"

"Still, it says a lot that he's here, even in his condition," Imogen speaks up, syrupy sweet. "Some men can't bear to think of marriage, even sober. How is Dickie, anyway?"

Fiona makes a huffing noise and flounces off.

"Good riddance," Imogen mutters, but I'm only half-listening.

"Hugh has a private jet?" I ask slowly, feeling an icy chill shiver down my spine.

"What? Oh, yes. Technically, it's his father's, but everyone keeps it hush-hush. You know, not a good look for his whole 'man of the people' political image," Imogen adds with a smirk. "Hugh and the rest of them use it all the time," she adds, distracted by something on her phone. "They're always jetting around Europe. It's miles better than flying commercial," she adds. "No waiting around at the airport or dealing with security. We all flew to Morocco for a rally a few months ago, were there and back in a flash. Why?" she asks, looking up.

I gulp. "Nothing," I blurt quickly. I lurch to my feet. "I, um, I need some air."

I slip away from the party before anyone notices, hurrying up the staircase, my heart pounding.

A private jet.

Why didn't I think of that before now?

Hugh's entire alibi for the weekend of Wren's attack was that he was giving a TED Talk in Sweden. We figured that with the travel, he couldn't have made it there and back in time. But if he simply had to get to a private airfield to be flown out at his leisure...

He would have had more than enough time to kidnap her from the party and stash her somewhere private, before jetting to Stockholm—and back.

I gulp. It was the perfect cover story, speaking on stage hundreds of miles away. But all it takes me is a quick internet search on my phone to see that the flight time is barely two and a half hours.

I feel sick to my stomach. The revelations about Ashford's fraud distracted me from Wren's attack, but she said it herself, they were connected. A threat, to silence her and send her running back to the States.

Now, the pieces finally fall into place. Hugh has the serpent crown tattoo, he was one of my original suspects, and—I realize to my growing horror—his father has more than anyone to lose if the falsified trials become public.

It's not just money. Lionel Ambrose has staked his political career on Ashford's success—and he's just weeks away from winning the election to be Prime Minister, the single most powerful position in the entire country.

A power worth killing for.

How could I have been so blind?

I grip my phone with shaking hands and send a 911 text to Saint.

'*Where are you? Meet me ASAP. Need to talk!*'

My mind is racing as I hurry down the echoing hallway.

Hugh Ambrose... My God. Out of all of Saint's friends, I trusted him the most. I liked his earnest manners and offbeat charm, and the way he was using his privilege for good with the Foundation's charity projects around the world.

And now...

Now I know it was all a lie.

I need to warn Saint—and fast. I try to remember where the usher said the groomsmen were gathering. Was it the Decker Suite, or the Darlington Hall? I pause in the hallway, lost, when footsteps come. I turn, about to ask for directions—

"Hugh!" I gasp, startled. It's him, strolling closer with a cheerful smile.

"Can't stop, I'm on a mission. Club soda," he says with a friendly smile. "Max's cousin managed to spill claret all over himself, poor sod."

"Oh, too bad." I blurt a laugh, trying to act normal. It's not easy, with my heart pounding in my chest, and every nerve in my body telling me to flee.

He hurt Wren. He locked her up, and did God knows what to her...

"Looking for Saint?" Hugh asks, pausing just in front of me.

"Yes, actually." I swallow, averting my eyes.

"Think he went looking for his parents," Hugh says.

"Although, I can't imagine why. Usually, he's fleeing in the opposite direction."

"I, umm, think it was a business thing. Ashford," I fumble an excuse.

"Is that so?"

I look up, and Hugh must see my true emotions radiating in my eyes, because his expression changes.

"So... That's how it is."

The affable smile drops, and something far more dangerous takes its place. Taunting. Smug. "Bad timing, my dear," he says quietly. "But then, you never did know when to keep your bitch mouth shut."

I feel a shot of panic. We're alone in the hallway, and suddenly, Hugh seems like a stranger to me, a world away from the earnest man I've known.

Run.

"I don't know what you mean," I say brightly, taking a step back from him. "But, umm, I should get back to the bridal suite. They'll be missing me!"

"They couldn't give two hoots where you are," Hugh says, moving closer. His eyes burn into me, chilly and full of disdain. "They're getting wasted on champagne and coke. Nobody will notice if you're gone."

I shiver, looking around for rescue. But this area is off-limits to guests, and the cathedral is so big, I can't tell if anyone is nearby.

"I really have to go," I say again, and he laughs meanly.

"You really are alike, you and your sister. Staying when you should have run. Trusting, when you already know it's too late."

Wren.

I freeze. "It was you," I breathe in horror.

Hugh smirks. "Took you long enough to figure it out. I

guess brains don't run in the family."

Rage consumes me. I lunge at him with a cry, furious, but I barely manage to scratch his face before he throws me against the wall and punches me in the stomach so hard, I'm sent reeling to the floor.

Fuck.

Pain blossoms, and I gasp for air. "Like I said, bad timing," Hugh says above me, as I lay in agony on the marble floor. "I was hoping you were really dropping this, but it looks like you're determined to cause problems for everyone."

I hear footsteps behind me. *Someone's coming!*

My heart leaps, and I struggle to my hands and knees, trying to turn. "Help me—" I start to cry.

Hugh lands a sharp kick to my gut, and I howl in pain, collapsing to the floor again.

"You brought the stuff?" he asks above me, as I lay there, reeling. Whoever it is, they're an accomplice, I realize, through my haze of pain. Nobody's here to help me.

Then a strong pair of arms drag me up from behind, and I feel a sharp prick in the side of my neck.

A needle.

"No... Stop..."

My voice comes out faint, and slurring. My head swims. I try to struggle, but whatever drugs were in that syringe, they're too strong.

"Help me get her out the back exit," Hugh is telling the other person. "I'll clean it up from here."

"Saint..." I whisper. My limbs turn heavy, and my legs give way, but I desperately try to fight it. *I need to warn Saint...*

But it's too late. My body sags. Hugh leans in close, smirking coldly. "Don't worry, we'll deal with him."

Panic swirls inside me, a desperate fear.

Then there's nothing but black.

Chapter 19

Saint

"Another round!"

"Easy there," I warn Max, amused. He's pouring whiskey shots for the groomsmen, although how he's able to drink in this hungover state, I'm not sure. "You do need to be able to walk back down the aisle with her, you know."

"Child's play," Max waves off my concern. "I'm made of sterner stuff, you know. Besides, how often does a man get to toast to his wedding day?"

"At least two or three, judging by your father," one of the other men cracks, and everybody laughs.

"Here's to Max and Annabelle," another says, raising his drink. "The perfect starter wife!"

"Hear, hear!"

I stifle a sigh and take a sip. Clearly, I'm going to need it to make it through the day. So far, the groomsmen have done nothing but crack crude, filthy jokes and egg on Max's worst instincts. Now, they're discussing when it's best to move on to Wife No. 2:

"Let her spit out a couple of kids first. You need that heir."

"She'll be so busy with the babies, that's when you get the mistress set up."

"But you don't marry that one, gives her ideas. You wait until after the divorce is final, so you can be rid of the both of them, and onto greener pastures."

"And by that, he means tighter pussy!"

There's a chorus of laughter, and I take another drink.

Fuck. When did these guys get so... bitter? I've known every man in this room at least half my life, if not more: boarding school, university clubs, and all the same parties. Our parents were friends, and so here we all are. But somehow, I barely recognize them anymore. Hairlines are receding, torsos are bulging with middle-aged spread, and there's a cruelty in their jokes I don't recognize anymore, complaining about their wives and children, like a prison sentence somebody forced them into taking.

When I think about the possibility of Tessa agreeing to marry me, giving me the chance to be her *husband...*

It takes my breath away. I can't think of a greater honor in the world than seeing my ring on her finger, and, *Christ*, her belly swollen with my child one day...

"See, Saint's doing it the right way," Max's cousin raises his glass to me. "Fresh meat every term up at Ashford College. Nice young fillies looking for an education."

"Lucky bastard."

"Got that American girl on rotation, isn't that right?" The cousin smirks. "Love the Yanks, they're always gagging for it. Filthy sluts."

I finish the rest of my drink, and slowly rise to my feet. "Care to say that again?" I ask quietly.

The man's smile crumbles, as he realizes I could easily tear him limb from limb. And I may well do just that.

"Woah there. Just a little banter, that's all."

I wait with a cool glare.

"Sorry," he offers, looking nervous. "Good for you. She seems like a lovely girl."

I sigh. Giving the best man a bloody nose wouldn't exactly help this wedding run smoothly, and God knows Annabelle has enough on her plate with the groom, so I restrain the urge to punch him in his smug face.

"Is there any coffee coming?" I ask instead, eyeing Max. It's time he sobered up. The man can drink like nobody else, but it would be better if he wasn't literally stumbling down the aisle.

"There's supposed to be a full wait staff," someone offers.

"I'll go see."

"Send the pretty one, that blonde!"

I leave them to their self-satisfied laughter. I feel restless, this damn formal outfit too constricting, and I know only one thing could make me feel like myself again.

One person.

Tessa.

I smile, heading to where the bridal party is gathered. Even in the midst of all this chaos, the thought of her is like a breath of fresh air. She's changed everything for me, I realize. She opened my eyes to the corruption and seedy lies soaked into the fabric of my privileged society.

I thought that simply turning my back on it and forging my own path in life was enough, frittering away my time with parties and women, like that was any better. Until she demanded more from me.

Justice. Honor.

Doing what's right, instead of the easy way out.

Now, I know I want to be that man. A man she can be proud to call her own.

"You're lost," Imogen's voice breaks through my thoughts, amused. "This is bride central. No boys allowed."

"I know, I know," I stop in the doorway, holding up my hands "I just dropped by to see Tessa. Where is she?" I ask, glancing around the suite. There are silk and feathered dresses everywhere; the bridesmaids all getting their hair or makeup touched up as Annabelle snaps selfies with her family.

"I don't know," Imogen shrugs. "I thought she went to find you."

I shake my head, getting a strange prickle of unease. "We must have just missed each other. This place is a maze. Text me when you see her, OK?" I ask, wondering where she is. I can't forget, we have enemies still out there. Maybe in this very cathedral.

"Sure. I'll let her know you can't go an hour without her," Imogen replies, smirking.

I walk away, keeping my eyes peeled for Tessa among the uniformed wait staff buzzing around down here, bringing trays down for the reception. I check the basement level, but there's no sign of her, even in the grand crypt area, beneath the main cathedral floor. "If you could please send coffee to the groomsmen," I ask, remembering my task, and pull one of the—male—servers aside. "And food, too. Thanks."

"Let me guess, my son needs something to soak up all that booze."

I turn. It's Max's father, Cyrus Lancaster, decked out in full white tie, complete with a top hat and tails. "Christ, it's a madhouse up there," he says, rolling his eyes. "This is the only spot I can take a call without being interrupted every five seconds. The VP's here... Wills and Kate... and that Deputy Leader is getting desperate," he adds with a smirk. "Had to invite him, of course. Bad for the optics if it's only Lionel here today. But everyone knows the PM position is sewn up. The

Ambroses will be taking up residence in Number Ten by the end of the month."

"My father says the polls are strong," I agree, as we stroll back upstairs.

"Everyone knows it's time to put this country in the right direction." Cyrus gives a satisfied nod. "With the right people steering the ship. The past points the way to our future," he adds, quoting from the Blackthorn Society lore. "Ensuring our legacies stand tall for another generation. Max will do his duty with the DeWessops girl," he adds. "He was chomping at the bit for a while there, but he knows what's expected of him. All you boys do," Cyrus says, slapping me on the shoulder. "I know you won't let us down, despite whatever *distractions* have been leading you astray. Family's what matters in the end."

I feel another bolt of unease. Cyrus's icy blue eyes are fixed on me, like he's waiting for some kind of answer.

"Of course," I reply vaguely. "I should actually go find mine."

"Over there," he nods, to where my parents are chatting with some other guests in the main cathedral. The crowd has swelled with new arrivals. Everyone from the British elite has showed up today, and half the international power players, too. "Now, I need to have a little chat with the French PM about those new online privacy policies..." He gives me another pat, then moves into the crowd—which parts for him like the Red Sea.

My unease grows.

If I would pick anyone to be my father's coconspirator, it would be Cyrus. His rise to media mogul has been meteoric, and he's achieved everything he has by crushing his business enemies without mercy. He's a huge investor in Ashford Pharma and getting rid of a few pesky whistleblowers would be nothing to him, not if it stood in the way of increasing his wealth and power.

And his talk about loyalty... Family... Duty...

Does he know I'm already working to expose them all?

Either way, there's no time to lose. I cut through the crowd and intercept my parents.

"Anthony, darling," my mother greets me with a bright smile. "Don't you look dashing? Isn't this a lovely event?" She adjusts my cravat, and I bat her hands away.

"I need to talk to you, Dad," I say urgently. He's dressed up for the occasion, but he has dark shadows under his eyes, and he seems distracted.

Is the guilt already getting the better of him?

"Now's not the time, Anthony," my mother answers for him, waving at someone across the room. "Louise! Let's catch up after!"

"Yes, now is the time," I say firmly, taking my father's arm. "It can't wait."

"But son—"

"You need to hear this too, Mum," I add. "And you, Robert."

My brother stops, looking surprised as he arrives with the wedding schedule in his hands. "What's going on?"

"Your brother's got a bee in his bonnet about something," my mother sighs. "But I'm sure it can wait until after the ceremony—Anthony!" she sounds a protest, as I grab her arm, too, and steer them away from the crowd, and into an empty vestibule. The small room is off a hallway, away from the main crowd, and I shut the door behind us.

Three confused faces stare back at me. "Honestly, Anthony, what an earth's gotten into you?" My mother complains.

I ignore her protests. She needs to know this. They all do.

"I know, Dad," I tell him, blocking their exit. "I know everything. You had the trial data faked for the Alzheimer's drug. Valerie found out, or maybe you made her do it in the first place, but she was blackmailing you, wasn't she? That's what the payoff was for."

My father's jaw drops. "That's preposterous," he tries to bluster, but I can see it in his eyes. Guilt. Shame. *Fear*. "I won't have you accuse me—"

"It's over, Dad!" I interrupt, getting angry. I don't have time for any more of his lies, not when every minute keeps Tessa at risk. "We know everything. It's time for you to confess and come clean. It's not too late to do the right thing," I add, urging. "I know you never meant to let it get this far. But these are dangerous people you're working with. You know what they did to Valerie. Do you really think they wouldn't turn on you, too?"

My father shakes his head, looking bewildered. "But Valerie... That was an accident."

"It was murder!" I exclaim, frustrated. "They killed her to stop her from revealing the fraud. Don't you see? They'll stop at nothing to keep this secret hidden."

"No!" my father protests again, pale-faced. "Maybe the first test results needed a little... *massaging*, but the rest of it? She was drunk driving. The roads were wet—"

"Honestly, Alexander. Don't be a fool." My mother's voice cuts through his excuses, icy calm. "The bitch got what she deserved."

What the fuck?!

I turn to my mother, shocked. She meets my eyes defiantly. "She brought it on herself, getting greedy, threatening to report the whole thing. As if morals mattered to her. She was happy enough to take the money and falsify the data to begin with. It was her fault the drug didn't work in the first place," my mother purses her lips in distaste. "If she'd been better at her job, then none of this would have happened."

I gape at her in disbelief. "You knew?"

"Of course I knew," she spits back at me, glaring. "Who do you think has been stuck cleaning up your father's mess? The company has everything riding on this new drug. Everything," she vows. "Our fortune. Our reputation. You think I would just sit back and let us fail? The Ashford name would become a joke. We'd lose it all," she adds, with a quiet fury. "Five hundred years of history. Our family's legacy, down the drain. Well, I won't let that happen."

I can't believe it. All this time I assumed my father was in over his head, swept along with someone else's evil plans.

He was.

I just never imagined it was my mother who was the one calling the shots.

"No," I tell her, the betrayal hardening to steely determination in my veins. "This ends. *Now*. I won't stand for it. We don't want this fucking legacy of yours. Do we, Robert?" I add, glancing over at my brother. He's been standing there silently through all of this, and I know he must be reeling from the revelations, too. "We're going to do the right thing."

But Robert puts his hands up, trying to calm me. "Just wait a minute," he says. "Let's talk about this."

"What the fuck is there to talk about?" I explode. "Didn't you hear what I just said? This is massive fraud. Conspiracy. Murder!"

"Which means we shouldn't be hasty," Robert says, looking nervous. "Just think of what happens if word gets out. There'll be consequences."

"You mean like a faulty drug going to market, fooling millions of innocent people who think it's their last hope of a miracle?" I shoot back, remembering that poor man outside

Ashford HQ the other day. He was desperate for a cure for his wife, and my family would go right ahead and sell him one, knowing full well that it wouldn't make a difference.

"The team is still working on the drug," Robert argues. "We're testing new formulations, we'll get it right soon enough, but not if we're just shut down."

"You can't be serious," I stare at him, confused. "You know this is wrong. People are getting hurt!"

"And who's fault is that?" Robert explodes suddenly. His face is red, shameful and frustrated. "If your girlfriend hadn't started digging around, if that sister of hers had just stayed dead, then none of this would be a problem!"

I stagger back, stunned at the anger in his voice. And that's when it hits me...

He knows Wren is alive.

Instinctively, I pull out my gun, and level it at my brother. I already fixed the silencer to the barrel, back at my house, and now it gleams a dull grey in the cathedral lights.

My mother gasps. "Anthony, what on earth are you doing!"

"Put that thing away!" My father adds, outraged.

I ignore them. "How did you get that shoulder injury, Robert?" I demand quietly.

"I... I told you. It was a squash match," he blurts.

"No, you said rugby." I flip the safety off, my grip steady. The pieces fall into place. Fuck, it's been right under my nose all along.

Phillip gave up Wren's location. He told his higher-ups at Ashford about the cottage in the country, and they sent a man there to kill Wren and Tessa. To stalk them through the dark woods, to terrorize and hurt them.

The gunman was someone they trusted. Someone athletic. Someone with everything to lose.

"It was you. You came after them, in the woods. You *shot* at her!"

I'm shaking with rage. My own brother. He tried to kill Tessa, fired a bullet right at her that flew only inches from her heart. "How could you?" I demand. "What the fuck is going on with this family?"

"He did what was necessary to protect us," my mother speaks up, still defiant, even after everything. "He put our legacy first and accepted his responsibilities to this family. Since you still refuse to play your part."

"You never do anything you're supposed to!" Robert spits, suddenly looking furious. "You're the oldest son, this is your future we're all fighting to protect, but still, you get to go off, partying, doing whatever the hell you want, while I'm the one who has to pay the price! You don't know the things I've done," he says, pointing an angry finger at me. "What I've had to sacrifice for this family..."

The haunted look in his eyes makes my blood run cold.

"It's over," I repeat, determined. "We have the proof, we're exposing everything. And you'll go down with them."

"Nobody's going anywhere." My mother sounds remarkably calm. "It's being handled as we speak."

"Handled how?"

And then I see it, the flicker in Robert's gaze.

Tessa.

"Where is she?" I demand, still pointing the gun at him. I already know in my gut that she's not just wandering the cathedral out there. They took her. Whoever else is involved in this has her, and I have to get her back, no matter what. "Where's Tessa?" I roar, my voice rising.

"She's being dealt with." My mother folds her arms.

I see red. "What the fuck does that mean?" I demand. "Is she hurt? Who has her? Tell me dammit, or I swear—"

"You'll do what?" Robert interrupts me. "Shoot me? This is

your family, too!"

I stare at them grimly. "You don't understand. There's *nothing* I wouldn't do for her."

Without hesitating another moment, I point the barrel of the gun at Robert's leg and pull the trigger.

The gun sounds a low whoosh, muffled by the silencer. Robert howls, falling to the floor and clutching his knee. "You shot me!" he cries in disbelief. "You actually shot me!"

"And I'll do it again, in a heartbeat," I vow, advancing. I raise the gun—pointing at his head this time. Fury and panic beat wildly in my chest, filling my ears with a dull roar. "Now tell me, *where the fuck is she*?!"

"At the house!" Robert blurts, eyes wide with fear. "In Sussex."

I keep advancing, until the barrel of the gun is pressed right between his eyes. "I swear it!" Robert sobs, crumpled on the ground in front of me. "Hugh took her. A half-hour ago! She's in the cellars there!"

My finger trembles on the trigger. Rage pounds through me, remembering what they did to Tessa's sister. What they plan to do to her. *And he helped...*

"Anthony, please!" my mother cries.

At the last minute, I force myself to lower the gun. There's no time. Not with Tessa locked up—scared, hurt, or even worse...

I back away, shooting them all a look of pure disgust. "You're dead to me now," I tell them, finality in my voice. "The Ashford name, the one you'll do anything to protect... It's yours. Keep it."

And then I turn and race away. Tessa is the only one that matters to me now. She's my family, my future, my everything. If I can reach her in time...

I only hope I'm not too late.

Chapter 20

Tessa

I wake, groggy. My head is killing me, and there's an intense pounding in the back of my skull. I moan before I've even opened my eyes.

Why does it hurt?

I try to roll over in bed, to grab a glass of water from the nightstand. Then I realize that I'm lying on the ground, with nothing but cold hard stone beneath me.

Where the hell am I?

I pry my eyes open, making my head pound even more. Dim light filters in, and I squint around, realizing to my horror that I'm in some kind of bare, empty room.

No, it's a dusty brick cell, more like a dungeon.

Oh my God...

Panic grips me as I sit up. There are iron bars on the door, a stone floor, and nothing but a small opening, way up by the ceiling, about fifteen feet off the ground. Bars block it, but I can see grass, and daylight filtering through.

I'm underground, somewhere. A mattress lays in one corner of the cell, along with a bottle of water, and a bucket.

My blood turns to ice.

This is where they kept Wren.

It's exactly the way she described to me, pieced together from her fragments of memory. The site of all her worst nightmares.

And now I'm the one locked inside.

How long have I been here?

I frantically try to remember what happened. I was at the wedding, with the bridal party. Imogen was saying something about private jets...

In a rush, it all comes back to me. *Hugh.* He attacked Wren. He's involved in all of this—and he's not alone. His accomplice injected me with something and helped him drag my body out of the building before anyone could see.

I shiver with fear, remembering the look in Hugh's eyes. He was terrifying. Just the memory of it chills me, so cold and unrecognizable.

What is he planning for me?

And what about Saint? The thought fills me with new panic. He doesn't know his friend has betrayed him. I didn't have a chance to warn him, and now...

Now he's in danger, too.

I scramble to my feet. I'm still strapped into one jeweled sandal, and I kick it away, standing in my bare feet as I scan the small cell again, desperate for some escape. Then I see something, high in the corner, mounted on the ceiling.

A camera.

The chill turns icy. What the hell? Is Hugh watching me right now?

Or is this for later, to record what's coming next?

I try to hold back the wave of nausea rising in my throat. I can't panic right now, not if I want to make it out of here.

Breathe. *Think.*

I need to find a way out—before Hugh comes back for me.

I search the cell again, carefully this time, tracing my fingertips over every wall, looking for loose stones or anything I can use as a weapon.

No luck.

I turn my attention to the door, instead. I grip the bars and shake them, hard. They're clearly old, the metal rusted with age, but they're embedded firmly in the wood, and don't budge an inch.

"Hello?" I holler into the shadows outside. "Are you there, Hugh? Are you watching this? You better pray to God I don't get my hands on you. I'll kill you myself! Bastard!"

My voice echoes uselessly. Wherever I am, Hugh wouldn't have been dumb enough to stash me where anyone would hear. I could be in a basement somewhere in London, or hours away. I don't even know how long I was unconscious.

Does Saint even know I'm gone?

He must. He'll be looking for me by now, I just know it. But will he find me in time?

"... Out there...?"

I freeze. There's a woman's voice, faint, coming from somewhere down in this dungeon. It calls again, a faded desperate screaming sound.

I lunge close to the bars and yell out into the darkness. "Is anyone there?"

There's a pause, and then the voice comes again, stronger now. "Hello?"

"I'm here!" I yell back. "I'm trapped here too. Where are you?"

"Tessa?"

I gasp. The voice is faint, but unmistakable.

"Wren?" I scream. "Wren, it's OK, we're going to get out of here!"

I rattle the bars harder, desperate now. They must have snatched her at the airport or tracked her somehow when she left. Has she been down here all this time?

They're eliminating all witnesses.

Through the bars, I catch sight of a heavy rusted padlock, hanging from the outside of the door, bolting it shut. Every time I shake the door, the lock makes a grinding sound of protest.

I whirl around, thinking fast. There's nothing I can use in the cell, so I pat myself down. The dress is nothing but silk and feathers, but my shoe... I grab it eagerly, turning it over in my hands.

The stiletto heel has a metallic tip.

I rush back to the door, and slide my hand through the bars, holding the shoe. It just about fits, and if I reach at an uncomfortable angle, I can slam the metal heel into the old padlock.

THWACK.

I hit it wrong, and the heel glances off the lock. I almost drop the shoe with the change in force, but I grip the strap just in time. Dammit.

Careful, I tell myself, my heart pounding in fear. It's our only hope.

I position the shoe again and bring it down on the lock. Hard. The padlock groans. I do it again, and again, hammering it with a barely-contained panic until my arm aches, and I'm beginning to lose hope that we'll ever—

CRACK.

The metal join on the padlock gives way. I hurl myself at the door with everything I have, and it swings open with a groan.

"Wren?" I yell, looking around. "Wren, where are you?"

There's no reply.

I race barefoot down the dark hallway, frantically checking around. There are a few more dusty cells, just like the one where I was being held, but they're filled with old boxes, and shelves of wine. "Wren?" I scream, panicked.

There's a faint sobbing noise. I rush towards the sound and find another cell at the end of the hallway. The door is barred, just like mine, and I can see my sister inside, huddled in one dim corner. She's dressed in the clothes she was wearing yesterday, when we dropped her at the airport, now stained and dirty as she sits, curled into a ball, shaking and sobbing in hysterics.

My heart breaks.

"Wren, it's OK, I'm here!" I call through the bars. But she doesn't even lift her head. She's having some kind of panic attack, brought on by the terror of being trapped here again. "I'm going to get you out!"

I check the door, but the lock is brand new and shiny. There's no way I can break it.

"There have to be keys, around here somewhere," I call to her. "I'm going to go find them. I'll be right back. I promise!"

I hate to leave her like this, but I know we're running out of time. Wherever Hugh has gotten to, he won't risk leaving us here for long.

I've already checked the rooms behind me, so I keep moving, deeper into the maze of narrow stone hallways and dim, dusty cells. It's dark here, with just the occasional bare lightbulb flickering in the ceiling, and I'm filled with fear as I creep onwards, wondering if the next doorway will bring me face to face with Hugh again. I desperately check another few cells, flinging open doors before—

Found it!

It's some kind of control room, with a desk, and filing cabinet, and bank of video screens, showing the inside of the cells. This is where the cameras are transmitting to! I can see Wren in her cell, still huddled and sobbing, so I wrench at the filing

cabinet drawers. It's locked, so I try the desk next, searching for-
-

There. An old-fashioned keyring, with a dozen keys on it. This *has* to be it.

I race back to Wren's cell. "It's OK, I'm here!" I call to her, fumbling with the keys. I try four different ones in the padlock, before the right one finally clicks.

I yank the door open, rushing over and pulling her into a hug. "It's OK, I've got you," I murmur, trying to soothe her. "Everything's going to be OK."

Wren lifts her head, looking at me with pure anguish in her eyes. "You can't be here. Please, no, he's coming back, you have to go," she sobs, shaking and clawing at me.

"I know, I know about Hugh," I tell her, trying to lift her to her feet. "I'm sorry, I know it's hard, but there's no time. We have to get out of here."

She stares back at me, limp and unmoving. I can't lift her, and we're running out of time.

"Wren! Please," I cry. "We have to go!"

The desperate sound of my voice echoing in the cell seems to snap her out of it. Her eyes come into focus again. She looks around and gasps a ragged breath. "You got it open..."

"I found the keys, in the control room. But we have to go. *Now*."

I pull her to her feet, and this time, Wren stumbles upright. She's weak but can manage to walk. I drag her to the door, and then down the hallway I just came from. "This way, I think there are stairs."

But she stops by the control room, staring through the open doorway at the bank of video screens. "There are cameras..." she says slowly, realization dawning in her eyes.

"Come on, Wren, there isn't time!" I pull at her arm, but she yanks free, lunging into the room.

"They recorded me," she looks around the room wildly. "If there's video, from before, then I can see what happened."

"Wren!" I glance anxiously to the stairway. "Please, we're so close to getting out of here."

"But I have to know what happened!" her voice breaks, raw and anguished. She looks at me, imploring. "Don't you understand, Tessa? Every time I close my eyes, the memories are haunting me. I have to see it. I have to know!"

Fuck.

I glance around again quickly, then join her in the room. "The filing cabinet," I point, "but it's locked."

Wren grabs a brick from the floor and slams it against the drawer. The metal buckles instantly. She tears it open, revealing stacks of CD cases, each containing a burned disc. "In here!"

Wren grabs a handful, and I do the same, flipping through them to check the handwritten labels. There are names, and dates, scribbled in different writing on the discs.

"Some of these are twenty years old," I say in disbelief. "Harold N, 1992... Peter J.... Lionel A..." I pause, feeling a new chill. Lionel Ambrose?

Wren shakes her head, frustrated. "I don't see it!" she exclaims, grabbing another stack of discs. "I'm not here!"

"What's on here, anyway?" I ask, feeling sick. I grab one of the discs. *Max L*, it says, with a date from five years ago.

Max Lancaster.

I shove the disc in the system drive and click to bring up the folder. Black-and-white video starts to play, one of the cameras from a cell. There's a man sprawled, unconscious on the mattress. A boy, really, he can't look more than eighteen.

The cell door swings open, and Max steps inside. Looking younger, reluctant. He speaks to someone outside the cell, but then the door swings shut.

He approaches the body on the mattress, unfastening his belt and pulling down his pants—

I click out of the video in a hurry.

"It wasn't just you," I tell Wren in horror, bile rising in my throat. "This has been going on for years. Countless victims."

She looks back at me, stunned. "What the hell have they been doing down here?"

"It's called loyalty."

The voice makes us spin around. Hugh is standing in the doorway, a grim smile on his face.

And a gun in his hand—pointed directly at us.

Chapter 21

Tessa

Instinctively, I move in front of Wren, shielding her from Hugh's aim.

"Loyalty," I repeat, furious. "What the hell does that mean? What kind of sick bastards are you?"

"I assure you, we take no pleasure from it. Well, not always." Hugh chuckles, a dark, unpleasant sound. "But certain assurances must be made. Old deals require new guarantees, you see.

"Guarantees about what?" I demand, curious—and stalling for time. If I can get him talking, long enough to distract him, maybe lunge for that gun...

"About *power*," Hugh replies forcefully. "What else is there? Raw, unfettered, unaccountable power. It's our birthright," he adds, sneering. "Never mind the façade of democracy. The powerful families in this country have run things for hundreds of years, and we will for hundreds more. As long as everybody remembers their duty," he adds. "That's where this little setup comes in. We have to ensure the bonds of loyalty don't fray with time. For each new generation taking the mantle, we need a little... insurance."

"You mean blackmail," I say, sickened.

"Privilege has its cost," he replies with a shrug.

"So... You're saying that these people, from powerful families, come here and..." I swallow back my horror.

"They do what it takes to prove their loyalty," Hugh finishes for me. "Call it mutually assured destruction."

The scheme is stunning in its evil simplicity, I realize. The crimes recorded on those discs could ruin anyone, if the truth ever got out. But if they're all guilty, none of them will ever tell.

My eyes fall on the cases, scattered on the desk. "Your father's on here," I say, my mind racing. "Max too. And you're here somewhere, with Wren."

"Yes, I am."

Hugh plucks one of the discs that's fallen to the floor and holds it up. "Is this what you're looking for?" he asks Wren, taunting.

She lets out a cry of anger and distress behind me, but I'm close enough to see the scribbled label. It's not just Hugh's name on the disc.

Robert.

"Saint's brother was there with you?" I ask, shocked.

"Of course," Hugh replies casually. "There's always a witness. And since Saint would never have agreed to play a part in all of this, Robert had to represent the family. Of course, the St. Clairs are always kind enough to offer up use of their lovely wine cellars here." He gestures around with the gun, and I realize, that's where he's been holding us.

The St. Clair Estate. Saint's childhood home.

My heart leaps with hope. Saint will put the pieces together. Somehow, he'll figure this out. But for now, it's just the three of us, and I can tell from the way that Hugh is waving that gun around that he's growing impatient. I'm not sure how much longer I can stall.

"They sent you after her, didn't they?" I ask him, hoping to distract him a little more. "Once she started asking questions about the Ashford drug trials, they ordered you to take Wren."

Hugh nods. "I was due to pledge my loyalty, so it was the perfect timing. The drugs were supposed to wipe away everything," he adds, talking to Wren over my shoulder. "But clearly, we didn't get the dose just right. Too bad. But you still should have kept your mouth shut and left us all well enough alone. But no, you and your sister just had to stir up trouble at the worst time. My father is weeks away from becoming Prime Minister, and we all stand to make billions from the drug launch. We can't afford any loose ends."

With that, he raises the gun again.

Fuck.

"Please don't do this!" I beg. "Have mercy on us, please!" I make my voice desperate, and inch closer, like I'm about to throw myself at his feet. "You don't want to hurt us; I know you don't. You're better than this! All your good work at the Foundation; you're a decent man, I know you are!"

Hugh pauses, smirking like he's enjoying this.

"I'll do anything!" My pleas echo, pathetic—and covering for the fact I'm still inching closer to him, playing at being hysterical. "I don't want to die," I wail, taking another step closer. "Please, just let us go. I'll do anything you want. Anything at all. *Please*!"

One more step, sobbing... Another, then—

I lunge for him, putting my head down and tackling him straight in the midriff.

"*Oof*!" Hugh sounds a grunt of surprise, stumbling back. He fires the gun, but I'm already sending the both of us hurtling to the ground.

BANG!

"Run, Wren!" I scream, struggling to keep Hugh down. He fires again, right beside my head, making my ears ring, and I can only hope it goes wide. "RUN!"

Hugh rolls, pinning me down, his hands moving to my throat. Oh God. He grips hard, choking me with a look of pure fury in his eyes.

I gasp for air, grabbling blindly for the nearest thing. The chair. It's just an old metal stool, but I grab it by one leg and swing wildly at Hugh's head. It cracks against the back of his skull with a sickening crunch, hard enough to send him toppling over.

I scramble out from under him and find Wren still cowering in the corner. "Come on!" I scream at her, grabbing her hand and yanking her from the room. We stumble over Hugh's groaning body, racing towards the stairs. "This way!"

I dash upwards, Wren following fast behind me as we sprint up the narrow, winding staircase. The door at the top is open, and I hurl myself through it, emerging in a dim hallway with light coming from a window at the end. There's a laundry room nearby... A tiled hallway, leading to more storage rooms...

The place is deserted. The whole family is in London for the big wedding, and they must have given the staff the weekend off.

"Which way?" Wren asks fearfully.

I look around, trying to remember the layout of the grand, sprawling manor house. I visited once before, for a party, but I'd been too swept up in Saint, focused on sneaking away for stolen kisses instead of clocking all the exit routes.

Now, I have a vague recollection of the servant's areas, leading to the kitchens, and a garage housing Saint's father's vintage car collection —

"Over here!" I blurt, racing for the far door. "If we can get to the garage, we can take a car and get the hell out of here!"

We bomb down another maze of hallways, past more utility rooms, until I find the entrance to the garage. It's a vast, echoing space, the size of a showroom, with glass doors at one end and rows of classic cars lined up, gleaming on display. Bentley, Porsche, Ferrari... But where the hell are all the keys?

Wren and I hurry down the aisle, pausing by a stack of gasoline cans and other auto equipment. "Do you see a valet box?" I ask desperately. "Any way to get one out of here?"

"No," Wren cries, looking around. "I can't see—"

BANG!

A gunshot ricochets, smashing the windscreen on one of the cars nearby.

Wren lets out a scream, and I grab her, knocking over crates and cans as we drive behind the nearest vehicle for cover.

BANG! Another shot rings out, too close.

"Nice try, but your little fun and games are over," Hugh's voice calls. His footsteps echo on the ground, moving closer. "There's no way out of here. And I can't let you leave... Not alive, anyway."

Wren and I exchange a panicked look. There's nowhere to run. We're cornered here, with nothing but solid brick behind us, and Hugh approaching from the only exit.

"When you get the chance, run," Wren whispers, giving me a shove. "I'll distract him."

"Wren, no!" I gasp.

"You're always the one trying to save me," she says with a sad smile. "It's my turn now."

"Please, no—" I try to stop her, but she's already rising to her feet, emerging from behind the car, hands raised.

"I'm over here!"

Fuck! What the hell is she doing? I look on in horror as

Hugh whirls around, training his gun on her. "Get over here," he barks, wary now. He's got blood on his face, and an unhinged look in his eyes. "Nice and slow. No fucking games this time."

Wren walks towards him, leaving footprints in the pool of gasoline spilling on the floor.

I peer out, horrified. I want to scream and shout, and stop her from doing this, but already, he's grabbing her and yanking her closer; one arm around her neck in a chokehold while the other waves that gun around.

"Now, where the fuck's your sister?" he demands. "Better get out here, Tessa, unless you want to see your sister's brains all over the floor. You're both dying today, but if you play nicely, I can do you the favor of making hers quick!"

I stay frozen there, torn. Wren told me to run, but I can't just leave her here. Hugh is losing it, unravelling before my eyes. There's no telling what he's capable of.

I look around me, searching for a weapon. The gasoline is spilling slowly, pooling on the floor at Hugh's feet. If I could just find a way to spark a fire—

CRASH!

There's suddenly an ear-splitting wrench of metal and glass, as a black Jeep careens through the garage doors and spins to a stop. And behind the wheel...

It's Saint!

Relief crashes through me, but it's quickly drowned out by fear as Hugh fires towards the car.

"Stay back!" he yells, still holding Wren in a headlock. He presses the barrel of the gun against her head. "I'll kill her, right now!"

Saint climbs out, his hands raised. He's got his gun in one of them, but when he sees Wren, he drops it to the ground, and kicks it clear.

"Calm down," he tells Hugh, his voice even. "I heard the gunshots, and thought you were the one in trouble. Your father sent me, to give you a hand with these two. And clearly, I got here just in time." Saint gives a snort of derision. "You couldn't handle two girls alone? Christ, it's no wonder you need a babysitter."

Hugh pauses, clearly confused. "I don't believe you," he says, aiming the gun at Saint. But his hand is shaking, and I can see the wheels turning in his mind.

Saint is bluffing, I know he has a plan, but how long will Hugh let him talk?

I look around, resuming my search for a weapon as Saint keeps him distracted, facing the other direction.

"I'm on your team," Saint continues. "Why else do you think I've kept Tessa so close? I had to find out who they told about the Ashford scheme."

"But your brother said—"

"Robert doesn't know everything. This was above his pay grade. After all, the way he failed in the woods, my parents knew they couldn't rely on him anymore. That's why they brought me in. Finally. You should have told me sooner," Saint adds, as I spot a glint of metal nearby, under the next car. A heavy wrench.

I crawl over to it, my heart pounding.

"You love her," Hugh's voice comes, sounding uncertain. "You chose her."

Saint laughs. "Over a billion-pound profit, and the entire Ashford empire? C'mon, no pussy's worth that much, even if she does fuck like a champion."

My hand closes around the wrench handle, and I slowly drag it closer, praying the sound won't carry over their voices.

"You know me," Saint is saying. "A little rebellion is one thing, but I was always going to do my duty in the end."

I slowly rise to my feet. They're twenty feet away from me, Hugh's back still turned with his gun in one hand, and Wren gripped against him.

Silently, I creep closer, brandishing the wrench.

Saint sees me over their shoulder. His eyes flicker wider in recognition, but then he talks again, louder, to cover the sound of my approach.

"So, how about you stop waving that gun at me, and let's get this mess cleaned up?" Saint continues, as I force myself to put one foot in front of the other. Creeping closer, *closer...* "God knows they'll already be missing us for the ceremony, but we can get back to London in time for the reception. A toast, eh? And a nice, solid alibi. Not that anyone else will notice those bitches are gone. They're not one of us, are they now?"

My foot slips in the gasoline, and I stumble, trying not to lose my balance. The sound captures Hugh's attention; he starts to turn—

"AAAAIIII!" I swing at him with everything I have. The wrench makes contact with his shoulder, and he fires, glass shattering nearby. Wren stumbles free as Hugh whirls to face me; he raises the gun to fire again straight at—

BANG!

Saint dives, pushing me to the ground. I see blood blossom on his shirt, but he doesn't hesitate: He rolls off and lunges at Hugh, tackling him to the ground and slamming a fearsome punch into his face, over and over again. Hugh gurgles helplessly, releasing his grip on the gun. Saint snatches it away, and stands over his body, levelling it directly at him. "Don't you fucking move!" he roars.

There's silence.

I gasp for air, and struggle to my feet again. We're surrounded by broken glass, and in the corner, I see flames; a fire started by a stray bullet, but it's the least of my concerns right now. "You're bleeding!" I cry. Saint barely glances down.

"It's just my shoulder. I'll be fine."

"Wren?" I turn. She's sagging against one of the cars, gazing at us with wide eyes.

"I'm... I'm fine," she stutters. I go to her and envelop her in a fierce hug.

"Thank God," I hold her tightly. "Don't you dare pull a stunt like that again."

"It worked, didn't it?" she manages a faint smile, pulling away.

I move to Saint, to check his wound. I could cry with relief when I see that bullet tore straight through his upper arm, a clean wound. "See, it's fine," he reassures me, as I grab a clean rag from nearby and tie it on to stem the bleeding. "We're alright, baby. Everything's OK."

"Is that what you think?" On the ground, Hugh spits blood from his mouth, laughing. "What are you going to do, call the police on me? We own the fucking police! The courts, the judges... Don't you idiots understand? Nobody will stand against us, not if they know what's good for them. We're untouchable!" he yells. "We're—"

BANG!

Hugh slumps to the ground, blood pooling from the back of his head.

Dead.

I let out a scream of shock.

Wren's standing there, calmly holding Saint's weapon, the one he dropped. She walks closer, until she's standing right over Hugh's body. Then she fires again, right into his chest.

"Wren!" I cry.

She finally lowers the weapon, like she's coming out of a

trance. "Every night, he's haunted me," she says, her voice dazed. "Every night. Not anymore."

"Tessa..." Saint's voice pulls my attention. He nods, the fire in the corner is catching now, flames racing along the spilled mess of gasoline.

Fuck.

"We need to put the fire out!" I exclaim, looking around. "Where's the fire extinguisher, or a hose? Your father has to have one in here, somewhere."

"No," Saint stops me, holding me back. "Let it burn."

I look at him in confusion. "But... The house... Your home."

He shakes his head, looking grim. "Wren was right. It's all haunted. There's no way of saving it. We have to burn it to the ground."

We lock eyes, and I nod, seeing the determination in his gaze. He's not just talking about the house. He means all of it.

The Ashford title, his family's legacy, his birthright. It's built on lies and a cruelty that have echoed through the generations, corrupting everyone they touch. But Saint is willing to burn all of it to ashes. He wants to be free of it.

The poisoned legacy ends, tonight.

"Wren, grab that gasoline," I tell her, my heart racing. "Come on."

With a fierce nod, she takes a can in each hand, and Saint and I do, too. He leads us through the vast house, turning on gas burners and emptying flammable liquid at every turn. We smash the liquor collection in the grand library; booze spilling on the antique rugs and tossing matches down to light the flames. Soon, there are fires burning in every room, catching blaze on the priceless curtains and roaring up the wood-paneled walls.

Smoke billows, thick from the windows, as we emerge back

outside. "Time to go," Saint says, as alarms start to wail. But I shake him off.

"Not yet. Wren, start the car, I'll be right back!"

I race back towards the cellar stairs, and of course, Saint follows. "Where the hell are you going?" he yells, as I skitter down the staircase and into the gloom.

"You'll see," I say breathlessly, racing back to the control room, which is in disarray after our desperate struggle with Hugh. I grab the CDs that are scattered around the room. "We need to take these," I tell Saint, who's appeared in the doorway. He looks around, quickly clocking the scene.

"Here." He scoops up a wastepaper basket from by the desk and starts throwing the cases inside. I make sure we grab every single one, before we race back upstairs again.

Wren is waiting out front, behind the wheel of one of the estate Land Rovers. "Get in!" she calls. The fire alarms from the house are wailing louder, in every room, and smoke is pouring thick from the windows; the grand house burning out of control.

It's an inferno.

We pile into the car, and Wren hits the gas, speeding down the drive. I cling on to Saint, his arms around me like he never wants to let go. Safe, at last.

Where I belong.

The flames burn higher. We watch Ashford Manor recede in the rearview mirror, until trees block our view, and the smoke is lost to the darkness, and we speed on, into the night.

Chapter 22

Tessa

We crash as soon as we get back to Saint's place in the city, but when I wake the next morning, everything aches.

I sit up, wincing. The sun is high outside the windows, so I must have slept late. I take a deep breath and look around the familiar room, filled with gratitude that I'm snuggled in soft linens, and not trapped in a cold, dusty cell—or worse.

I almost can't believe everything that's happened. My blood spikes with adrenaline as the memories from last night flood back to me, and I focus on my breathing to block it all out.

It's over, I repeat to myself. *You're safe.*

Slowly, my heartbeat slows, but there's one image that lingers, one I know that I won't be able to shake in a hurry:

Hugh's body slumped, bloody on the garage floor, and Wren's calm expression, standing over him.

Justice.

"Here you are: coffee, toast, and freshly-squeezed juice."

I sit up in bed, yawning, as Saint brings in a tray. His hair is wet and rumpled from the shower, and he's wearing a soft cotton tee and sweatpants. "Wait, what are you doing?" I protest, realizing. "You're the one who's injured!"

"A couple of stiches," he shrugs, nonchalant. "I'm fine. How are you feeling?" he asks, setting the tray down, and sitting beside me on the bed. He cups my cheek tenderly. "Still shaken up?"

"No," I reply immediately. He gives me a dubious look. "OK," I admit, reluctant, "I'm pretty sore."

I have marks all over my body from my desperate struggles with Hugh, but the worst of them is the ugly purple bruise spreading on my stomach. I touch it gingerly, wincing at the ache. "You need an ice pack for that," Saint says, his jaw tightening with protective anger. He gets up to go, but I catch his hand, and hold it tightly.

"Stay a minute?" I ask, full of emotion. I want to hold onto him, to reassure myself that he's safe, and here with me.

Watching him take that bullet for me... It made me never want to let go.

Saint immediately sits back down, and holds me gently, so he doesn't hurt my bruises. "How's Wren?" I ask, taking a welcome sip of coffee.

"Still sleeping," he replies. "I knocked to take her breakfast order, but I think she's still out cold."

"Good." I exhale. "She needs the rest."

"You both do," Saint tells me, kissing me softly on the forehead.

"What's the news, with everything?" I venture. The last we saw of Ashford Manor, it was going up in flames. I'm guessing there's been some serious fallout, even if nobody knows the reason why it burned.

Yet.

Saint shakes his head. "We'll deal with it later. For now, you should just relax."

"That means there's something to deal with," I point out.

He smiles at me. "You're stubborn."

"And you're stonewalling," I point out, smiling back at him. Even with my body bruised and aching, after everything I've just been through, I can't help glowing with happiness.

We made it through. Together.

"The fire is in the news, but so far, there's nothing about why it went up in smoke," Saint tells me. "The tabloids are all too distracted by gossip from the wedding. Apparently, some minor royal got plastered at the reception, and danced on the tables singing Kylie with some guy from *Eastenders*."

"Good." I exhale. I know there are still plenty of loose ends for us to tie up, but I'll take a moment to relax before the final battle. I glance over at Saint, who looks lost in thought as he idly strokes my hair. "And how about you?" I venture. "How do you feel?"

"I told you; my shoulder is fine."

"That's not what I meant," I tell him gently. He filled me in on everything that happened with his parents and Robert back at the wedding. I can't imagine what he must be going through, learning that his entire family was part of this twisted conspiracy.

But Saint looks surprisingly calm for a man who just burned his inheritance to the ground.

"I'm... alright," he says, giving me a slow nod. He leans closer and kisses me, soft and tender. "I'm always alright when I'm with you."

"Saint..." I reluctantly pull back, concerned. "Really?"

"Really," he smiles back at me, and it's a quiet, sincere expression; his eyes shining with peace. "I'm not saying I won't have a few things to discuss in therapy soon," he adds with a wry look, "But knowing that it's all over, that's you're safe, and we're together..." He lifts my hand to his lips and presses a tender kiss on my knuckles. "That's all I really need. Truly."

I sigh with relief—and happiness. "That's all I need, too," I whisper. "I love you so much."

"I love you, too."

Saint kisses me, deeper this time. It's the kind of kiss that makes me want to tell him *Yes* right now to that question he floated yesterday. *Yes*, there's nobody like you in the world. *Yes*, my heart is yours.

Yes, I want this forever.

Saint finally releases me and gets to his feet. "Your breakfast is getting cold," he says, teasing.

"You're right," I smile and reach for the toast, my stomach rumbling. "Where are my priorities?"

He chuckles. "I need to get on the phone, to my lawyers, for starters, to make sure the police aren't asking too many questions about the fire. Then the other calls we discussed," he adds, with a determined nod.

"I'll be down soon," I promise. "I just need to take the longest shower known to man."

He chuckles. "Take your time. I'm not going anywhere."

He leaves, and I sink back into the plush pillows for a moment, still processing the past few days. Hell, the past few months. After everything we've been through, a small part of me doesn't quite believe Saint's reassurance yet; I'm still braced for some new disaster, but I know, that will fade in time.

We can face anything and make it out the other side. *Together*.

AFTER LUXURIATING under the hot water for a good half-hour and using pretty much every product lined up on the shower ledge, I finally dress in cozy sweats and my favorite of Saint's oversized sweaters. Wrapped up in the faint woodsy scent of him, I make my way downstairs.

"Is there any hot water left in the known universe?" Wren asks me, teasing. She's curled up on the sofa with a mug of tea, looking tired—but clear-eyed and calm.

Saint wasn't the only one who slayed his demons last night.

I go to her and smother her with a hug. "Wait! My tea!" she laughs, trying to keep it from spilling. I draw back and settle beside her on the couch.

"Did you sleep OK?" I ask, searching her delicate features.

Wren nods. "Straight through the night. No nightmares, nothing." She smiles. "I feel like a whole new woman. No, scratch that. I feel more like myself again."

"Good." A knot of emotion wells in my throat, I'm so relieved to see her smiling again. "Have you eaten? Do you need anything? Do you have any bruises, or—"

"Woah, easy there, *Mom*," Wren says with a smirk. "I'm good. Your boyfriend has been fussing over me enough this morning. You picked a good one, there," she adds, with a grin. "Makes a mean bacon sandwich, and he'll take a bullet for you. I say, keep him."

"I'm planning on it," I smile back, as the man himself joins us. He folds his tall frame onto the couch beside me, immediately stroking my back, like he's reassuring himself I'm really here.

Clearly, I'm not the only one who wants to hold on tightly and never let go.

"So, what now?" I ask, looking between them. "Time to deliver a message to Ashford Pharma, and Lionel Ambrose?"

"And Cyrus Lancaster, and Max," Saint ticks them off on his fingers. "And whoever else they recruited into their evil conspiracy."

"Just a few of Britain's elite," I joke lightly. "No big deal."

Saint chuckles, but Wren sips her tea, eyes down. I feel a wave of compassion for her, forced to confront the very stuff of her nightmares. She's been through so much, and all because she stumbled on their secrets—and gave up her old life to protect me.

"How would you feel about going home?" I ask her softly.

Wren's head snaps up. Her eyes shine with emotion. "Can I?" she asks us eagerly. "I mean, would that even be possible?"

"I don't see why not," Saint replies. "You're safe now. Ashford Pharma, and anyone connected to this is going down, and in a few hours, they'll know it, too. You're not the threat to them anymore. Nothing's going to stop us exposing them now."

Wren exhales a sigh of pure longing. "I can't wait to see Mom and Dad again," she says, smiling at me. "But..."

She pauses, a shadow flitting across her face.

"What is it?" I ask.

"I don't know if I can be Wren Peterson anymore," she answers slowly. "Go back to my old identity, I mean. There'll be so many questions," she adds. "Everyone knows I died, and if I have to keep explaining what happened..." Wren shakes her head. "I don't want that. I don't think I could take it. I want a clean slate, to leave all of this behind me, and just move on."

"We can make that happen," Saint speaks up.

We both turn to him, hopeful. "How?" I ask.

"The usual ways," he replies with a wry smile. "Money, power, connections... We might as well use them for good, before the St. Clair name is ruined beyond all redemption."

"I wouldn't need much," Wren says eagerly. "Just a new identity, to start over. I could tell Mom and Dad the truth, and then... Pick a new town, by the ocean. Maybe somewhere I could teach or do my research. I'd love to keep working on the Alzheimer's problem," she adds. "Even if Dr. DeJonge's theories didn't work, I know we're just a few years from finding a cure for the people who need it the most."

My tears well in my eyes again. That's my sister, always thinking about everybody else.

Saint squeezes my shoulder. "I'll make it happen," he vows. "You deserve your life back, after everything you've had to sacrifice. You know what? I bet that hacker, Charlie, will have some connections for building a new identity," he says, rising to his feet. "I'll call her, right away."

We spend the rest of the morning planning Wren's fresh start, while Saint contacts his parents, and sets up a meeting for us all. The details of her new life come together quickly, and I love seeing her face lit up with excitement, musing over possible cities and places to go.

"North Carolina has some great research universities," she says, as we eat lunch in the kitchen. "But I've always wanted to live on the West Coast, near the ocean..."

"Are you going to take up surfing?" I tease. "Start preaching to me about the flow of the earth, and letting go?"

She giggles and tosses a potato chip at me. "Maybe. Or maybe I'll quit medicine altogether and open a bookstore-slash-tea shop on the coast somewhere, and spend my days baking scones."

"And flirting with hunky fishermen," I add.

She grins. "Sounds good to me. I can do anything," she adds in wonder, and I can tell that she's still taking in the options, wide open to her after a year of fear and hiding, when every door seemed shut.

I pause.

"What?" Wren knows me and she knows when I have something on my mind. I don't want to ruin the joyful vibes, but there's something still weighing on me.

I go to the hallway and retrieve one of the security video

discs that Saint and I rescued from the fire. It's Wren's video, with their names scribbled on the front in black Sharpie.

I place it on the table between us.

"You said you needed to see what happened to you," I say slowly. I look at her, torn. "I thought about destroying it, but... It should be your choice, what you do. If you want to watch it, or..."

I trail off anxiously.

Wren takes a deep breath, and picks up the case, turning it over in her hands. "I thought I needed to watch it," she says, looking thoughtful. "Those gaps in my memory have been driving me crazy, and I thought maybe, if I filled them in, I could finally be free. But what happened last night, with Hugh... That's the end of the story. *I ended it*," she adds fiercely. "I don't need to know what happened in that cell, because I made sure that it'll never happen again. To anyone."

I breathe in relief.

She opens a couple of drawers, until she finds a lighter. It's expensive, silver, engraved with the insignia from one of Saint's fancy clubs, and it feels fittingly ceremonial when Wren opens the case and pulls out the security disc, burned onto a CD. She snaps the lighter, and a flame rises. Holding it to the edge of the disc, we watch as the fire melts the plastic, until it's just a warped, twisted mess. Wren drops it in the sink, smoldering.

"There," she says with a smile. "Good riddance."

"Nothing but freshly baked scones and hunky fishermen ahead."

Wren chooses not to come with us to the big meeting at Ashford Pharma, and I don't blame her. She's focused on her future now; Saint and I can take care of the past. As we approach the towering building, I squeeze his hand, suddenly nervous.

"These are a lot of powerful people we're about to tell to go to hell," I murmur.

He gives me a reassuring look. "Nobody's going to touch you again. They'll have to fire a hundred bullets to get past me."

"You're not invincible," I point out, even as I feel a glow over his stalwart protection. Wren's right: The man threw himself in front of gunfire to protect me. That kind of love is about as committed as it gets.

"But I feel like I am when you're next to me," Saint says with a dashing grin.

I laugh, feeling better as we enter the vast marble lobby. The place is still buzzing. To every other employee, it's just another ordinary workday. We're the only ones who know that Ashford Pharma is about to burn, just like the manor house last night.

As we make our way to the elevator, and up to the executive floor, I feel a twinge of guilt over all the people we're about to make unemployed. "They don't know what's about to happen to their jobs," I murmur, looking out across the office floor. "Or the company. They're innocent in all of this."

"And I'll make sure they get help finding new positions," Saint promises me. "Working for companies that are actually making a difference, instead of feeding them lies."

We stride down the hallway, towards the conference room. This part of the office has been cleared out of people, I notice, spotting the empty desks and gathering spaces. Clearly, nobody wants this meeting to be overheard. As we approach, I can see everyone is already assembled inside: Saint's parents, Lionel Ambrose, and Cyrus Lancaster.

We told them to come alone, no lawyers or staff, and they

complied. They don't need any witnesses for what we're about to discuss.

"Ready?" Saint asks me, arching an eyebrow.

I nod, determined. "Ready."

We open the doors, and walk in. Every head turns to look at us, and I feel the rage in their glares like a sharp slap. But it's not just anger on their privileged, aristocratic faces.

It's fear, too.

Good.

Saint leads me to the head of the table, and stays standing, looking out over the room. His parents are pale faced, but the others bluster and rage.

"Whatever this is about, I had nothing to do with it," Cyrus Lancaster announces. "And I'll sue you to hell if you say one word otherwise."

"My solicitors are already applying for an injunction," Lionel agrees, "If you dare try and connect us with any... irregularities that may have been going on here at Ashford."

"Fucking liars," Saint's father grumbles furiously. "You were the one who told me to keep it quiet, just for another few months."

"Shut your mouth!" Cyrus booms. "They could be recording this!"

"And who's fault is that?" Lionel pitches in.

Their arguing is interrupted by Saint slamming his palm on the table. They fall silent.

"So much for loyalty," Saint remarks, scathing. "I thought you all were bound together, by duty... and blackmail."

Their faces change.

"Oh yes, we know all about the dungeons at Ashford House," I speak up, furious. "And all the sick, twisted things you've done. So you better listen to what we have to say, or our next meeting is with the editors of *The Sun, the Mirror*, and *The London Times*."

That gets their attention.

"Good," Saint says coolly. "Now, Ashford Pharma, and our miracle Alzheimer's drug. You'll draft a statement today, Dad, announcing that the trials were fraudulent, and the drug will not be released to market."

His parents gape. "You can't possibly be serious. The share price will collapse!"

"The money is the least of your problems," Saint replies, harsh as steel. "You'll give a full confession, both of you. About everything. The drug, the lies... and Valerie's death."

His mother sounds a sob.

"Lionel, you'll withdraw from the leadership election, and resign your seat in Parliament," Saint continues. "People will understand. After all, you need to be with your family at this difficult time."

Fear flickers on Lionel's face. "What do you mean? Where's Hugh?" he demands, looking stricken. "I've been calling him all morning. Nobody's seen him."

"You mean, since he drugged and kidnapped me, and tried to kill us all at your instruction?" I counter. "He died in the fire."

Lionel sags back, shocked.

"It was a tragic accident," I continue. "At least, that's what you're going to make sure the coroner's report says. Unless you want a certain video of his loyalty test made public..."

I'm bluffing, of course. Now that Wren's destroyed the disc, there's no proof of Hugh's crimes. But his father doesn't know that. He crumples, starting to sob.

I don't feel a shred of emotion for him. He's corrupt and evil, just like Hugh.

"What about me?" Cyrus ventures, looking nervous.

I look at him with disdain. He'll be implicated in the Ashford fraud, and Valerie's murder, too. I have no doubt he was the one pulling plenty of strings, along with Saint's mother. But that's not enough. His position and power will be useful to us in other ways.

"For starters, you'll help cover-up the fire, and make sure nobody asks any questions about Hugh's death," Saint instructs him. "Your newspapers will sell the official story and shut down any investigation."

"And then you're going to be overwhelmed with a charitable spirit," I continue. "And donate your massive fortune to good causes."

Cyrus snorts. "Over my dead body," he vows, shooting me a look of such cold disdain that I gulp. But Saint squeezes my shoulder in support.

"It's funny you should mention bodies..." He produces a disc case from his jacket and slides it across the table to Cyrus.

"That's Max's video," I remind him helpfully. "A copy. And we have yours, too. All of you," I add, looking around the room. "So if you try to fight us, or hide from the truth, the world will see exactly what kind of monsters you really are. In fact, the first recipients of your generosity will be the victims of your crimes," I add, shooting Cyrus a glare. "We're going to track down every one of them, and make sure they're compensated for what you put them through. Very generously compensated."

Wren, Saint, and I debated what to do about the rest of the videos. Saint wanted to turn them over to the authorities right away, so the perpetrators could all be hunted down and brought to justice.

But Wren pointed out, that wasn't our decision to make. The victims of those attacks deserved to make their own call about what happens next. Some of them may not even remember what happened to them, some may have spent a lifetime trying to move on. If we handed the tapes over for criminal prosecution, then they wouldn't have a say in this, either. Their names would leak, be splashed across the headlines around the world in a salacious frenzy.

We agreed that we'd handle this privately. Saint will hire investigators to track down every last victim, so they can choose for themselves what to do. And if they wanted retribution...

Well, accidents happen. Just ask Hugh Ambrose.

"Is that it?" Cyrus demands. He's red-faced, gripping the disc case.

"For now," Saint replies coldly, pausing as we turn to go. "Remember, Dad, you have until the end of the day to release your statement. Then we're turning all the trial data over to the authorities and letting them take it from here."

"Anthony—Saint, please, you'll ruin us!" Saint's mother, Lillian, lets out a wretched cry. She's stricken: Her life of status and luxury slipping away before her very eyes. "We'll lose everything."

"Ironic, isn't it?" he tells her coolly. "You sold your souls, and it was all for nothing in the end."

"You have to understand, we did this for you," his father pleas. "For the Ashford legacy—*your* legacy!"

"We're your family!" his mother adds.

Saint pauses there in the doorway, and shoots them a final, furious look. "No, you aren't. Not anymore. Tessa's my family now."

And he takes my hand, and we walk out, and away from Ashford for the last time.

Chapter 23

Tessa

Sunlight falls through the palm trees, a gentle breeze whispers my bare skin, and the only sound I can hear is the gentle swish of waves lapping the shore.

Paradise.

I let out a blissful sigh, lounging in a luxury cabana right on the waterfront. The beach is deserted, white sand sparkling under the South Pacific sun, and there's nobody in sight—aside from a discreet waiter, who materializes with another icy drink as soon as I slurp the last of the old one.

"Can I get you anything else, ma'am?" he asks.

"No, thank you. I'm great."

He nods, retreating out of sight again. I sit back, nibbling a chunk of pineapple from the rim. Great? How about completely, luxuriously perfect...

Saint surprised me with a trip, after everything exploded back in England. The downfall of Ashford Pharma was front page news, and suddenly, there were reporters camped outside his house, braying for answers. After everything we'd been through, he said we needed a break. I was expecting an escape to the countryside, maybe, or even a little getaway in Europe, but instead he whisked me first-class across the world, to one of the most exclusive resorts around. No reporters stalking our every move, no lawyers blowing up our phones all day; nothing but miles of white sand and turquoise waters, and total privacy.

Even clothing is optional.

My phone buzzes with a familiar ring tone, the only one I'm picking up these days. I answer, smiling. "Wren!

"I take it that you made it to the island okay?"

"How do you know?"

"I can hear the smile in your voice."

I laugh. "Well, it's kind of impossible not to, when you're surrounded by this kind of luxury," I admit. "We have a massive villa with a private pool, right on the beach, and we've been here a full day already, and I haven't seen a single other guest."

"You'll get used to it," Wren teases. "Soon, you'll be expecting caviar with every meal, and turning up your nose at any bedsheets that are less than two thousand thread-count!"

"Believe me, I'm not taking anything for granted. Not one single day," I reply. "Nearly dying a half-dozen times will do that to you."

"Oh, I know. I'm making it a habit to eat ice cream every day," Wren reports with a giggle. "There's a place just down the street from my new apartment, and I'm working my way through the flavor list. Life's too short to skip the double-chocolate chunk."

"Amen!" I agree, smiling. "So how are you getting settled in?"

"I'm great!" she exclaims. "I finally got my new furniture delivered, so my apartment is starting to feel like a home. You should see this place. It's too big for me, but I love it. My balcony has a view of the ocean, and I'm even thinking about getting a dog. They were doing adoptions at the farmer's market, on the weekend, and I fell in love with this one puppy, a golden Labrador."

"Like Buster!" I say, naming our childhood dog.

"Exactly. I got the details of the adoption place, so I'm going to visit this week, and see if we bond."

"You have to send me all the photos," I say immediately, and she laughs.

"I'd say the same about you, but I'm guessing they're a little racier than puppies and waffle cones."

"Maybe..."

We laugh. I love hearing her so happy. With her eye-popping 'gift' from Cyrus, she decided to set up home on the West Coast—after a stop back at home, to reunite with our parents. They were stunned by the news that she'd faked her death, and had a million questions—for both of us. But in the end, their joy at having Wren back has outweighed their anger and confusion over what happened to her. I know it may take a while for them to process everything, but they're already scheduled to visit Wren this week and help her get her new place set up, and I can't wait to bring Saint to meet them, too.

It's a fresh start, for all of us.

"So, do they get the news on that fancy island of yours?" Wren asks.

"You mean, have I seen the latest round of headlines? Yup. There's nothing new though," I add, reassuring her. "It's all just about the falsified trial results, and Ashford Pharma crashing and burning."

"Literally," Wren adds, with a wry twist in her voice.

News about the drug scheme sent the press, and markets, into a frenzy. The company share price collapsed overnight, and word is, they're heading straight for bankruptcy. Not to mention, jail. Rumors are swirling about fraud convictions for

Alexander and Lillian St. Clair—and Robert, too, since his name was all over the paperwork. The public will never know the depths of their twisted conspiracy, but it's good that they're facing justice for this part of their crimes, at the very least.

"Just curious, but how is Mr. Fancy Pants planning on paying for all that luxury travel, now that his inheritance is basically gone?" Wren asks.

I smile. "Saint's rebellion against his family included the company, too," I confide. "He told me the minute he got access to his trust fund, years ago, he yanked all the money from Ashford, and invested it elsewhere."

Lucrative places, like his friend Sebastian Wolfe's hedge fund, which has skyrocketed since Saint signed on as one of the original investors. Which means he's still eye-poppingly wealthy.

"Smart man." Wren sounds delighted. "I hope he's planning on keeping you in the height of luxury." The sound of a doorbell comes. "That's my take-out," Wren says. "There's a Thai place here you're going to love. I'll call you tomorrow. Love you."

"Love you!"

I ring off, in time to see Saint approaching, sauntering from the tropical gardens in nothing but a pair of swimming trunks—and the sexy, wolfish grin I love so much.

"Wren's getting settled," I report happily.

"That's great." he joins me in the cabana, stretching with a yawn. "I just talked to Imogen."

"Things are still crazy in London?" I ask.

He nods. "The ripple effects of Ashford's collapse are still making their way through society. But she did have some news for us," he says, with a smirk. "Annabelle's dumped Max. Sent him packing, the minute news hit that they were all going down. She's filed for an annulment, and last anyone heard, she was on a yacht, heading for Brazil with some famous soccer star."

I burst out laughing. "Good for her," I say, pleased. She tried to help me and Wren, in her way, and I'm glad she's getting out unscathed.

"You're looking a little sunburned, sweetheart," Saint says, reaching for a bottle of sunscreen. "Let me help with that."

"You're so generous," I coo, flirty. "Always looking out for me."

"It's my pleasure."

I applied some just a half-hour ago, but I lay down on my front, melting under the feel of his hands slowly massaging every inch of my body. And in my tiny blue bikini, there's plenty to touch. Saint's fingertips brush my back slowly, skimming over my waist and hips until I'm practically melted into a puddle on the chaise.

He leans in, brushing the back of my neck with a slow kiss. "Are you happy?" he murmurs.

I roll over to face him, only inches away. "Very," I whisper, kissing the edge of his neck... His sexy, stubbled jaw... His mouth...

Saint captures me to him, deepening the kiss until I'm gasping and boneless in his arms. His tongue slides over mine in a sensual dance, body hardening against me as I instinctively wrap my legs around his waist, bringing him into the cradle of my thighs.

Saint groans against my mouth as I rock against him. "Baby... *Fuck.*"

"Excellent idea," I tease him with a smirk. "It's been all of... Two hours since you were inside me."

Saint's eyes flash with heat. "How remiss of me."

In one smooth motion, he nudges aside my bikini bottoms and sinks two fingers inside my wet core.

I gasp in thrilled surprise. "Saint..." My cheeks redden, and I glance around, but of course, the beach is empty, and the gauzy drapes of our cabana flutter around us, blocking his wicked touch from view.

"Is that a 'Yes, Saint? More, Saint?'" he teases, curling his fingers deeper, and starting to pulse.

I moan in pleasure, sinking back into the pillows. His fingers feel incredible, palm applying the perfect pressure on my clit as he strokes and pulses, but soon, I'm hungry for more.

I reach for him, palming the hard length of his cock through his trunks and pumping in time with his strokes. He breathes faster, his movements turning more urgent as our eyes lock, his expression a mirror of my own fevered lust.

"More," I moan, shoving his trunks down and parting my thighs wider. Inviting. "I need all of you. *Now*."

"God, I love it when you beg for this dick," Saint hisses a breath, his cock springing free. Straining. He pulls me on his lap, so I'm straddling him, and guides my hips as I sink down, taking every inch of him inside.

"*Yes...*" I throw my head back in pleasure, reveling in the deep, dragging friction, and the way his thick girth stretches me, filling me all the way up. Saint tears my bikini top aside, burying his face in my breasts and licking the sensitive swell of my chest, sucking at my nipples until I'm whimpering in bliss.

I rise up, then sink down again. deeper. Harder. *Fuck*. Another moan falls from my lips, and I gasp for air, riding him hard now. "I love it. God, you feel so perfect inside."

"You're the perfect one, baby," Saint vows, gazing up at me with an expression of pure, reverent lust. "This sweet cunt drives me crazy. I can never get enough."

"Prove it," I smile, feeling the pleasure and power roll through me. "Show me how good it feels."

In an instant, Saint rolls us, laying me out flat on my back, and thrusting so deep I howl with pleasure. "Yes!" My voice echoes, high with pleasure through the palms. "Oh God! Right there. *Yes!*"

He fucks into me again, gripping one knee and pressing it back against my body to angle even deeper. Even sweeter. *Fuck.* It's a wild, relentless rhythm, and I rise to meet him, matching every stroke. We don't need words, we never do when our bodies are in perfect conversation like this: gasping and groaning, lost in the delicious grind of friction, sweaty and rabid and raw. He fucks me into the pillows, wild and unleashed, and God, I love it.

I love him.

"I forgot to say, I ordered us some lunch," Saint murmurs, as he pins my wrists above my head.

I blink up at him in confusion, my mind hazy and consumed with lust.

"It's a three-course meal, they usually send a whole team to set up the table," he adds, thrusting into me again, holding me down and grinding his cock high inside me so I can't help but sob with pleasure. "They should be here any minute." His smile spreads, knowing. Wicked. "In fact, they might already be out there, enjoying the show."

Oh God.

My body floods with a rush of wild, thrilling shame at the thought of it. People, hearing us. *Watching.*

"Saint," I gasp in protest, struggling against his grip. "We can't—*oh*—"

My protest melts into another moan. My climax is already rising, wild and out of control, and it's too late to hold back the tide of release, not with my body tight and pulsing, and Saint fucking into me, over and over, a relentless pace that blots everything from my mind but the thrill of discovery and the exquisite bliss of his cock filling me up—

I come with a wail, pleasure exploding so brightly, I swear I scream his name.

"Fuck, Tessa!" Saint pumps faster, groaning, until he explodes his own release in a deep shudder as I cling to him, gasping for air.

"You can't *do* that!" I cry, playfully smacking his arm when I finally come back down to earth again. I peer outside the cabana drapes, relieved to see that there's still nobody around.

"What are they going to think of us?"

"That you're a brilliant, incredible, kinky-as-fuck goddess?" Saint suggests, breathing hard. He gives me a sweaty kiss, then lolls back, smug and satisfied. "You loved it though, didn't you?"

"That's not the point!" I laugh, flushed and glowing.

"Your pleasure is always the point," he vows, and my heart swells with love.

How did I get so lucky to find him?

"You look like you need to cool off, before I make you scream again," Saint says, tracing my flushed skin.

"Good idea." I scramble up. "First one in the water gets to pick dessert," I challenge him with a flirty grin.

Saint laughs. "That's hardly motivation," he points out, as I back away, feet bare in the warm sand. "You're the one with the sweet tooth."

I smirk. "I didn't say it had to be on the menu."

With that parting shot, I take off, sprinting for the water. But I barely make it a few paces before Saint sweeps me up, throwing me over his shoulder and wading the rest of the way into the shallows. "Victory is mine!" He drops me with a splash, and the water closes over my head in a rush, cool and refreshing against my naked body.

I surface, laughing. "Somehow, I think I'll be the one winning in this bet," I tell him, drawing closer.

"Let's call it a tie."

Saint wraps his arms around me, kissing me slow and sweet. The tide swells around us, and I lose myself in the joy of this moment, with him.

Always him.

My heart suddenly pounds in my chest, and I know exactly what I'm supposed to do next. "Yes," I tell him, pulling back.

Saint looks puzzled. "Yes to what?"

I feel giddy, but my smile has never felt wider as I loop my arms around his neck, beaming up at him. "Yes, I'll marry you. If the offer is still open," I add, laughing.

Saint's jaw drops. "Yes, it is. A thousand times, yes." He kisses me again, lifting me up and spinning me around, sending splashes of water glittering in the sun. "I mean it, Tessa," he adds, setting me down, and cradling my face in his hands. "I'll love you, forever."

"Forever," I agree, flushed with happiness. Who could have known that a journey which began under the shadowy spires of Oxford, fueled with anger and vengeance, could have led me here: standing in the sunshine with this incredible man, sharing a love filled with trust, and tenderness, and—yes—a passion that I never imagined was possible.

And our forever has only just begun.

THE END

(Almost...)

Imogen

I know what you're hiding.

The note arrives in a heavy cream envelope, delivered to my home address in the regular morning's post. I think it's a wedding invitation or PR mail before I tear it open. Now, I stare at the single line of printed text, chills running down my spine.

Who sent it? I search the envelope for clues, but there's nothing else marked on the paper, no clue or hint where it came from. Just those five little words, that have the power to bring my world crashing to the ground.

Someone knows my secret.

And they want me to know it, too.

TO BE CONTINUED...

Imogen's story is coming... But what secret is she hiding, and how far will the mystery letter-writer go to expose her?

Sign up to my newsletter and be the first to know about my next release, plus sales, and other sizzling romance news.

**** www.roxysloane.com ****

And keep reading for your sneak peek at my spicy billionaire series, FLAWLESS >>>

Discover Roxy's spicy billionaire romance trilogy - available now!

Are you ready to surrender?

Flawless... Caleb Sterling is seductive. Commanding. *Revered.* And he's hiding a dark secret that could bring his luxury jewelry empire crumbling to the ground.

Glittering... He gets what he wants, and he's set his sights on me. But I have a secret of my own.

Forever...? The game is set. The stakes couldn't be higher. But who will claim the ultimate prize?

Find out in this steamy contemporary romance with a sprinkle of glitz! Featuring a dominant hero, wild plot twists, and plenty of spice.

THE FLAWLESS TRILOGY:

1. Flawless Desire
2. Flawless Ruin
3. Flawless Prize

Prologue

Desire is a powerful thing.

People say that it's ambition, or love, or rage that makes the world turn. That sends armies to wage war, and brings empires crashing into dust. But desire... Desire is a force greater than anything.

The craving deep inside that demands satisfaction—no matter what the cost. It doesn't matter if you're begging for surrender or aching for control. Dreaming of the hot slide of friction, lips parted in a desperate gasp of pleasure.

Desire will make a fool of you.

You feel it now, don't you? Your heart beating faster, that shiver of lust curling down your spine. Your nipples tighten into stiff peaks, aching, as that tell-tale rush of heat spirals lower, slick between your thighs.

What will it take to satisfy you now?

A soft touch? A firm grip?

A hard, unyielding fuck?

Facedown in the bedsheets, sobbing with need. A fist in your hair, unfamiliar weight bearing down. You never thought you'd go this far, but still, desire will urge you on. Past reason. Beyond pride.

And it will never let you go.

Because desire is never truly satisfied. Even as you lay claim to everything you've wanted; even as the thick waves of pleasure ebb away, you feel it. Calling again.

Wanting more.

It's how my family built its luxury jewelry empire. Under my control, Sterling Cross has made desire into an art form. Turned craving into a billion-dollar brand that spans the globe.

The glitter of jewels, tempting in the darkness. The cold press of platinum on hot, flushed skin.

I thought I was above the fray. I knew how to keep my needs in check: nameless women in dark rooms, pretty little things on my arm, as much an ornament as the exquisite jewels caressing their skin. Never getting close. Never once threatening my control. Always unravelling under my expert touch, until they begged for more.

I was the master of desire.

Until *her*.

Chapter 1

Juliet

Do you ever wake up in the morning and feel like today, everything could change?

Maybe it's wishful thinking, but the moment I open my eyes on Friday morning, *something* feels different. The grey New York skies are gleaming a bright blue outside the windows, my alarm is playing my favorite song, and my roommate hasn't made it home from her latest walk of shame, so there's plenty of hot water still left in the shower. By the time I've dressed in my smartest pencil skirt and blouse, aka, the Interview outfit, and headed on the subway downtown, I'm just about ready to believe that fate—or the subway—is on my side this time.

And after the year I've had, I could use the break.

But today, I'm determined to change my luck. I even make it to Tribeca with twenty minutes to spare, so I duck into the nearest Starbucks for a pre-interview caffeine jolt. Taking my place in the line, I try to give myself a pep talk for the battle ahead. An assistant position at a luxury jewelry company like Sterling Cross isn't like answering the phones at the local dry cleaner, so I'm going to need to polish up my experience as bright as the diamonds they sell. Sure, I've been stringing along basic admin jobs for the past few years, but that just means I'm good at multitasking. I'm *scrappy*. *Resourceful*.

Or dead broke and at the very end of my rope.

My phone buzzes with a call, and I wince when I see the number. Meadow View Residential Home doesn't have a view of a meadow, but it's the nicest facility I could afford.

I let it go to voicemail, then brace myself to listen to the latest 'concerned' message from the billing department.

"Miss Nichols? We've been trying to reach you. If you can call me back as soon as possible, we need to discuss your late payments that are past due."

Payments. As in, more than one. My mom's Alzheimer's is advancing fast, and she needs round-the-clock care. Expensive care. The proceeds from selling our house lasted a couple of years, but now, I know the latest bills are piling up—and the facility won't be patient for long.

Which is why I need this job... Not because an executive assistant salary can even come close to covering the cost. No, once I'm in the door, there's a whole different payday on the table.

One that could solve all my problems.

Just thinking about the shady mess I've gotten into gives me butterflies in my stomach and shaking hands. Hmm... Maybe I should get decaf this time.

The line is inching forwards at the coffee shop when my cellphone buzzes again. It's Kelsey, my roommate, who must have finally made it back from her late-night hookup.

"I'm freaking out," I tell her.

"They're going to love you, Juliet. Obviously."

"If I don't say anything stupid out of sheer exhaustion," I sigh. "I hardly slept last night."

"Oooh, that's right. You had a date! How were things with whats-his-name?" Kelsey perks right up. But I just give a hollow laugh.

"I don't want to talk about it."

"That bad?"

"Worse." I wince at the memory. "He still lives with his parents."

"Well, that's not so ba—"

"—And he doesn't seem to want to *leave*." I continue. "All he did was talk about the gaming magazine he writes for. There's only so much *Call of Duty*-talk I can take. And, worst of all.... He's a bad kisser."

"How bad?"

"*Bad*." The line starts moving again so I turn, knocking into the person behind me. I turn to apologize.

And all my senses go haywire.

Because standing there, just inches away, is a wicked fantasy in a custom suit. Over six-feet-tall, with strong, angular features and sensual lips. He's got slate blue eyes, and the kind of hair you want to run your fingers through, tousled and dark.

Or maybe that's just me.

I blush, I can't help it. "Sorry," I murmur quickly, but the guy hasn't even noticed I bumped him: He's scrolling through his phone, with Airpods stuffed in his perfect ears.

He's totally oblivious to my existence.

Story of my life.

"Juliet?" Kelsey's voice breaks through my lustful haze. "You were telling me about your bad make out. Maybe it wasn't a dealbreaker?" she asks, ever the optimist. "You could train him, if he's hot enough. And rich enough. Is he?"

I have to laugh. This is why Kelsey has a date every Saturday night, and I... Don't. "You can't teach a guy to kiss, not so you feel it right to your toes." I tell her. "You know when a guy reaches for you and time just stops? And everything disappears, and it's like you and him are the only two people on earth?" I sigh wistfully. "You can tell *everything* by the way a guy kisses. *Especially* how he is in bed."

And let's just say, if last night was anything to go by, I would be in for three minutes of sloppy, beer-flavored action if I gave this guy another try. Call me a romantic, but I can't help feeling there should be more to life—and make outs—than that.

I finally reach the counter to order. "Got to go!" I tell Kelsey. "Wish me luck!"

"You'll be perfect."

I hope so. But Kelsey doesn't know that landing this job is only the half of it.

Because 'assistant' wouldn't be my only task.

But that's getting ahead of myself. I hang up and order my iced mocha, trying to focus. Wow them in the interview first, worry about the rest of it later. But as I'm striding confidently to the doors, gripping my mocha, someone jostles my elbow. My arm lurches, the cap flies free, and a wave of cold, dark coffee hits me, square in the chest.

"Noooo." I wail in dismay, looking down at my no-longer-white blouse. I'm soaked to the skin, with cream smeared down my front and caramel sauce dripping from the mess, just to taunt me with my extra treat add-on.

I look a total mess.

And I have exactly ten minutes until the biggest interview of my life.

I quickly run through my options. I can't go back home and change—I don't have the time. And all I'm wearing underneath is my lucky pink lace bra, not exactly interview material. Can I find a store open to grab a replacement? Not likely, before nine a.m.

I can't believe it. So much for turning everything around.

Tears well in my eyes. Everything was riding on getting this job today.

Everything.

"I apologize."

A voice beside me breaks through my misery. "That was my fault.

"I apologize. Let me cover your dry cleaning."

I look up and find my day has just turned from 'bad' to 'humiliating' because, of course, it's the handsome man from behind me in line. But I'm freaking out too much to care. This is an emergency, and I'm about to lose it: my pride, my self-control, and my future job.

"No... You don't get it," I nearly sob, looking around helplessly. "I have a big interview. I can't show up looking like this!"

The man looks around, and then briskly begins to hustle me to the lobby of the building next door. I'm all out of options, so I follow blindly behind him, but unless he's taking me to an Ann Taylor outlet, I'm all out of luck.

It's not a store, but the ladies' restroom. He guides me inside, locks the door behind us, and then orders:

"Take off your clothes."

"Umm, what... ?" I stammer, flustered. My cheeks burn hotter as he strips off his suit jacket, unknots his tie, and he starts unbuttoning his shirt.

I gape. This can *not* be happening.

Am I dreaming? Did someone spike that mocha with some hallucinogenics? Because my walking fantasy is slowly undressing in front of me, totally unconcerned.

He shrugs off the shirt, revealing a set of mesmerizingly solid muscles, gloriously tight and cut. He has the lean physique of an athlete who worked hard for it, too hard to keep it covered with a suit. Broad shoulders taper to a narrow waist, thick biceps and just a smattering of a treasure trove right at his belt buckle. It's a feast for the eyes. I can't look away, even if I wanted to.

I don't want to. That's a buffet I could happily gaze at for hours. *Days*, even.

"You can do something with this, right?"

Oh, yes. I can. Many things.

It takes me a moment to realize he's holding his shirt out. It's only when one corner of his lip curls up in a knowing smile that I finally get it. He's offering me a replacement for my ruined blouse

I take it from him. "But what about you?"

He shrugs. Like handing over fine Italian linen is no big deal. And to him, it probably isn't. "I'll manage. You clearly have someplace important to be."

For a moment, I can't recall where. My blood pulses.

Then it hits me. If I don't get a move on, I'm going to be terribly late for my job interview. And yet, I can't seem to convince my eyes to get with the picture. All they want to do is drink him in.

And the rest of my body... Well, it wants to do a whole lot more.

I feel a shiver of sexual awareness, my nipples tightening. The man's smirk grows wider, and I realize, he can see the stiff peaks, right through my wet shirt.

My cheeks burn hotter. "Turn around," I snap, embarrassed.

He does it, so I quickly yank the ruined blouse over my head and start buttoning his shirt up. But I'm just tucking it into my skirt when I catch sight of him in the mirror, his eyes on my reflection.

I gasp. He was watching me undress the whole time!

"So much for chivalry," I say pointedly, trying to hide my embarrassment.

And giving thanks that I wore a good bra.

The man turns to face me again as I straighten up. "I just gave you the shirt off my back," he says, sounding amused as he shrugs on his jacket again.

"Right. Thanks," I blurt. Glancing at my reflection, I can see, he really did just save the day. His shirt is oversized in a cool, stylish way, and I might even look better than I did in my sale-rack blouse. "Well... I should go."

"Wait."

He doesn't block my path, but somehow, I find myself pressed up against six feet of taut, toned muscle.

"Wha—"

My question is cut short as he takes me in his arms, pushes me firmly back against the sink, and kisses the living daylights out of me.

Holy shit!

His mouth is demanding, hot and hungry as his hands grip my waist, pinning me in place. My brain short-circuits. One minute, I'm wondering if I buttoned this thing right, and the next...

The next, I'm in sensory overload.

He eases my lips open and slides his tongue deep into my mouth. My legs give way. Heat rushes through me, tightening at my core, and I have to grip his lapels and hold on for dear life as he kisses, and probes, and *undoes me* with his mouth.

Oh my God.

I can't get enough. It's hot, and wild, and totally overwhelming, and I arch up against him, eagerly reaching to—

He releases me.

Just as quickly as it started, the kiss is over. I blink at him in disbelief, my heart pounding, my blood boiling from his touch. I'm unraveled, but the man looks totally unaffected as he gives me a smug grin.

"You can tell *everything* by the way someone kisses," he says, smirking. "*Especially* how they are in bed."

And then he saunters out, leaving me reeling there alone in the restroom.

He heard me!

I recognize the words, and let out a groan. He was listening to my conversation with Kelsey, back there in line at the coffee shop. All my blabbering about my date, and the job interview. What must he think of me?

Enough to land the hands-down best kiss of your life.

Good point.

And if the kiss was that good, sex with him would be...

Nope! I can't be thinking about this right now. I grab my bag and hightail it across the street, trying to put that weird and wonderful encounter behind me and focus on what really matters right now:

Landing this job.

I TAKE a deep breath as I approach the building, windows gleaming in the morning sun. Sterling Cross is *the* most exclusive luxury jewelry company in the world, crafting the kind of exquisite creations that adorn movie stars and royalty, with waiting lists a mile long. Their headquarters here in New York is like a work of art on its own. When I take the elevator up to the fifteenth floor, the doors open on an incredible atrium sparkling like one of their priceless jewels, all light and crystal, with display cases showcasing gorgeous necklaces, and stunning prints of their gems.

This place screams style and exclusivity. Mere mortals not invited.

Except I am, today.

I approach the front desk. "Hello, I'm Juliet Nichols, here to interview for the executive assistant position?"

The terrifyingly chic blonde barely glances at me. "To your left. Wait with the others."

I follow her directions to a packed waiting area, full of equally stylish-looking people. I find a spare corner of a bench to wait, and try to get my head in the game, but it's impossible with my heart still racing and my whole body alive with adrenaline after that kiss.

Who was he?

I fan my face with a copy of *Fortune* magazine, and listen to the young man beside me mutter to himself.

"Founded in 1945 when Levi Sterling fled Europe... Originally a watch-mending business... partnership with Charles Cross expanded into jewelry..."

I gulp. I cribbed the same research to prepare, but I'm not sure what's going to set me apart from the crowd. This is a big-deal company, and the CEO, Caleb Sterling, is the biggest deal of all.

Ruthless. Respected. Even *revered*, if the press is to be believed.

I tried to research him, but the guy stays out of the spotlight. Somehow, he's got everyone talking about him, without actually showing up anywhere. No posed photos, no red-carpet appearances... The most I could find was a years-old PR photo showing a stern-looking man half-hidden under wire-rimmed glasses and too-long hair.

He's a mystery.

I would be nervous at the best of times—even if I didn't have a whole lot more than just a job on the line here.

"Juliet Nichols?"

I bolt to my feet, and follow a brisk-looking red-headed woman down the hallway to the corner office. "I'm Victoria," she says. "Mr. Sterling's *first* assistant. You'll have ten minutes," she says, looking me up and down. Clearly, she isn't impressed with what she sees, because her lip curls slightly, and she adds: "Or less. Mr. Sterling doesn't suffer fools lightly."

Then she opens the door and gives me a light push that I'm not expecting, so I stumble into the room. I struggle to keep my footing—and my grip on my leather-bound resume.

"Sorry, hi! Pleased to meet you—"

I start—and then stop dead. Because sitting on the other side of a long conference table, flanked by serious-looking people in suits, is the man from the coffee shop.

The one who kissed me senseless in a bathroom not twenty minutes ago.

The one who is staring icily at me like we've never met before.

"You're late." He says shortly, disapproval clear. "Sit. Speak. I don't have much time."

I stare at him—at the way the other people in the room are all turned to him, like he's the freaking sun—and I finally put two-and-two together and come up with *holy hell*!

This is Caleb Sterling. And I need to make him hire me in the next ten minutes—or my whole life will fall apart.

To be continued...

What happens next? Juliet and Caleb's sizzling story is just getting started. Discover the FLAWLESS trilogy, available now!

Roxy Sloane is a USA Today bestselling author, with over 2 million books sold world-wide. She loves writing page-turning spicy romance full of captivatingly alpha heroes, sensual passion, and a sprinkle of glamor. She lives in Los Angeles, and enjoys shocking whoever looks at her laptop screen when she writes in local coffee shops.

~

To get free books, news and more, sign up to my VIP list:

www.roxysloane.com
roxy@roxysloane.com

Also by Roxy Sloane

THE FLAWLESS TRILOGY:

1. Flawless Desire (Caleb & Juliet)

2. Flawless Ruin (Caleb & Juliet)

3. Flawless Prize (Caleb & Juliet)

THE RUTHLESS TRILOGY:

1. Ruthless Heart (Nero & Lily)

2. Ruthless Games (Nero & Lily)

3. Ruthless Vow (Nero & Lily)

THE PRICELESS TRILOGY

1. Priceless Kiss (Sebastian & Avery)

2. Priceless Secret (Sebastian & Avery)

3. Priceless Fate (Sebastian & Avery)

THE TEMPTATION DUET:

1. One Temptation

2. Two Rules

THE KINGPIN DUET:

1. Kingpin

2. His Queen

Explicit: A Standalone Novel

THE SEDUCTION SERIES:

1. The Seduction

2. The Bargain

3. The Invitation

4. The Release

5. The Submission

6. The Secret

7. The Exposé

8. The Reveal

Printed in Great Britain
by Amazon

36672082R00155